# MY DEAD BODY

**DEL REY** *BALLANTINE BOOKS   New York*

# MY DEAD BODY

## A NOVEL

## CHARLIE HUSTON

A Del Rey Paperback Original

Copyright © 2009 by Charlie Huston
Maps copyright © 2009 by David Lindroth

All rights reserved.

Published in the United States by Del Rey,
an imprint of The Random House Publishing Group,
a division of Random House, Inc., New York.

DEL REY is a registered trademark and the Del Rey colophon
is a trademark of Random House, Inc.

ISBN 978-0-345-49589-1

Printed in the United States of America

www.delreybooks.com

2 4 6 8 9 7 5 3 1

*Book design by Jo Anne Metsch*

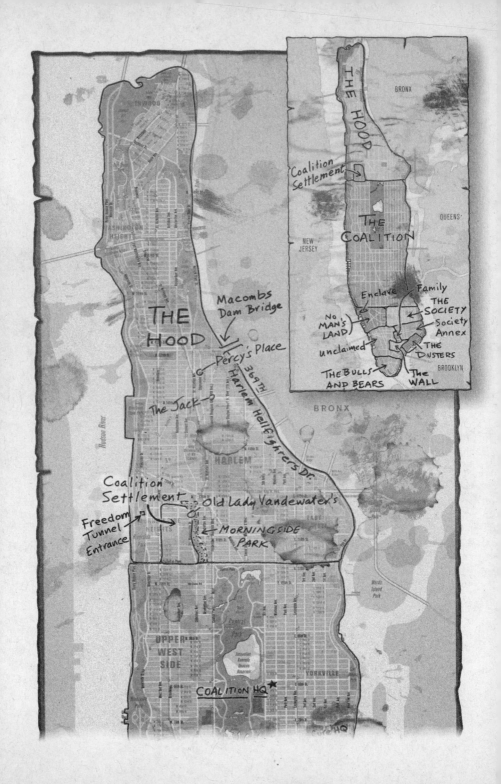

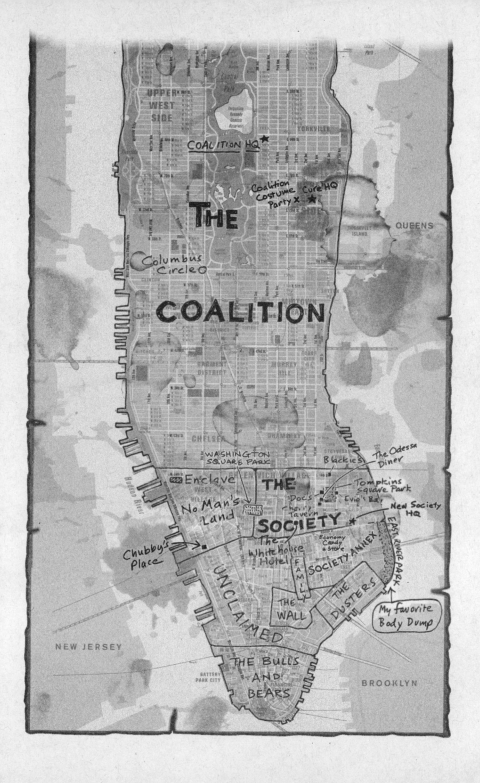

# MY DEAD BODY

If you're listening to this I'm dead.

(*laughter*)

Could be that's maybe only funny to me right now. Listen to a little more of this and could be it'll be funny to you too. But probably not. My guess, anyone listening to this won't find much amusement. If you believe it, that is. You don't believe it, you'll probably just about die laughing. I would.

I wonder how I did die.

So many goddamn options. The mind fucking boggles. But probably I just got plain shot. Course, seeing as how many times I've been shot before, it must have been a well-placed bullet. Or just a lot of them all at once. Then again, I knew a guy in my line who got machine-gunned more than once and lived to tell about it both times.

(*laughter*)

*Lived to tell about it.* That's funny. But you got to be in on the joke.

I was put in on the joke when I was sixteen. Happened in a bathroom at CBGB during a Ramones gig in '77. What it was, a guy was paying me twenty bucks to hand-job him, and while I was doing it he chewed a hole in my neck and started slurping.

(*laughter*)

Okay, maybe you had to be there.

That guy, if I could have ever got my hands on that guy. I got my hands on plenty of other people I had a problem with. But I'm not the type to keep score.

(*laughter*)

Trust me, the jokes don't get any better the rest of the way.

What I notice about getting older, things that seemed funny before just seem boring or stupid or sad. Things that shouldn't seem funny at all suddenly have a lighter side. No, that's not it. Nothing lighter about it. More that things you never thought you'd laugh at you find yourself laughing at because you got no other choice. Like the alternative is you go digging under the sink for some Drāno to guzzle.

(*laughter*)

See what I mean.

Tell the truth, this is the most I've laughed in forever. Not literally *forever*, I'm not that old. But, yeah, something about this is hitting the funny bone.

Probably it's the idea of you, whoever you are, listening to this. For you, this is one of two things. Either it's the lamest prank ever, or it's too little too late. If you're listening to this, either everything has blown up and everyone knows everything, or it hasn't. Either way, I'm gonna tell it.

So.

So, hey, here's some trivia for you. Did you know a pregnant woman has about forty percent greater blood volume than a woman who's not pregnant? Take a woman, she's a hundred and ten pounds. Her blood volume is about seven percent of that. Seven point seven pints. Or thereabouts. Call it eight pints. Over her first two trimesters she's gonna add forty percent more volume. Little over three pints. Going into her last trimester, she's hauling eleven pints.

More than a fat man.

That much blood, you can stretch that two or three months. One body in the ground and you're above it for another sixty to ninety days.

Well, two bodies in the ground.

What's that worth, that extra forty percent, over a regular person and their seven to ten pints, what's that extra worth?

The blood of a pregnant woman and her baby, what's the price on that?

(*laughter*)

I'm not laughing 'cause I think it's funny. It's just I'm all out of Drāno.

So.

*Just tell it like it happened.* That's what she said. Like talking is a gift I have or something. Well, better talking than writing. You had to make sense of this by reading my chicken scratch you'd be crying not laughing.

So.

And that wasn't a rhetorical question by the way. I know the price. The blood of a pregnant woman goes for about twenty grand. That's the price in dollars anyway.

There's all kinds of prices you can pay for such a thing. Parts of yourself that will never grow back.

But that's the story. And I'm supposed to tell it. Like it happened.

So okay.

So I'm a Vampyre. Spelled with a Y instead of an I. Capitalized like it's a name. Don't ask me, just tradition I guess. Anyway. Vampyre with a Y, that's the real deal. With an I, that's for scaring babies.

I'm the kind that scares everyone.

And when this started, I was a secret. Lived in an apartment, just like you. Well, just like you if you kept a mini-fridge of blood.

When it ended, I was living in a sewer. Downward mobility being a danger to my kind.

Should be a punch line for something: Vampyre in a sewer.

But it's not.

It's my life.

(*laughter*)

Still, it makes me laugh.

So.

This is what happened.

I can feel it, that little extra bit of heat. And smell staleness in the air. Heat and carbon dioxide, a combination that equals life. Something breathing and exhaling, the air filling its lungs, the oxygen being absorbed. Something warm and breathing, you can count on at least one thing about it. It's full of blood.

Ahead of me in the dark, something alive.

Alive for now anyway.

I didn't expect him to be so much trouble to find. When he ran down Freedom Tunnel he was soaked in the cripple's blood; so not like there was much chance I'd lose the scent. I figured to stroll after him, kick some garbage every now and then to let him know I was there, keep him running until he keeled over gasping and wormed his way into some crack in the walls. I figured the hardest part would be deciding if I wanted to let him cut me a little while I reached in to drag him out, or if I wanted to look around for something I could ram down his hiding place a few times until I cracked his head open.

Then he went shit-diving.

I don't know if it was a plan he had, the way he went spastic and cut up the cripple makes me think planning isn't his forte, but when he dropped out of the train tunnel and wallowed in a bank of sewage that had washed up in the storm drain below he put me off the scent.

Went from tracking a guy who smelled like an abattoir to a guy who smelled like a porto-potty. Which pretty much describes the way everything under Manhattan smells.

Got dicey after that. Cagey little fucker realized I wasn't right on his ass, he started to calm down a bit, caught his breath some, stopped panting so much, stopped stumbling so much, started picking spots he could hole up a minute at a time and be quiet. If there'd been any kind of light at all I'd just have started throwing rocks at him until he went down. All I needed was one of those odd reflections you get down here sometimes. Sunlight filters through the grates over the train tunnels, a spear of it finds its way down a sluice, it reflects in some runoff from the sewers and you find a whole section of drain takes on a haze of light. Enough so you might see an idea of your hand if you held it an inch from your eyes. That's you. Me, I'd see a damn sight more than my hand. But even my eyes need *some* light to work with. Something to reflect off the surfaces and show me what they are.

Instead I'm blind. Whether that means it's night up top I couldn't say. Been some time since I've kept track of the hour. Used to be I knew sunup and sundown like my own heartbeat. But after you miss a couple hundred of each you start to lose that sense.

The guy ahead of me is just as blind, but he knows the drains. Been down here I don't know how many years. Since he was a kid most probably. Since someone kicked him loose to make his way on his own and he realized the tunnels might be dark, but they were a better place for not getting fucked with than the streets. In the land of the lost, no one empties a gas can over you and lights a match just to see what happens next. Sure people kill each other, but not for no reason other than you're sleeping in a gutter in their neighborhood. Everyone down here has slept in more than one gutter. They got nothing to prove. When they kill down here it's for something that matters. Stove fuel. A bottle of wine. A dead guy's good boots.

What the guy breathing out carbon dioxide up ahead of me killed the cripple over I can't say. What it was made me take off after him is a little easier to figure.

Figure it was because he did it near the mouth of Freedom Tunnel not far from where the graffiti kids come crawling around to see the work that Amtrak never bothered to paint over when they started running trains through there again. Figure there's no telling if one of those kids might have seen it happen and might be up top right now talking to the cops about murder in the tunnels. Mostly the cops are pretty fucking happy not to do any enforcing down here. Let justice take its own course. But a nasty slashing witnessed by a Columbia fine arts student might encourage them to put together a squad of troopers with helmets and shields to come down here, break up the shanties, club some skulls and drag some asses up top for a grilling and a few days in one of *their* holes.

Not that I'm any too likely to get caught up in a sweep like that, but I have an interest in the moles maintaining something like a stable community. More stable it is down here, the less likely they'll get spooked and spread out. More stable it is, the more moles get drawn in. The more moles, the more camouflage for someone looking to be lost.

And the more to eat.

I'm not fattening up or anything. Far from it. Rarely been leaner have I. But in a population dominated by drunks and junkies, it's generally not too hard to find someone passed out or on the nod who you can tap for a pint in the darkness. Don't get greedy and you can hit a vein just about any time you need one.

So figure that's one reason I took off after the guy. To keep my good thing from getting fucked with. But figure it was probably more about all that blood hitting the wall in a spray. The smell of it was a punch in the face. My eyes and my mouth watered and I was on my feet and running after the guy before I even thought about cops. Before I thought about anything else, I was thinking how nobody was gonna care what I did to this guy. How it was gonna be dark in the tunnels while I ran him down. How good it was gonna be to rip a hole in him and drink until I was so full I was gagging on him. How I wanted a damn drink after all the sipping I'd been doing.

No, I don't know why he killed the cripple. And I don't much care. I just care that I'm blind right now and he knows the drains better than me and he's just there, him and his blood. Question is, did he stop because he hit a dead end, or because he thinks he's got a play he can make.

Cold shit is bumping against my ankles and flowing toward him. There's a loud gurgle and suck a few yards ahead.

My first month down here, I found myself in a drain like this, just trying to map out the new turf, thought I was as deep as it goes, took a step and found out it goes deeper. Dropped straight about eight yards, hit brick and cobbles, a shard of rust snagged the back of my thigh and ripped it knee to ass. Lost enough blood before the wound started to clot that I went spinny-headed. That time I had a flashlight on me. Hadn't been using it because I wanted to learn how to work the dark, but I had it on me. If I hadn't, if it had broken in the fall, I'd maybe never have found my way out.

I don't have a flashlight this time. I go down a suck hole and I'll be gone. Little fucker up there, laying for me, thinking he's got this wired now that we're on his turf, he's got me wanting to make things hard for him. But I got to know where he is first.

I wonder how crazy he is.

And I make a play to find out.

—Hey.

Nothing.

—Let me ask you something.

Still quiet.

—Why'd you go and kill the cripple?

He inhales, like a guy about to say his piece, then lets it out, says nothing.

I keep up my end of the conversation.

—Mean, just because he was a cripple, that doesn't mean you didn't have a reason for killing him. Just 'cause the guy didn't have a lower body, that doesn't mean he didn't do something to deserve it. I knew a guy, blind, blind as a bat blind, couldn't see shit. Know what being blind did for his personality? Nothing. Guy was a prick. A blind prick. A drunk, blind prick. Closing time at this bar I used to work the door, someone had to always walk this blind prick home. When I drew that short straw, I'd walk the fucker to a vacant lot, let him pass out on the ground. He'd come in the next night, be a prick about the deal, tell people what I'd done. Know what they did? They patted me on the back. All of them knew he deserved it. A guy's a cripple, that doesn't mean he's charming.

I hear him licking his lips, just dying to say something. But he doesn't.

I do.

—Maybe not, though. Maybe your cripple was a great guy. Could be you're a crazy asshole who lost his shit and cut up a perfectly good cripple for no reason other than you got tired of listening to his wheels squeaking.

—He stole my fucking girlfriend.

That was really all I need, just the sound of his voice, the echo behind it as it bounced off the drain walls and ceiling, that pretty much pins him down for me. Close enough I can jump over anything between us, a few yards maybe, no worry about going down a suck hole. Once I'm on him there won't be anything at all to worry about.

But my curiosity gets hold of me.

—He stole your girl?

—Yeah. Motherfucker. We've been shacked five months. Fucker, that chair, man's got not just no legs, got no stomach, nothing, fucking pathetic. Sits up on Fifth Ave and just rakes it in. Everyone else going broke, legless motherfucker always has a bottle to wave at the ladies. Asked her, what he's got I don't got. Already know what he ain't got. Got no fucking dick.

—What she say?

I hear his spit hit water.

—Says he got class.

We both think about that for a second. His curiosity gets hold of him.

—Why the fuck do you care? Fuck you run after me? Seen you around, one-eye, never had a beef. Never saw you chum up with the cripple. Why the fuck you chase me down here? Motherfucker, into my drains. Been in the tunnel how long? You know *shit* down here. Come after me. You're fucking the crazy one. Come after me in the drains. Why'd you do that?

I check my footing, make sure there's nothing to slip on under the soles of my boots.

—You got something I want.

He laughs.

—Motherfucker, you got the wrong man, I ain't got shit. All I had was a girlfriend. Cripple got her. Now all I got is a blade. You want to come and get it?

—No, you can keep that, I got my own.

I jump, push off, arms out, leaving my feet as if to make a tackle in a football game, except leading with a fifteen-inch amputation blade I found in the rusted tangle of an old shopping cart at the mouth of an outlet three months ago. I used a river stone to hone away the rust, losing about two millimeters of the blade's width in the process, but after wrapping a quarter of a roll of yellow friction tape around the tang to replace the bone handles that had rotted away, I had a serviceable piece of cutlery that could fend off most trouble just through the act of slipping it from the drop sheath I'd rigged inside my jacket with a section of bicycle inner tube and more tape.

This guy never gets a chance to see it. Not unless the sensation of it coming in under his rib cage and pushing up into his right lung is so distinct that it paints a picture in his mind's eye. Normally I'd jerk it around a little once it's in there, make sure things get settled quick, but we go down hard with me on top and the blade making a new hole for that carbon dioxide to hiss out of and that knocks the blade around more than enough. He's not exactly dead when I pull it out, but near enough not to quibble with me when I poke a hole in his neck and catch the last few strong pulses of blood from his carotid before things become official. After that I have to get a good seal with my lips against his skin and suck pretty hard. When my mouth pulls off, it sounds like the half-clogged drain nearby.

Do I feel bad about it, killing a sad man who just went a little nuts when he lost the only thing he cared about to maybe a sadder case than he was? Yeah, I do feel bad about it. Thinking of where I've been in my life, where I could be right now, the kind of plays I've made over the years that put me down here, I feel very bad about it.

I'm not saying I'm better than this, just that I don't like where I've come to. Even if it is my own fault. I'd been the type to get along and go along a little more, I'd be doing OK.

Not that it matters.

I changed who I am, I'd have to change everything. I changed who I am, I'd never have made it as long as I have. I changed who I am, and likely as not she'd never have looked twice at me.

Thinking about her while I'm drinking this guy's blood in the filthy dark makes the taste go sour in my mouth. Not that I stop. I'm no fool. Eat what you kill.

I finish it, as much as I can take, then roll the corpse toward the sucking sound and feel the current grab him and pull his foot from my hand and he's washed down to a lower place. I find the wall and use it to guide me back around the hole and out the way we came. It's too dark to know how bad I look, how much blood is coating my mouth and cheeks and chin and neck, but I've looked at myself in the mirror before so I have a pretty good idea. When I find some light I'll clean up a little. Not that it'll require a great deal of grooming.

Standards down here being what they are, a man only has to do so much to pass as human.


There's not much to know.

A guy living in the sewers, what do you need to be told that you can't figure out for yourself?

Figure he fucked up somewhere along the way. More than once. Figure he's got enemies. Many. Figure he's got reasons for not just running far away. One reason is, he's got nowhere to go. Never been out of the City. Another reason is, he has certain minimum requirements as far as living conditions.

Anonymity. If not crowds to get lost in, then a place where no one cares who you are or what you've done.

Darkness, he needs. Night is best, but protection from solar UV rays will do. Too many of those and he erupts in a welter of pustules and wet scabs. Seen pictures of guys with severe eczema? Picture that in your mouth and ears and nose and on your eyes. That's what the sun does.

And people, he needs. Not to practice his social graces, but as a food supply. Blunt, but there it is. Not like I'm hiding anything. No food supply, he starves in short order, goes crazy just before he dies, crazy strong and crazy fast and woe betide the motherfuckers in his immediate proximity when it happens.

Sound like something's been left out of the equation?

Yeah.

Figure there's a girl.

Guy living in a sewer. There's got to be a girl in the story somewhere. My story, it's thick with them. Lost girl, rich girl, smart girl, dyke girl, crazy girl, tough girl, pregnant girl. Over the years, I've dealt with all of them. Dead girl. Yeah, her too. But only one matters. My girl. A girl worth sitting in filth for. Waiting. Watching. Feeling the walls of the tunnels for vibrations that will tell you something about what's going on up top.

What the hell is going on up there? Who's bought it? Who's still kicking? How are the cards coming off the deck and where's my play? Confused? Well come late to a tale, you got to expect to have to tread a little water.

Last thing is this, I'm not the way I am because of god or the devil. I'm like this because it's who I am. I'm a bastard. That I happen to be a bastard that got infected with something called the Vyrus that turned me into something called a Vampyre, that's just bad news for a lot of people who happened to cross my path over the years. Not because I'd have left them alone if I wasn't infected, but because being infected makes me a damn sight harder to put down than I'd have been otherwise. Some people, they'll argue against that. They'll tell you there's something mystical about the Vyrus. Some will tell you it's nothing but a bug, a bug that makes us special, makes us dangerous. Some will say it makes us sick, makes us need to stick together, makes us better off if we went public and got help. Some will say that we need a cure. Some hover around the top of the fence and put off making a choice about which yard they'll jump into.

Those people, they're all at war against one another.

My bad.

I'd have kept my mouth shut, it wouldn't be happening. But that girl, I needed to see her, and I needed a distraction to make it happen. Starting a war seemed what the occasion demanded.

Looking back, I maybe made a mistake. Not about starting the war, but listening to the girl. When she said to leave her where she was, I shouldn't have listened. I should have dragged her out. I'd done that, we'd be gone from here already.

So I like to think. In the dark. With nothing else to think about. Sit and brood on what I should have done. What lives saved. Which throats slit.

Even a guy like me, we get one go-round, and regrets come with the ticket.

Just I never had time to entertain them before. And now they're all that's come to the party.

Makes me want to kill.

Chubby Freeze finds me curled in a ball in the shack I took over from Q-line Dave after he went under the tracks of the Hudson Valley Express.

Chubby makes a lot of noise coming up on the shack, which is good. It keeps me from acting rashly and slipping the amputation blade behind his windpipe and pulling it toward me. But it *doesn't* keep me from putting it at his throat while I ask him what the fuck he's doing down here. What *does* keep me from

putting the knife to his throat is the gun his boy Dallas is holding on me.

Probably for the best. Me and Chubby, we've always been
friendly for the most part, I'd hate to kill him without a good reason. Of course, the fact he's found me is a pretty good reason. But
I'd maybe like to know if there's anyone else knows I'm down
here.

If there's killing to be done, I'd just as soon have a complete
list.

—You don't look well, Joe.

Some people, they feel strongly that the obvious must be
stated. Me, I'd take it for granted that some poor son of a bitch
holed up in the tunnels was gonna look like shit and spare the
commentary. Not that it hurts my feelings, just that there's only
so much time in a man's life, so why waste it stating what's clear
to start with.

Chubby squints and purses his lips.

—No, you do not look at all hale.

I point at the grease stains on the trouser cuffs of his three-
thousand-dollar custom-made suit.

—You're gonna need some sprucing up yourself, Chubby.

He fingers the material gathered in pleats at the front of what
passes for a waist on a man that big around.

—I made a point of wearing one of last year's. I generally give
them to a charitable organization when my new wardrobe arrives
from Hong Kong, but I've found it's wise to hold back one or two.
For grubby work.

I nod at Dallas, the pretty boy with the well-defined muscles
and the gun.

—That what I am these days, *grubby work?*

There's more gray in Chubby's afro than when I last saw him. More fat being held in by the five-button vest he sports. More wrinkles around the eyes. It's cold in the tunnels this time of year, our breath puffs out white. Even so, Chubby's top coat is draped over the arm Dallas isn't using to point his gun. The fat man has worked up a sweat coming down here.

He fingers a handkerchief, a plain white one, not the blue and white silk that fans from his breast pocket, matching his tie.

—I'm not certain I could say what kind of work you are these days, Joe. It's been some time since we crossed paths. Some time since anyone has crossed your path. I'd hazard to say that the nature of your work these days is a subject for wild conjecture.

The place is lit by a fluorescent bulb Q-line Dave scavenged from a demo site somewhere up top. It hangs from a hook of coat hanger that's been twisted around the scrap-wood beam that supports the sagging sheets of waterlogged Sheetrock over our heads. Power comes from a daisy chain of extension cords that snake and tangle through the shantics; little more than bare wires wrapped in electrical tape in some places, they disappear into the darkness, running to a source I've never bothered to explore. The head of our Nile down here. There's a dozen blackouts a week from people tripping over cords in the dark. The lifers live in fear of the real thing: some city engineer noticing the drain and cutting the juice.

I wouldn't miss seeing the surroundings, but I don't have much to pass the time other than reading the moldy paperbacks that get passed around. Right now the light is bright enough for me to see that Chubby's eyes aren't just decorated by new wrinkles, they're also cracked with red.

I move for one of the patch pockets on my Ben Davis mechanic's jacket. I took it off a greaser who came down slumming. Clinking along the tracks with a sack of Thunderbird pints, looking for an experience he could impress his friends with. He left in his underwear and a pair of yellow plastic flip-flops someone with a kinder soul than I gave him so he wouldn't shred his feet on the broken glass and ballast lining the tracks. I got the jacket mostly because he was a big guy and it didn't look to fit anyone else. Which is to say that I got the jacket because I'm pretty much the biggest guy down here. I had another jacket, about the only thing I owned that I cared about. I left it topside.

Better not to think about that jacket. Or who's holding it for me. It's a distraction. Something I don't need when Dallas lends a little more emphasis to the way he's pointing that gun at me because he doesn't like me sticking my hand in any pockets he hasn't gone through first.

I put my hand in the pocket anyway.

Dallas wags the barrel back and forth a little, like the thing is shaking its head at me.

I nod my head at him.

—You go ahead and pop one off.

I fill my hand and it comes out of my pocket.

—I'd rather take the bullet than go another second without a smoke.

He flinches when he sees the fluorescent flash off what's in my hand, but give the kid credit, he's not half-cocked, gives himself enough time to see the light's just reflecting off the cellophane on my pouch of Bugler. Truly, I'm grateful he's a touch gun-shy. I want the smoke, sure, but I was just talking big about the bullet being a fair trade.

I pull a paper from the cardboard sheaf tucked inside the pouch and fill it with cheap dry tobacco. Given my choice, I'm a Lucky Strike man, like my father before me, may he and my mom both be suffering in a miserable ditch somewhere. Not that I want to introduce a note of bitterness to the story. In any case, store-bought smokes come dear, and I can't make a pack last more than an evening. I can tease out a pouch of Bugler for a couple days. If anything might drive me to the surface and into the eye of the shit storm up there, it's the taste of a Lucky.

I lick the strip of glue at the top of the paper, roll it up, strike a match from a pack with an advertisement for a phone sex line on the cover, and get the thing going.

Chubby pats some more sweat from the back of his neck.

I tear the spent match from the book and flick it into a corner littered with a couple thousand of them.

—Tell me, Chubby, who is it up there doing all this conjecturing about me?

He refolds his handkerchief and slips it into his pocket, smoothing the front to be sure no bulge shows to ruin the hang of the material. Not that is really hangs on him. Clings, more like.

—I'm not one to name names, Joe.

—Unless it's a name you'd like to see dealt with.

He takes a moment to consider his manicure.

—I've never been one for spite or rage. Any dealings I've had with you have concerned business. And I don't recall either of us ever expressing any squeamishness about how matters were closed. Not I when I asked for details. Not you when you've been paid.

I'm still sitting on the ground, a chunk of broken concrete digging into the back of my thigh. I reach under my leg to move it.

Dallas, a little more relaxed after the tobacco incident, doesn't wave his gun around this time. Which makes me feel better about my chances when I whip the chunk of concrete at his head. It doesn't bounce off his skull, more like it skips off it when his head is snapped back. Either way, he drops the gun without shooting me, and he drops himself immediately after. I don't bother to go for the gun. Dallas won't be making a move for it anytime soon. And if Chubby decides to make a play, I trust I can reach over and scoop it up a full minute before he manages to bend his knees to stoop.

I blow some smoke his way.

—Sorry, Chubby, I know he's your boy and all. Just the gun was a distraction.

I grind out the butt end of my cigarette, get out the pouch and start rolling a fresh one.

—So about those people you'd hate to name, what were those names again?

He clears his throat, shakes his head.

—He was only doing as I instructed him to do, Joe.

—You should have known better.

He nods.

—Yes. Yes, I suppose that is true.

I light up.

—Never had guns between you and me before, Chubby.

He looks around the trash and debris in the shack for something he might sit on, but it's all half-rotted, so he stays on his own two feet.

—That's also true. But then you were always a somewhat known quantity. As I said before, your actions and intents are mired in uncertainty now. And these are dangerous times. I didn't know what I might expect from you, having found you in circumstances such as these.

He waves his fingers at the place.

—A man could come to anything down here.

I scratch the side of my nose with a broken thumbnail rimmed with someone else's dry blood.

—How'd you find me, Chubby?

He shakes his head.

—Joe.

—I need to know how you found me.

The shake travels from his head, his cheeks tremor, the roll of fat at the collar of his shirt, his whole body begins to wobble.
—Joe. If you could.
I push myself into a squat.
—Chubby?
Tears are starting from the red eyes, filling the wrinkles, washing down to his chins.
—I think I need.
I get to my feet and cross the space between us and catch his arm before his legs collapse.

Recently fed, I'm strong, I can break bones, shatter teeth; called upon, I could tear a healthy man's leg from his body. But still I have to strain to keep from dropping Chubby when he goes limp. I manage to ease him to the ground, half-sprawled on his side, sobbing.
—I need to sit. I need to sit. I'm sorry about the gun, Joe. I. Oh, Joe.

I pick up Dallas's gun, in case this is a play to get his hands on it. But I know it's not. Just that the gun makes me feel better.

Chubby rolls onto his front and pushes his face into the dirt and cries louder.

I walk back and forth a few times, smoke. Keep touching the gun.

Chubby wears out after a while, gives a heave, and rolls to his back. I reach out and he takes my hand and I pull him forward as he scoots, then he leans his back against the four-by-four at the middle of the shack. It groans, some hunks of plaster drop, the whole structure lists an inch or two to the left, and it settles.

Sitting strains his trousers at the waist. Unable to get a hand in his pocket, he pulls out the blue and white handkerchief.
—She's gone, Joe.
I grind the cherry of my cigarette between my fingers.

—Who's gone, Chubby?

He wipes snot from his upper lip where it's turned the dirt to mud.

—My girl, Joe. My daughter, Joe. My little girl. I can't find her.

Sitting there in the ruined suit he wore here for grubby work, wiping at the dirt that's given him a tear-streaked Kabuki face.

Saying it over and over, about his daughter.

Like it should mean something to me.


I maybe owe Chubby.

Was a time he did me a solid when I found myself on the wrong turf. Vouched for me. Put his name behind mine. Backed me when DJ Grave Digga, president of the Hood, would just as soon cut my windpipe out and blow a tune on it while I bleed all over him.

I did him back for it, some errands that qualified as grubby. Could be we're all square.

Then again, could be, you put a hard eye on those books and they show an outstanding balance still due.

I maybe owe the man.

Still, I wanted to, I could just rip that page right out from the book. I have the blade, I have the gun. Where I come from, either one closes all accounts.

Better yet, neither one of these guys is infected. Neither one carries the Vyrus. They know enough to do a little business with us, but they're both clean. Truss them up, find some place cool to stash them, they could last weeks. Fit as Dallas is, fat as Chubby is, they'd last. I could be better fed than I've been the whole last year.

I think about it.

But it's just the tunnels talking to me.

It's not me. Not really.

That's Chubby Freeze there in the dirt. Crying about his lost daughter. Looking at me like I can help.

And I know there's no question of how things lie between us. I ain't gonna kill the man.

I look up at the crumbling ceiling. Think about the thousands of tons of stone and concrete hanging overhead. The City above. I think about the war I started up there. What would be waiting for me if I went up top, started poking around, showed my face.

Chubby is watching me, waiting.

I look at the cigarette between my fingers.

—I can't help you, Chubby.

He spits into the dirty handkerchief and rubs it across his forehead, leaving a smear.

—Yes. Well. To be expected.

I shrug.

—In your line, a missing girl, you know plenty of people for something like that.

He raises his eyebrows, exhales, long and tired.

—Surely. The pornography business is rife with young ladies disappearing or wishing to be disappeared.

—You've had to find them before.

—Yes.

—You know people.

—Yes.

—You know everyone, Chubby.

A slight smile, the first since he came in from the dark.

—Yes, I do. And yet. And yet.

He waves the handkerchief at the decaying interior of the shanty.

—Here I am.

He nods at Dallas, still inert other than deep breathing.

—With my favorite young man.

He touches the handkerchief to each corner of his mouth, first one, then the other.

—Bearding the wounded lion in his den.

He gives the handkerchief a shake and a little flip and tucks it back in his breast pocket, fanning it perfectly, filthy or not.

—Why, I wonder, would I do such a thing? Take such a risk. When I could simply hire the detective of my choice.

I think about life with a sky overhead. Governed by the sun. The way we perform up there, shadow-puppet lives. Hiding what we really are. Hiding it from the world, from ourselves. Down here I'm almost myself. Almost my nature. Almost the predator the Vyrus would have me be. It comes easy. What's up there always came hard. Even before I was infected.

This man, what he's lost. Trying to find the lure that will tease me to the surface. Into the air. Where I might drown.

I clear my throat, dry as dust.

—I get it, Chubby. But it doesn't change things. She's found some trouble on my side of the street, gone lost with the infected, I can't help that. It's bad news for her, but it's got nothing to do with me. Hell, I didn't even know you had a daughter.

He dips a hand inside his jacket, draws out a photograph pinched between his index and middle fingers.

—Would you like to see her?

I raise a hand.

—It won't change anything.

He offers the photo.

—I have a father's vanity.

I don't take the bait.

He gives it a little shake, dancing the line in front of my face.

So I look, to get it over with, to say *no* one last time, to make him leave, to be alone again.

He raises his shoulders.

—I won't say I was shocked, a man in my line, as you say. I certainly know all there is to know about the birds and the bees. Not exactly disappointed either. As little time as I've spent with the girl, I can't afford to disapprove of her choices, not if I want to have any kind of relationship with her. But still, a father has feelings about these things. At first I thought she'd come to me for the obvious reason. If that had been the case, I could have solved her problem in any number of ways. But she didn't consider it a problem at all. The young today are so very different than we were, eh, Joe?

I'm still looking at the picture. Young, very young and pretty girl, Chubby's beautiful gold eyes, otherwise she must take after her mother. Slender limbs and face, but round in the middle. Say about seven months round.

Chubby nods.

—It makes a difference, Joe?

I don't say anything.

He nods again.

—Evie said it would make all the difference to you.


Chubby knows everyone.

He knows a one-armed barber named Percy. Percy's got a bad case of being a Vampyre. Runs with the Hood. One of Grave Digga's people. How most people know him. But he runs sideways too, like most people deep in this life, runs connected in ways that can't be seen.

Percy is Enclave.

He doesn't hole up with the rest of them in that warehouse they keep downtown. Starving themselves, letting themselves be warped by the hunger of the Vyrus, striving for some kind of

transmutation no one but them understands. Even so, he's Enclave going way back. Way I gather, some years back when the
Hood was coming together under the original man, Luther X,
Percy got inspired. Felt the color of his skin more than the con-
tent of his blood. Left Enclave turf, split uptown. But like a man
who left the church to fight a war on foreign soil for reasons that
have nothing to do with his god, he can't get the stink of religion
off himself. Once Enclave, always Enclave. And he knows some
things about what goes on with them, what goes down in their
warehouse.

I know a little about what goes on in that place, myself.

I know a little about some of the people in that place.

Evie.

Girl with my jacket. Which is only right. She gave it to me.


Chubby's tied both his handkerchiefs together so he can put
them around Dallas's head. Dallas himself is too fuzzy to get his
fingers to tie the knot themselves. But not so fuzzy that he
doesn't remember who threw the concrete at him and put a gash
in his forehead that is most definitely going to fiddle with his
prettiness. He's sitting on the ground, trying to throw me nasty
looks, but his eyes keep going crossways, ruining the effect.

Chubby stands behind him, having gotten to his feet with just
a little help, arranging the makeshift bandage so that it doesn't
pinch the boy's ears.

—Her mother was a contract player from several years ago.
When we still worked in VHS. The dark ages. Before instant grat-
ification became imperative. To think porno was once a commu-
nal event. Stag parties. Adult theaters. Do you remember Times
Square, Joe? Forty-second Street? The Deuce?

I remember the Deuce. The block of Forty-second between

Seventh and Eighth. Wall-to-wall peeps, skin shops, XXX marquees. I remember being thirteen, things so loose back then I didn't even have to pretend I was sneaking in, just put my money on the counter. Setting up shop in the back row. Hand jobs, five bucks a pop. Business overhead was a jar of Vaseline and a pack of Handi Wipes. Got myself through a whole summer of squatting that way. Somewhere in there was a bust, passed back to Child Services, another foster home. Back out the door after a few weeks. Now the Deuce is franchised end to end. I haven't been there in years, it's off my turf, but I've seen the pictures.

I'm not nostalgic. It's no better or worse than it was. Different whores, different johns. Some people get off on fucking, some get off on fast food. People can ruin themselves however they want, it's not my business.

But it is Chubby's.

He spreads his arms.

—Adult film was for the aficionados in those days. Men who made an effort to seek it out. Or it was a right of passage. Boys with their collars turned up, trying to find out what their teachers were talking about in sex ed class. Looking to glimpse some tittie. Ass. A *beaver* shot. And getting so much more than they had imagined.

He lowers his arms.

—Now, entirely amateur. Not only do they all know what a rim job is by the time they're eleven, but they're considered uptight if they've not webcammed themselves giving and receiving one and posted it to their Facebook page.

I'm sifting gravel through my fingers, thinking about buried things, against my will.

—You were talking about your girl, Chubby. And how you found me.

He pats Dallas's shoulder and moves away from him.

—I was, I was. Just illustrating a point about her mother. That, while she postdated the era of celluloid, she was nonetheless of a more civilized generation. And she raised our daughter well. My little girl is not one to be involved in sordid matters. Her predicament is an affair of the heart.

A cracked jewel of green bottle glass lies in my palm. Same color green as a bottle of Cutty Sark. I think about a drink.

—You want to tell me your girl's no slut, just say so. You're getting wordy in your old age, Chubby.

He raises his eyebrows.

—Joe, the way your boot bends when you squat, I'd say you've lost a toe. Your knee sounds like broken crockery when you walk. You have one eye.

—Your point?

He lowers his eyebrows.

—You ain't the motherfucker to be talkin' as to how a man is or isn't agin' his best.

I smile.

—Ah, there's the Chubby Freeze I know.

He snorts and adjusts the knot of his tie.

—Well, bid him farewell. That is the only appearance he will be making in this concern.

I drop the bit of glass.

—How you found me. That's my concern.

—Yes.

He reaches inside his jacket and takes out a leather humidor.

—While not of loose morals, my girl is adventurous. Romantic. Overly so. Not weepy about it, but a touch light-headed in her desire for something . . . poetic. And a child of her generation, she is also wired. She met a boy online; having chatted with him at length, she was not the type to balk at meeting him in person. In a public place, of course. She is no fool. And while that may not be the prologue one would expect for even the most modern interpretation of *Romeo and Juliet,* she did fall in love with him. The courtship, I gather, was brief. As is typical these days.

He slips the top from the humidor, pulling it loose with a slight pop.

—The boy.

He takes the end of one of the cigars between his fingers and draws it free.

—Was not.

He studies the length of the cigar, inspecting it for tears.

—He was not.

Satisfied with the quality of the cigar, he offers the business end to Dallas, who bares his perfect teeth and nips away a tapered quarter inch.

Chubby grunts, thumbs a bit of leaf from the end of the cigar.

—The boy was not . . . typical.

He offers me the humidor.

—I don't suppose?

I shake my head and roll another cigarette.

—Not my thing.

He nods, caps the humidor and puts it back inside his jacket, his hand coming out with a silver lighter roughly the size and shape of a .12 gauge shell.

—You're missing out on a fine smoke.

I light my own.

—You were telling me the boy was infected.

He ignites the lighter, holds the end of the intense blue flame just below the end of the cigar and gives a few puffs, rotating the cigar to bring it evenly to life.

—Yes. That was the point I was driving at.

—And she found out.

He releases the button on the side of the lighter with a snap, the flame dies, and he wraps it in a fist.

—Yes, she did.

—And she dug it.

He takes the cigar from between his lips and lets loose a cloud.

—Against all better judgment, yes she did.

I stand up, brushing dirt from my backside, not that it makes me look any cleaner.

—A girl would have to be pretty adaptable to take something like that at point-blank and roll with it. I mean, tell a girl you're a Vampyre, out of the blue, that's generally an invitation to be considered a nut job. Most girls, they exit laughing or screaming. Depending on the type.

He doesn't say anything.

I do.

—Unless she had some idea that things like that are real. She have some idea that things like that are real, Chubby?

He's studying the cigar again.

—It is possible, that in an effort to entertain and impress her, that I may have told her one story too many. With too great a level of credibility.

He looks up from the cigar.

—Fathers, whether they admit it or not, do so want to be thought cool by their children. And vampires have quite the pop culture caché. Forbidden fruit of every shape and hue. I was able to suggest, without telling her more than the basics, that there might be more to the myth than capes and fangs or dewy teenage boys.

I start poking in some corners of the shanty, looking for odds and ends I've tucked here and there.

—Out of curiosity, you happen to know what kind of site they met on?

He makes a gesture with the cigar, sketching a vague notion in smoke.

—Something to do with *damned* or *insatiable thirst* or *eternal languor* or something. Dot com.

I find one of the things I'm looking for. Two small steel rings attached to each other by twenty-eight inches of braided steel wire. This I got from a tunnel camper. Urban explorer type. What he expected to use a wire saw for down here I can't say. Maybe it was part of his normal camping kit. Maybe he thought he'd use it to saw his own leg off if it got pinned under something. Anyway, he made out OK. Never knew what knocked him on the head. Most likely never missed the pint I took from his veins. He was too well equipped and carried too much ID for me to empty him. Probably had a whole crew who knew he was going spelunking in the tunnels. Missing a day too long, search parties would have started. But the saw looked useful, so I pocketed it. Figured he be happy he woke up without having fallen and broken his neck. Wouldn't notice one item gone.

I haven't had occasion to use it yet, but the strangest things come in handy in my line.

I put the wire saw in my pocket.

—*Damnedinsatiablethirsteternallanguor.* Dot com. So fair to say she was looking for something specific.

He looks at the floor.

—Fair to say, yes, fair to say.

—And the boy. One of those infecteds likes to cruise Goth and vampire sites looking for a Lucy? He out trolling for someone he could tap for easy pints?

Chubby looks up.

—No. No. I don't think so at all. I think, forgive me the sentimentality, I think the boy was looking for someone to talk to. He struck me as, if anything, annoyingly earnest. I think, perish the thought, that he was lonely. With, perhaps, some tendency to overplay the roll of doomed and undead, he was certainly feeling genuinely isolated. Confused. Desperate, I would say, for something resembling normalcy. I am not at all unacquainted with the type. My business draws them like flies. Young men and women, out of their depths, looking for something they can cling to. It has long been one of the hallmarks of my professionalism that I aggressively vet my applicants and accept only those who I trust to be most willing, able, and adaptive to the rigors of a life in porno.

It's not actually bullshit. Everyone knows Chubby is a cut above pornmeister. No junkies. No self-mutilators. No bipolars. No chicken. He runs a clean shop. Hi-tone freaks who like to fuck on camera, and coldhearted pros. And he takes care of his people. Full-time staff and freelancers. Chubby doesn't leave anyone to swing in the cold if a bust comes down. Or any kind of stalker trouble. I ran security on his studio more than once. I won't lie and say it was a happy place, but I never found anyone shooting up to get loose for an anal gang bang, or being slapped around because they didn't want to do a face fuck.

All in all, Chubby's a gentleman scumbag.

I find the other item I was looking for. A one-foot length of bicycle inner tube packed tight with sand, stitched shut at both ends with heavy thread. Lighter than you expect when you heft it, it'll drop just about anyone when you lay it across the back of their skull. It goes in the pocket opposite the wire saw.

—Sure then, you know a lost soul when you see one. The boy was a helpless kitten looking for acceptance in a cold world. So why'd he take your daughter somewhere you can't find?

He shakes his head.

—It's not me they ran from, Joe. The boy.

He brings the cigar to his lips, realizes it's gone out and lowers it.

—The boy was pledged to the Coalition.

I'm looking at the gun I took from Dallas, checking to see if it's anything I can rely on. I look up from it.

—Shit.

Chubby nods.

—He crossed onto Society turf to meet my daughter. And stayed.

—Shit.

He takes a step my way.

—Things up there. Joe. In the past, if I wanted to know anything about what was happening, it took an effort. Subtlety. One had to mind one's Ps and one's Qs. Simple awareness of the Vyrus was a threat. Now. It's . . . hectic. Word of bizarre goings-on reach my ears unbidden. There are rumors. Not among the straight citizens, not yet. But at the borders and fringes. Things are being said. In barrooms, massage parlors, shooting galleries, after-hours clubs, street corners, and, I'd dare say, in police precinct rack rooms when the bottle is being passed about. Things are being seen. Disbelieved most often, but they are seen. And reported on. Blogs. The tabloids even. *Serial killings unlike anything since Jack the Ripper.* That is the tone. There is a palpable tension on the street. Anyone who lives close to the edge of things feels as if something is coming. The straights itch. A second shoe is expected. An ill wind. Metaphors of every kind. In an atmosphere such as that, it takes very little for tempers to flare.

The gun is OK. It's an automatic. It's black. The barrel has a hole at the end big enough for something serious to come out of it. The clip is loaded. And I can't find *Made in China* stamped on it anywhere. It'll do what it's supposed to.

I stick it in my belt at the small of my back and pull the jacket down over it.

—What happened, Chubby? Straight.

—What happened.

He snaps the cigar in two pieces and lets them drop from his fingers.

—Terry Bird accepted the boy into the Society. He cannot compete with the Coalition in terms of troops and arms, but he is an effective propagandist. Young man crosses battle lines for love, to the only place where such love will be accepted. Society turf. Infected and uninfected.

I grunt.

I can hear Terry pitching it in my head. *It's, you know, Joe, it's exactly what we've been talking about. A story of acceptance. This is the kind of thing, this is a uniting kind of thing.* Or some shit like that. Playing with his John Lennon specs and his ponytail, selling his version of the revolution. Years of old blood dripping from his hands the whole time. A show I've seen before.

Chubby places the toe of one of his formerly well-shined shoes on half the broken cigar and grinds it into the dirt.

—It raised Dexter Predo's ire, having one of his own raised up as a Society poster child. And then things became rather more complicated.

He places his hands on either side of his belly.

—She started to show. Needless to say, the idea of this baby has generated passionate debate. Bird seems to think it could be the thin edge that would allow him to take the Vyrus public. Predo sees the opposite. Interrace breeding has always been a taboo that takes many blows to shatter. A certain air of imminent danger crept into the debate. It appeared they might become targets for kidnapping or assassination.

He drops his hands from his belly.

—And they disappeared.

—And you called Percy.

—Someone I care deeply about is missing in the midst of Vampyre warfare. There is only one person I want looking for her.

And that person has dropped from sight. So, yes, I called Percy.
He knows people. And he is an old friend. I was born and raised
in Harlem. When I was a small boy, before they went underground, the Hood were our Black Panthers.
—And he told you about Evie.
—He suggested there was a young woman, Enclave, who might
have a line on you.

I shake my head.
—You went to the warehouse?

He takes a step back.
—Oh no. I am trying to find my daughter. Being eviscerated
would not advance the cause. Percy spoke to the lady. And she
came to see me.

Does my heart skip a beat? I can't say. I don't count all of them.
But it seems so.
—You saw her?

He nods.

I don't want to ask. I don't want to ask. I don't want to ask.

But I do.
—How'd she look?

He casts his eyes to the ceiling.
—She looked, Joe, both perilous and beautiful.

He brings his eyes to mine.
—As I imagine death must look.


Evie knows me. If anybody does. Possible she'd rather she didn't,
but there it is. Some things, by the time we know they're bad for
us, we're already hooked.

She gave Chubby the bead on where he might find me. Hard
to say how she knew for sure where that was, but figure she
started with the idea that I'd be underfoot and went from there.

However she sussed it, Chubby took the lead and poked. All the former street kids he has passing through his doors, he was able to put some feelers out. He knows what kind of setup a guy like me would need down here. And there's only so many places like Freedom Tunnel. Asked some questions of some of the inhabitants who travel up top, got a description of some of the newer faces on the scene, and hit on mine.

Big guy, limp, attitude, eyepatch.

I keep to myself, but it's not like I'm invisible.

And here we are.

The gun butt is poking me a little so I shift it.

—She say anything?

Chubby is holding a hand out to Dallas, letting the young man pull himself unsteadily to his feet.

—She said you would take an interest.

—Not what I mean.

He lays his palm alongside Dallas's cheek.

—I'm sorry, my dear, I should not have involved you in this.

Dallas gives me a look and touches the bandage on his forehead.

Chubby winks.

—Don't be concerned about that. A small scar, a slight blemish on your great beauty, it will only highlight perfection. And it wouldn't hurt to add a little of the rough stuff to your resume, would it?

Dallas juts his chin, frowns at me, turns and walks out the door.

Chubby shrugs.

—Temperamental. Like all talent.

—What else did she say?

He shoots his French cuffs, fiddles with the links a bit.

—She said I should tell you she wants you to help find them.

The gun still isn't right. I move it again.

—She thinks they're important? The baby and all that?

He licks his lips, pushes out the lower, sucks it back into his mouth, and bites it.

—She said they're kids and they need help.

I stop messing with the gun.

—I want to see her.

He looks at the floor.

—She says no.

I watch him.

—There something you're neglecting to tell me, Chubby?

He shakes his head.

I step close.

—Is she in trouble?

He shakes his head.

I step closer.

—Only if there's something you're leaving out, and I dig to it later, I might be upset if it turns out to be important.

He looks up from the floor.

—She said to tell you to *crawl out of your fucking cave and do something, you son of a bitch.* She says find them. She says maybe then she'll see you.

I nod, adjust the gun one last time.

—What do you got for me?

He sticks his hand inside his jacket and comes out with an envelope.

—Money. Their names.

I take the envelope and look at the scrap of paper inside.

Ben Forest.

Delilah Cooper.

—Your real last name Cooper?

He adjusts the knot in his tie.

—My name is Freeze. As everyone knows.

I look at Mr. Chubby Freeze.

—Any idea where they'd run to with the heat on?

—Having failed to find safety in the Society, it would be natural for the children to seek it within a racially familiar community. The Hood.

I slap the envelope into my palm.

—There a reason Percy isn't dealing with it himself?

—He is occupied with Hood politics. And since telling me how I might track you down, he has stopped answering calls.

—So the kids might already be on Hood turf?

He shrugs.

I shake my head.

—Not where I'm most welcome.

—From what I gather, Joe, you no longer have any turf at all. In any case, if that's where they are, you'll not have far to go.

I stick the envelope in the pocket with the cosh full of sand.

—Walking under Harlem is one thing. Walking on top of Harlem is another. Grave Digga may still have issues with me.

Chubby makes for the door.

—Who does not, Joe? Who does not.

Can't argue that, so I follow him out.

Find the kids and maybe she'll see me.

First thing I've had worth dying for in a long time.


I don't have any goodbyes to say. Nothing to keep me from following Chubby and Dallas up the tracks toward the north entrance to Freedom Tunnel. The locals give me the same wide berth they always have. I took care of some trouble once or twice down here, but they won't be sad to see me go. Couple days after I'm out, they'll figure Q-line's shack is vacant again and someone will move in and start renovating. Bring in a new color dirt or something.

Neither Chubby or his boy are doing too well with the rail ties and rocks in the darkness. Chubs isn't built for it, and Dallas is still a little sloppy on his feet after the concrete to the head. Still, I'm not in a hurry. I dawdle behind, letting the flashlights they brought show the way. Now we're on the tracks, I can see it's night up top. The vent shafts are blue-black, moonlight washed out by what the city is shining up there itself. Come late morning, bright columns will cut the dust. You can see the edges of them, sharp and clear. See the line exactly where you'd cross into that light and start to fester.

One of the flashlight beams picks out some letters on the wall: OBSOLETE MACHINE. Further, the American Way mural. A Dick Tracy figure pushing an armed man out of frame, shouting, *Drop the gun, mole!* The cover from *Dark Side of the Moon,* captioned: *You shout and no one seems to hear.* A Unibomber portrait. Always one of my favorites.

I smoke and kick some rocks. I'd say I was thinking about Evie, but that would be redundant. She's my white noise. Always there, crackling static in my brain. Inescapable. Mostly you tune it out. The second you focus on it, it drowns out everything else. This occasion, it drowns out the one guy down here I should maybe say goodbye to. Swallows up the thought of him right until Chubby pauses to loosen his tie.

—Is it getting hotter down here, Joe?

I feel it then. Should have felt it before the fat man, but I feel it.

Heat and carbon dioxide reveal life, and the thing panting in the darkness beyond the reach of the flashlight beams is screaming in this silent language that it is fucking well alive.

Or about to die.

Close at the edge of both.

I freeze.

—Chubs, you and your boy go on ahead.

He turns to look at me, the beam of his light rippling over rocks.

—Speed, Joe, is of the essence.

I'm looking at the darkness, wondering if it will explode.

—Pace you two are making, I should be able to catch you up.

—I'd not like to lose track of you after just finding you.

I take a step into the heat and the darkness.

—Chubby, go fuck off up the tunnel. Now.

No one ever accused Chubby Freeze of being a stupid man. He catches my drift, spares further comment, takes Dallas's hand and fucks off up the tunnel at a much better clip than they'd been making before.

I keep my hand away from the gun. I don't have any weapons to deal with this. Besides, I don't think he means to kill me. A pretty big assumption when dealing with the mad, but all I can go on here is past experience. He's never killed me yet.

There's a flutter in the air, it gets hotter, a white blur, and he's in front of me.

—Buddy, hey, buddy, leaving somewhere, buddy?

He's dispensed with clothes since the last time I saw him. Can't say why that is. Could be he finally realized that wearing whites down here was a losing proposition. Could be he finally got so skinny there just wasn't anything he could put on that wouldn't slip right off. That last time, all he had on was a loin-cloth and some dirty white rags wrapped around his limbs like bandages. Could also be that he's white enough now in his own skin not to need to wear any kind of uniform.

Subway tile white. Glossy porcelain with a thin layer of soot.

*Emaciated* doesn't do him justice anymore. I can see the fibers of his muscle under his skin. His circulatory system so vivid, it looks like a long branching tattoo laced over his entire body.

He's at the limit.

What the Enclave are after as they starve themselves, he's at the frontier.

I saw the guy who went furthest. I scooped him off the street when he walked into the daylight believing he had been absorbed by the Vyrus, believing that would make him something the sun didn't want to kill. He was wrong. But even he, even Daniel hadn't gone this far.

The man in front of me shimmers. Like when I was a kid and I'd lie down on the blacktop in summer and watch the air wiggle above it at the end of the playground. He shimmers like that.

Part it's the Vyrus, fighting itself and him. Fighting to tear him apart from hunger for blood, and to keep him together so it won't die with him. Driving him to kill someone and drink their damn blood. And part it's the heat of that fight.

He's what's behind the *missing* poster that describes how an MTA worker disappeared in the tunnels. He's that ghost you see flicker outside the scratched Plexi windows as you rocket down the A express, the one you don't see clear at all, but still it crawls into your nightmares. He's what eats the alligators in the sewers. This fucker, he's the boogeyman.

He scratches himself and hitches a shoulder at me.

—Roll me one of them, will ya, buddy.

I roll him a smoke.

—Keeping an eye on me are you?

He laughs. Sounds like a cat coughing up a hair ball.

—An eye on you. Buddy, no, no buddy. Just I heard you were leaving is all, buddy, an I thought I'd come send ya off is what.

I hand him the cigarette, half-expecting the paper to ignite when he takes it, but it doesn't.

—Must have gotten advance word. Just found out myself.

I snap a match and he flinches at the light before dipping his face into it to puff the cigarette alive.

—Don't need advance word. Got ears, don't I. Hear it all down here. Want to or not, I hear it all. Hey.

He cocks an ear, bit of gnarled skin on the side of his head that looks kind of like an ear anyway, hand cupped to it.

—Hear that, buddy? Course you don't. I do. I hear down at West Fourth, I hear a platform announcement that the uptown F is running on the downtown track. I hear over at One Eighty-one, I hear a couple rats fighting over a pork rind someone dropped on the track. Hey, and, buddy, hey, Canal Street, I hear a guy, he's got his hand in a woman's back, about to push her in front of a train.

He takes a drag and the cigarette is consumed in one long crackle.

—I hear everything down here, buddy.

I start rolling him another smoke.

—You hear anything up top?

He spits dry, no moisture left to him.

—I hear up top, buddy. I hear an asshole parade marching in the alleys is what I hear. Buddy, I hear wolves what were meant to be, dressing in sheep's clothes, baa-baa-baa.

He takes the new cigarette. He doesn't have lips anymore, just a hole slashed in the hide sucked back onto his skull.

—Buddy, I told you once, I told you a hundred, I told you we don't belong up there. Walking their walk, talking their lingo, living their rules.

He cat-coughs again.

—Know what's funniest in it, buddy?

I spark another match and he lights up.

—No. Tell me what's funniest. I could use a laugh.

A tremor rattles through his bones, his body blurs for a moment, then he resolves again.

—What's funniest is now they're fighting a war for the right. That's what's got me up late slapping my knee, buddy. Idea of all them, them and their values, killing each other over which color sheep they're gonna dress as. What kind of prey they want to pretend to be for the privilege of living in the flock.

He takes a drag, only sucks down half of it this time.

—Should be ripping their skins off, howling, running pack mad, buddy. Just for fun.

I light my own smoke.

—Old man, got to tell you, you're getting a little weird being down deep all by yourself.

That laugh.

—Buddy, I'm the real thing. Or close to it. I'm just about the end of the road.

He's been squatting, knees up by his ear, elbows out, looks like a spider someone sprayed with the wrong chemicals. Now he rises, spider morphing into a skeleton, assembling itself from its own jumbled bones.

—Want to see the future, buddy, look into my eyes.

I'm game. But there's nothing to see. They've gone black. Blacker than the deepest tunnels below our feet. Light sucks into his eyes. Black like I've seen only once before. I look in there, and something rises toward the surface.

A cold lance cuts through the heat of him.

I step back, cigarette dropping from my fingers as my hand goes to the gun.

—Right, buddy, pull the piece. That'll help ya.

He smokes the second half of his butt and exhales.

—We all got it inside, buddy. Waiting to come out. Just it needs to be nurtured some.

I take another step back.

—It's dark. I didn't see anything. You're crazy.

He raises the notched bone of his finger.

—Two of those three is true, buddy. Pretty good average, two out of three. But the one that's a lie, it's a doozy.

My hand is still on the gun. Just because it likes being there.

—You're crazy. You don't know what you're talking about. I don't even know what you're thinking.

He looks up at the vents.

—Me buddy? I'm thinking about what I always think about. Daylight.

—Then you're thinking about dying.

He looks back at me.

—Too late for that.

He takes a step toward me.

—Hey, buddy, know why we burn? Know why we get so damn hot when we finally embrace the Vyrus?

I take a step away.

He comes closer.

—It's 'cause of what's growing inside. Buddy, it's so cold, it just drives the heat out of you. Tell you, it's like winter in my bowels.

I'm leaving, I'm walking backward, some lesson about never turning your back on the mad, but I'm leaving.

—There's nothing inside of you except crazy. Nothing growing except your own stupid death.

He's still following, shimmering at every step.

—You got one too. Stick around, let it come out. It's what we're for. To become what's real, buddy.

I'm not walking backward anymore, I'm just going, I'm just leaving.

—It's not in me, old man. I'm infected, not possessed. I'm diseased, but I'm me.

Cat coughs behind me.

—Ain't that what I'm saying, buddy? Ain't that the joke of it? It is you. What we are, it's what we are inside. Just you have to work at it to make it come out.

I'm down the tracks now, looking at the rails to where they fade into darkness ahead of me, meeting at a point I can't see yet.

He's crazy. That wasn't a lie.

It's dark down here. That wasn't a lie.

And I didn't see anything when I looked in his eyes.

Enclave are mad. None madder. And they kicked him out for going apeshit and killing a bunch of his brothers and sisters. The maddest of the mad. What he says carries no weight. Mad and starving and alone in the dark, he's making up stories to scare himself. The boogeyman, making up ghosts to haunt himself.

Wraiths.

If I saw something once that I can't explain, that doesn't make them real. And if a trick of the dark gave me a chill, that doesn't make them real. And if a madman says what's at the core of us all is a senseless, flapping quiver of black shade, that's just one more reason not to believe.

The only killer I'm carrying around is the one I was born with.

I didn't see anything when I looked in his eyes. I didn't.

But I see plenty as I run down the tracks.

That memory, it doesn't sit on top waiting to be picked up and put down. It's at the bottom. Something digs it up from down there, everything else gets knocked over and spilled about.

Think of the Wraith, think of Amanda Horde and her crazy parents.

The original lost girl. Her mom hiring me to find her. Apeshit daddy Doctor Horde and his biotech millions and his plan to infect people with a fucking zombie bacteria that only he can cure. How I got trailed around on that gig. Something left no trace, left an absence behind itself. Enclave called it a Wraith, I called it bullshit. How I got kicked and stabbed and shot on the gig, starved when the thing with no trace stole my blood bank. Running dry in a basement, I died. Yeah, the real thing. And the Vyrus raised me up. Said, *Not fucking yet!* Threw all it had left into me, sent me buzz-sawing through dangerous men. But I took too much. The mad doctor had me. Dying the second time in minutes.

And the Wraith.

Black fell over that room and when it lifted, I'm there with a frozen corpse in my hands.

Still pissing myself years later.

Remember that, more comes tumbling.

The Count. Loser rich boy Vampyre causing trouble. Dealing anathema; infected blood getting Vampyres high. Exposing the community. Me taking a job with Terry and the Society for the privilege of putting a proper beating on that punk.

Evie getting sick. HIV sick. AIDS sick. Never knowing what I was. Me never copping to the fact. Never knowing if my blood would kill her or cure her.

Little Amanda coming back around, launching her own crusade. Clan Cure, all comers welcome. Feed the hungry, while the little super genius tries to save them all.

Mad as her father. Twice as smart. Drunk as her mother. Twice as beautiful.

Things heating up with the Coalition.

Me in the middle.

Evie getting sicker, and me making the play.

Taking her to Enclave just in time to see the old master die. Daniel. In the sun. Dying to believe.

Ready to bleed into her myself, and having it taken away. The Count taking my place. Infecting her. Keeping her down there. Taking over Enclave.

Badness.

Running years. The Bronx.

Coming back for a shot at something, and finding . . . What? A hole. A pit. The secret beneath it all.

Using it, spilling the secret, launching a war.

And running to Evie.

Finding some things don't get forgotten. Forgiven. A killer I may be, but I'm worse. I'm a liar. Lied to the only person I cared about, I can live with the blood, but talk about fucking up.

Into the ground.

Go low.

Hide.

Wait.

Now.

Run.


Coming out the entrance of the tunnel at One Twenty-three, the city almost blinds me. Just like she always has.

Far west side, traffic packed both ways on the Hud. Rush hour they call it, even when it's never been anything but stuck hour. People coming into the city I understand, people leaving it I don't get. Then again, I don't know a thing about what's out there. Could be paradise, but I doubt it. Other side of the Parkway there's a little glitter coming off the water between the patches of scum floating down the Hudson River to the sea. Above on my right, the tree line topping Riverside Park gets highlighted by the city glow. G. W. Bridge upriver, all lit up.

Picturesque as hell.

A horn blasts down the tunnel, hits my back like a shock wave, and I step from the tracks to let the train through. I could argue with it, but you have to pick your battles.

Headlights flash in the trees above from the shoulder of Riverside Drive. I scramble up the slope and find a black 1978 Riviera parked there. Dallas behind the wheel, Chubby occupying the bulk of the couch-size, black velour bench seat.

His window rolls down.

—All well, Joe?

I lean against the car.

—Just saying my farewells.

—To whom?

—No one you know.

He spreads his hands.

—I know most people.

—Not this guy.

—Why so certain?

—You're alive.

—Like that, is he?

I watch the traffic below.

—Talking about him, Chubby, is liable to attract his attention. And then you can get to know exactly what he's like.

He nods.

—Another topic, then.

I push off the side of the car.

—Idea where I might find Percy?

He shakes his head.

—As I said, Percy is absent. Start with Digga.

—Sure, I enjoy climbing in the bear's mouth. Makes it so he can just chew. Where do I find him?

He purses his lips.

—Commanding the siege.

I look down at the entrance to the tunnel.

—The siege.

—You'd like details.

I look up from the tunnel, up and through the trees, east.

—No. I don't think I need them.

—You know the place, then?

The empty socket where my left eye used to be itches. I'd like to scratch it, but I'd need an ice pick to dig deep enough to make it stop.

—Yeah, I was there once.

—Ah. On your previous uptown visit.

That itch gets a little worse.

Chubby strokes his goatee.

—Well, there should be no need for you to get too close. I understand the Coalition resistance has been rather intense. Digga will be nearby the park.

He goes in the glove box and comes out with a cell phone and offers it to me.

—My number is programmed.

I take the phone.

—Don't wait up.

I look for an opening in the traffic on the drive.

Chubby sticks his head out the window.

—Look out for her, Joe. Look out for my little girl.

I see my opening between the cars and start across.

I don't say anything to Chubby as I go. Promises don't keep, and he already knows how this is most likely to finish. He wouldn't have dug me up otherwise.


Middle of the park I hit Grant's Tomb. Coming out of the trees beyond, I'm just north of Columbia. I look down Broadway toward the campus, but I don't go any closer.

Siege.

Technically, it's all Hood turf above One Ten. Water to water it belongs to Digga and his people. But the Coalition, they only give up hard what they got. And what they got up here is the top of the rock: poaching rights on the campus, a few blocks of old money addresses, and a school for training their elite enforcers.

Way I know it's sideways here is because no one has killed me before I got this close.

But I don't need to test things any further.

I roll downhill on One Twenty-three, going east, and roll right into more of those riled-up memories. The past likes to haunt you, and I've come this way before.

Old city full of my ghosts.

Morningside Park on my right, rising steep to the high ground, empty. Street the same. Wind rattling bare branches. The butt of the pistol cold in the small of my back.

There should be people here.

Early in the evening, there should be students in the park, climbing the steep path winding to the top. Should be a couple drunks on the benches at the bottom, adding up the day's change, mentally converting it into 40s. But there's no one.

All parks in Manhattan used to be like this when the sun went down. Straight empty but for two types of people: mean people and the stupid people they loved. But by the time I went under, every inch of the Island had been gentrified. Tots played in the parks at midnight.

Seems the tone is different here.

Seems this park has redeveloped its reputation for being a place to avoid after dark. Or maybe at all hours it's this empty. That would make sense. With what I smell on the breeze, it would make a lot of sense if no one came near this park unless they were profoundly stupid.

As I'm the one wandering into it now, figure I win the stupid crown.

What I smell on the breeze smells like me. Like my blood. In large quantities. Spilled in puddles, dried and frozen over for someone to slip on and break their neck. The fuckers. The stupid, stupid fuckers. They've been fighting in the open. Fighting and killing one another out where it can be seen. Thinking on it, I feel the edge in the air. The one Chubby was talking about. Tension. Radiating from behind closed doors and drawn blinds. Showing in the empty sidewalks. A feeling that people are catching. The city isn't safe. It's not theirs anymore, if it ever was.

The path I'm following bends around a boulder. I pass behind it, a guy drops from a thick knot of branches overhead, and I step out of the way. As he tries to recover from hitting the pavement instead of me I loop the wire saw around his neck and pull tight and put my knee in his back and ride his face into some broken glass. I draw the saw once to the right, feel it bite through his windpipe, see the bright red splash on the ground, pull my face back as the acid burn of Vyrus hits my nostrils, tense my muscles to see if I can get through his whole neck in one more good yank and a log hits me in the side of my head and I fly off the guy, the saw still clenched in one hand, wire whipping free along with some of his throat, and I slam into the boulder and feel my right shoulder pop out of its socket. That kills my arm and I go for the gun with my left hand, bringing it out, looking for the guy with the log, but all I see is a man with taste in threads to make Chubby jealous.

—Pull that trigga, make a muthafucka angry.

I don't want to make a motherfucker angry, so I pocket the piece and work on getting my shoulder where it belongs.


—Should tell your people not to wear perfume on patrol.

—Told my people to shoot first on big white guys is what I told they asses. Muthafucka has a thing for ninja movies. Sittin' in a tree. Thinkin' he gonna get all silent assassin on some enforcer ass.

—He might have had me if it wasn't for the personal scent.

D.J. Grave Digga, president and warlord of the Hood, keeps his eyes on the video screen he's watching and kicks the seat back it's mounted in.

—Hear that, Jenks? Boy says your eau de cologne tipped him off. Watchin' that chop-sockey, how many those ninjas splash on some Calvin Klein before they go out to get they kill on, muthafucka?

The guy sitting in the front passenger seat doesn't say anything. That being a symptom of having most of your throat torn out. He does make a noise, something between a gurgle and a grate, but the mass of cartilage and skin in the middle of his neck is going to need some untangling before it's of much use.

Digga takes his eyes from the screen and leans forward a little.

—Muthafucka, you best not brought your bleedin' in here. I know you finished that shit before you climbed your ass back in my Escalade. Oh shit! Take that nastiness outside! Now, muthafucka!

Jenks and his nastiness climb out and close the door, leaving me and Digga alone.

Digga leans between the front seats, licks his thumb and rubs at a spot of blood on the cream leather.

—Use is it, his throat heals enough for him to breathe if his ass can't swallow? Answer me that. *No use.* All that blood he just lost. Starve by the end of the week. Start going batshit in a couple days. Need one more like that is what I need. One more batshit muthafucka starvin' on our turf.

He drops back into the seat next to me.

—Shit.

He runs his hands down the tops of his thighs, smoothing the black wool of his trousers.

—An like I need another harbinger of how shit is fucked up, your ass comes wanderin' by. Shit.

He redirects his eyes to the video screen.

—Look at this.

He touches the screen and a control bar appears at its bottom. He rewinds the picture, hits play, and we watch a twenty-second clip of a starving Hood launching herself from a second-story window into the path of a bus on the street below. The bus catches her before she hits the ground and she flies fifteen feet and smashes into the security gate covering a storefront. She gets up, broken bones jutting every direction from her shredded skin, and runs down an alley.

Digga shakes his head.

—Fuckin' YouTube. Muthafucka caught it with his phone an shit. Had it posted in minutes. See the title? *Crazy PCP Bitch Won't Die.*

—What's YouTube?

He looks at me, shakes his head.

—Muthafuckin' Joe Pitt.

He points at the screen.

—This your fuckin' fault, this shit is.

I lean forward and look at the screen, shake my head.

—Never saw the crazy bitch before.

He has me by the back of the neck, bounces my forehead off the screen, the picture fractures, screen goes black. I don't see anything else for the moment because of the gun stuck up against my remaining eye.

—Tell you about that crazy bitch. She a lady. Good lady. Got a high school diploma. College degree. She a pillar of our community. Works with young people new to the life. Helps with they get adjusted to how things is. Loves them kids. Loves them kids so much, when shit gets tight up here last few months an I got no choice but to institute rationing and a strict policy of no more killing the normal muthafuckas till further fuckin' notice, she lays off her rations on some of her kids. So that they be more comfortable an shit. That who that bitch is. Was. Cuz now that bitch put down with a bullet I had to lodge in her fuckin' skull on account of this crazy shit we see here. Muthafucka! Muthafucka!

He pistol-whips me a few times. My nose breaks. Again.

He stops. Looks at his gun. Reaches over and wipes the blood onto my jeans.

—Shit.

I pinch the bridge of my nose and force it into place.

—Hey, Digga.

He doesn't say anything.

I go in my pocket for my tobacco and start rolling a smoke.

—Just like old times, huh?


Digga's suit is black. Trousers, jacket, shirt, tie, socks, shoes and cuff links. Solid black. Just that much blacker than himself. A good color for hiding the blood that sprinkled him when my nose broke. Still he doesn't like it.

He dabs at a blood spot with a damp paper napkin.

—Had to make noise, didn't ya, Pitt? Keepin' yo mouth shut just a lost art where your ass comes from, is it?

I keep my mouth shut.

He looks at me.

—You bein' cute?

I shrug.

He shakes his head.

—Cute. Know what happened? You went off half-cocked last year? Know what the result of that action came to be?

He balls some used napkins and throws them into the footwell.

—Society emissary comes up here. Lydia Miles. Comes up here, secret communiqué from the Society. My ears only. Whisper-whisper. Some shit about how they finally found where Coalition gets they blood. How it is they asses always got enough. How they supply the masses between Fourteen and One Ten. Do tell, says I. Thinkin' this is gonna be some valuable shit to know. Years now we been relyin' on Coalition to supplement what we got up here. Years we have to put up with they asses holdin' top of the rock. Payin' what price they set. Market monopoly. Twistin' my tits. Then this chick, she leans to my ear and she tells me where they get it.

He's stopped blotting, scrubbing now, little white bits of paper tearing off a napkin and sticking to his jacket.

—Says some shit about Queens. Says some shit about a hole in the ground. Asks me, all drama like, *Know what's in that hole, Digga?* Shit!

He throws the napkin into the front seat.

—Like I'm supposed to know that shit. Asks like maybe I know. Muthafucka! Like she's checking my shit out to see how I jump. Thinkin', *Did he know or didn't he?* Like it's a fuckin' question if I knew or not.

His hands are fists now, he shakes them in front of his face.

—Like there was a question what I'd have to say on that shit.

He pounds the fists into his thighs.

—War! War, I say, muthafucka! War on they asses! War! War! War!

I've got a cigarette rolled. I put it in my mouth and light it and inhale some smoke, then blow it back out.

—Yeah, well, that was kind of the point.

· · ·

That hole.

About that hole in Queens. Not trying to be coy or anything. Just some things I don't feel like talking about much. And some people, they get uncomfortable thinking about some things.

Veal.

Veal makes some people uncomfortable to think about it. Baby calves in pens so tight they can't turn around. Milk-fed, tender-muscled, raised to young slaughter and the table. Put a plate full of it in front of someone, don't say a word, most folks tuck right in, rub their tummies and say *mmm*. Same plate, same person, tell them a little about those big-eyed calves and their short and miserable existence, and they're like as not to go off their appetite.

I go into too much detail on this, I'm liable to get distracted. Start thinking about things I can't change. So take the above as context, and see what kind of picture gets painted when I mention the following:

Hole in the ground.

Chains.

Breeding cells.

Anticoagulants.

Incubators.

I.V. hose.

Truncheons.

Vampyres.

Veal ranch.

Rape factory.

Paints a vivid picture don't it? Illuminates some of the strong feelings people might display. But, yeah, guess I kind of buried the lead at the beginning of the story.

•  •  •

We're only human. At least that's what I think. Just people got infected with this thing that needs blood to survive. We're not evil. No more than other folks. We're not soulless creatures of the night. Sure, yeah, mostly anyone can get used to mostly anything if that's what it takes to survive. And sure, tap enough veins and you start to get a little casual about the process. Still, when I look at the people around me, I don't feel like I'm looking at cattle. They're people, sure enough. The fact that I'm looking for a person who's an easy mark doesn't mean I think any less of them.

Pretty damn hard for me to think any less of humanity than I already do.

Digga, he's plenty human himself. He's a vicious thug, but he likes dogs and children and all that usual stuff. No wonder he took it hard when he found out what he'd been drinking hadn't been given up by Vampyre-loving volunteers or bled off packs of kiddy-fondling Klansmen.

Sensitive boy.

What he's got to be sensitive about could be debated.

Me, I was in that hole. I saw. I got through it without blinding my remaining eye, and you don't hear me complaining.

But Digga's his own man with his own concerns.


—What color?

—Not sure I follow.

He puts a finger in my face.

—Don't pull that ignorant white bullshit with me, muthafucka. You know what I'm askin'. What color them kids down there in that damn hole?

I pick a flake of loose tobacco from my lip.

—I only saw a few.

—Give a shit how many, give a shit what color.

I flick the tobacco flake from between my fingers.

—Color of naked rats raised underground. That color.

He takes his finger from my face, looks me over, leans back into his seat.

—Muthafucka. An you ran away.

I know what I did, so I don't contradict him.

He looks out his window, up the slope of the park.

—Uh-huh. Joe muthafuckin' Pitt. Uh-huh.

I smoke.

He fiddles his cuffs.

—People lookin' for your ass. Be happy to find you in the open. Where they can get a clean shot off. Wrap your ass up, sell it to the highest bidder. Rake some much needed coin for up here.

I nod.

—Maybe swap me for some of that Coalition blood.

He makes fists again, but doesn't use them.

—Muthafucka always got to be pushin' shit. Can't let it alone. Try to tell a muthafucka a thing and he's got to open his mouth and let out whatever stupid smart-ass shit in his head. Make a man want to pummel. Paste your ass right on the sidewalk. Smear you all over for the dogs to lick up. Damn!

I nod again.

—Yeah, sounds like me.

He opens his fists.

—Shit. Predo and the Coalition. Terry and Society. Every other muthafucka wants to get they hands on your ass. Fuck 'em.

He looks at me.

—Did alright by me. Alright by the Hood. Last time you were up, did what you said you would. Played your part in complicated business. I don't like you, that's beside the point of this shit. You did alright by me. And I don't pawn the asses of people do alright by me. Mamma didn't raise me like that.

He squints.

—Just tell me what your ass is doing up here and get that shit over with.

I adjust the strap of my eyepatch.

—I'm looking for a girl.

His eyebrows go up.

—Shee-at. A girl. Joe fucking Pitt looking for a girl. What a girl got to have to get your ass interested?

I hold a hand in front of my stomach.

—This one has a baby.

His lips go thin. He shakes his head.

—Shit. That chick. Should have known.

His head shake shifts to a nod.

—Cuz don't trouble just like to run around with trouble

—Could use you in this.

—Negotiation isn't my strength.

—Like I want you openin' your ass to talk. Could use you to fill in for muthafucka with his throat tore out.

I turn my head to look at the small group of young men and women on the sidewalk. Pacing, bouncing on toes, chain-smoking Kools. Black Ecco down jackets. Timberland boots. Baggy jeans. Informal uniform of the Hood rhinos.

I look back at Digga.

—Seems like you have an escort already

He looks at his people.

—*Escort.* Gonna be me escorting their asses is what it's gonna be. Soldiers got to feed an I keep em fed. But not all what they need. An they all cherry anyway. Hardly a one done the deed. Frontline rhinos almost all takin' dirt naps already. We staked our position, said straight up we were standing with the Society, and Coalition dropped hammers on us. Went all tense on the border down at Fourteen, but they didn't cross the line, not in any fuckin' force. But us? Like they was ready. Jumped One Ten and muthafuckas was all up in our shit before we turned around. Had our shit scouted deep. Safe houses. Doors busted in, enforcers came through. We were flat fuckin' pants down for almost a week. The smoke cleared, all we had time for was to get the bodies in the river before they could start to stink. Keep from attracting too much attention. Some gun killin' uptown, the law doesn't pay too much mind. Lets that shit settle itself out. Think it's all drugs anyhow. But some of the shit enforcers were layin' down, that would have drawn some long looks those corpses had turned up. Had to go whole hog after that shit. *They* had addresses, *we* had some of our own. Sent some heavies down. See how they like gunplay on the Upper East. See how Predo bags that shit an keeps it out of the paper an off the police blotter. How long his payola keeps a lid when some muthafuckin' co-op boards and neighborhood commissions start they bitchin'.

I rub my bad knee.

—How'd that go?

He smiles.

—Not too bad. Lost some boys I couldn't spare, but sometimes you need to sacrifice a knight to knock off some pawns an shit. Get the other player's attention. Let his ass know good an well you ain't above doin' some foolish shit if it means you can draw a little of his blood. Predo got busy hisself, dealing with some community relations, ditchin' some stiffs. Eased off on those incursions. Mean, we still light the shit up, but ain't no nightly event like it was for a while.

The knee is stiffening up, too much time sitting.

—And downtown?

He doesn't smile at that.

—*Downtown*. Fuckin' Terry Bird. Sends that Miles chick up here, gets me all riled an shit. Then what? Sits on his ass and says, *Actions need to be coordinated and timed for maximum effect*. Shit like that. We're getting our asses starved, an he's fuckin' co-ordinatin' an shit. Muthafucka. If I didn't have issues with the man before this shit, I got them now.

I flex the knee and it feels like gravel.

—Lydia has a tendency to rile shit up more than Bird wants.

He bats the air with the back of his hand.

—Lydia muthafucka and her *systemic misogynism of the African American male* bullshit. Give me that, *no judgments, but the fact of alternative lifestyle intolerance in your community is indisputable*. Make a man want to shoot. An bullshit anyway. We got the gay up here, no doubt.

The knee doesn't feel any better. I need to walk it around.

I put my hand on the door.

—Not that I don't enjoy catching up and all, but I was asking about the pregnant girl.

He's looking out at his people.

—Yeah, yeah. Got your own griefs, huh? *Pregnant girl*. Pregnant with what is the issue. Shit we don't know an don't understand about ourselves, any wonder we're still fightin' each other? Vampyre on Vampyre violence, whatever the color, it just makes shit sense.

He tugs at his lower lip.

—Somethin' like this comes out of the woodwork, bound to stir up feeling. Uninfected girl with an infected baby daddy. I'd already heard the nonsense being talked downtown about them. Nothing like a baby to make people see visions of the future. See salvation or new Armageddon. Me, I don't read it that way. See just plain trouble. Horny kids got themselves a baby they didn't plan on. Everyday trouble up here. Least the boy seem like he wants to stick it out. They always do till the first diaper. But those two, living in a fantasy land. Feedin' the noise. Bird may think he can use 'em as a symbol, but they got their own damn ideas. Come up here talkin 'bout how that baby is a *bridge to the future*. Saw them, the look in their eyes, like they just got out of church, full of the Lord, said, *Aw no, fuck this shit*.

He lifts his hand, drops it.

—I told Percy to keep 'em wrapped. Too hot to have that shit at my elbow. People all worked up about that shit. People lookin' for signs and portents, all they need is to hear that girl talk about her baby being *The Uniter*. No chance. Told Percy they could stay, but keep 'em down low.

—Percy was with them?

—That's where they started. Found Percy, he brought them to me, I told him to keep 'em quiet while more pressing issues get resolved. Percy the man to keep a lid on shit. Meditate on it and drop wisdom regarding the affair. Counselor to the king, that's his deal.

I open the door and step out.

—Thanks.

He's still looking out the other side of the Caddy, studying his people.

—Not sure where your ass thinks it's going.

He never shook me down. Didn't bother looking for my weapons. Didn't care what I was holding. He doesn't have to. He's a badass. But I'm out of the car now, space to work with. Never got that pistol where I wanted it, but I think I can whip it out before he digs his from the floor where he set it.

I don't touch the gun, not yet.

—My ass is going to see Percy.

He's still looking out that other window.

—Uh-huh. You know the way?

—Been there before.

—Mhmm. Assuming he ain't moved.

A fish, when the hook is set, does he feel it?

I sure as hell do.

I felt it when Chubby told me Evie wanted me to find his daughter. And I'm feeling it again right now. And I'm wondering how many more barbs are gonna fill my mouth and snag my gills before this deal is done.

—If he's moved, I guess I'll have to depend on the kindness of strangers to point the way.

I watch the back of his head nod, see a flash of white teeth in the glass where his face is reflected, as he presses the tip of a finger to that glass, pointing up at the top of the park.

—I ain't no stranger to you, Joe, an it sure as shit ain't no kindness, but his ass is right up there.


The rhinos ride herd on the three people with black bags on their heads, while me and Digga bring up the rear.

—Funny how shit works itself out.

I'm not laughing.

Digga observes this fact.

—You not laughin', Pitt.

I pause in the midst of sucking the life out of another cigarette.

—Just wondering.

—Do tell.

I toss the butt into some frost-dead weeds at the side of the path.

—Just wondering how I come out from under my rock after a year, try to mind my own business, and still find myself doing exactly what someone else wants me to do.

He shrugs under his topcoat.

—Like I say, some shit just funny as a muthafucka.

He flips up the collar of the coat.

—Ain't that big a big anyhow. We got what-who they want. They got what-who we want. It's Friday fucking evening before prime-time TV. No one wants to cause a ruckus. Why we do it out here. Lessen the itch in a muthafucka's trigger finger.

I hook a thumb at the cars at the bottom of the park.

—That why Jenks tried to drop me?

—Our half of the park down there. Figure they ass come that far, they get what all they got comin'.

My new smoke is ready, so I put it to work.

—How'd they get Percy?

He grunts from his chest.

—By bein' scumbags is how. Percy come up here under a truce flag. Negotiate some shit about how and when we can engage. Rule of law in war and shit like that. Shit right up Predo's alley. War on the Q.T. But this muthafucka up here.

He makes that same grunt, deeper.

—This mutha is crazy. Rule of *pay no mind to nuthin'*.

He casts his eyes my way.

—Which is why, open-air meeting an all aside, I can use a cruel gunsel like yourself this fine evening. Cuz this is a muthafucka jumps eccentricwise.

The cigarette is working.

—Who they got up here now?

—Old lady Vandewater went missing 'bout a year back. Know anything on that?

I know. I know the word *missing* is a good enough metaphor for *beheaded,* but I don't feel like covering the details for the man, so I keep the cigarette busy.

He doesn't need a map.

—Yeah, thought so. Thought that might have involved you.

I don't tell him it wasn't me made her gone. Hate to ruin his good impression of me.

He tilts his chin up the hill.

—Since she got lost somewhere, Coalition decided to dig deep in the crazy hole. Came up with something must have been stuck at the bottom for a lot of years.

I try to picture someone crazier than Vandewater.

Digga points to where the path levels on a bend just ahead.

—And here we go.

I look up.

Fate laughs at me again.

Half a dozen enforcers. Large to extra large, the only sizes the Coalition goes for. Black suits that would get them past any wardrobe check in the city. Small flat black firearms of the type that like to empty themselves when the trigger is breathed on. I get that much of an impression of the overall scene before a voice drags my eyes to a slightly lower plane.

The bottom of the crazy barrel. Or maybe the thing that lives in the mud under it.

Looks like he's wearing the same crusted bathrobe and pleated tux shirt as the last time I saw him. Bent nearly double in his rusting wheelchair, tufts of long greasy hair springing from his scabbed scalp.

Spittle flies off his lips as he opens them.

—You, I know you. Shiftless, yes. That's your name.

He spits a thick wad of yellow mucus at me.

—*Shiftless.*

He points at Digga.

—It resonates so naturally with nigger.

Digga takes it in stride.

—Fuck you, Lament. Where the fuck's Percy?

Seeing Lament, lots of things start to itch. My missing eye.

The stump of my toe. Places in my memory. But mostly my trigger finger.

And it turns out I have the gun in the exact right place after all. I get it out and put it to use before anyone can stop me.

Once the first three bullets are in Lament's chest, Digga knows the score and doesn't waste time scolding me. His hands come out of his pockets, each with their own ebony-handled revolver, and he starts plugging. The enforcers are the next to catch up, but we're already dropping bodies. Digga and I are splitting wide of each other, laying down fire, running low on bullets. The enforcers fire at the middle of our group, cutting down two rhinos and two of the guys with bags on their heads. I'm dropping my gun now, closing on an enforcer with a shotgun, no time to go under my jacket for the blade, free hand comes out of my pocket with the cosh and I swing it uppercut and it splits as it hits his jaw, teeth spraying with sand. Digga's got himself a new gun. The revolvers haven't hit the ground before he's scooped a machine pistol from the dead hands of a dropping enforcer. I go for the ground myself as bullets fill the air. Facedown, I miss the guy coming at my back, turn only when he grunts as Jenks drops from the tree, lands on the guy's back and uses one of those short samurai swords to stab the guy in the mouth, down his throat. And then Digga's cleaning up. Putting bullets in the heads of the ones that are just grievously wounded. Making sure they don't get back up.

I'm busy myself, putting my blade to work on Lament. I have his scalp halfway down his throat before Digga kicks me and points out the bastard is already dead. I keep at it anyway. It's something I promised myself I'd do when I got the chance. And you don't get second shots at these things.

•  •  •

Percy's not dead, but he's gonna be.

—Fuck, Percy.

—Where's Lament?

Digga looks at me.

—Pitt went all Geronimo on his coif.

—He dead then.

Digga widens his eyes and nods.

—Oh, muthafucka dead ah'ite.

Percy tries to nod himself, but too much of the muscle on his neck has been flayed away with his skin.

—Almost die a happy man, hearin' that.

He looks at me. He's still got his arm, but only the ring finger hasn't been mashed by pliers. He points it at me.

—Pitt. 'Member what I say when we last spent some time together, 'bout cigarettes?

I'm standing a ways away, outside the van we found him in at the top of the park. Black windowless van, we didn't exactly need a treasure map. We haven't moved him from the back. Digga started to rip off the razor wire that was wrapped around him, but Percy told him to stop. He'd healed a little, skin had grown back around the wire in a couple patches. And it wasn't like it was going to change things. It hurt less to just be still, I guess.

Now the younger man is huddled in the back of the van with his dying vizier.

I step a little closer so I can hear him better.

—Yeah, I remember.

His lips part, broken teeth inside, broken smile.

—Look at me.

I'm looking.

—Look at me, set up ta leave it all behind. An dyin' just as much ta have a damn smoke.

I start rolling one.

His eyes close. Open. He looks at Digga.

—Lament layin' ta hang yo ass. Literal like. Sonofabitch had it in mind ta off yo rhinos, take you in charge. Lynch you. Highest tree. Top of the rock.

Digga frowns.

—Don't care. Don't matter.

—Lissen yo ass.

Digga listens.

—I came up for to do some talkin'. Not like I stepped outta line. He just made up his mind his own self. Take me down. Cuz what I figured.

He looks at me.

—You got that ratty ass thing spun yet?

I lick it closed, lean in, put it between his lips and strike a match.

He inhales.

—Give half my immortal soul for a damn Pall Mall.

He exhales.

—But this'll do. Take it from me so's I can talk some.

Digga takes the cigarette from his mouth.

—What'd you figure, Perce?

His chest starts working like a bellows. We can see the bones of his rib cage, gaps in the cartilage and muscle between them, expanding, contracting. Air whistles around his broken teeth.

—Damn. Damn. Damn. Ah hell. What I figured. They *done* up here. I went in, he had his boys and girls runnin' they's asses in and out all about. Tryin' to make it look like they's in they's dozens. But they not. Got one arm, not one eye.

He looks at me.

—Speakin' on which, you seen better days, Pitt.

I look him over.

—Look who's talking.

We all have a little laugh. Percy's laugh hurts. Hurts him to make it, hurts some to hear it. No use lying about it.

He smokes a little more.

—Saw the same faces runnin' in an out. An Lament, he crazy, but not stupid. Not like that. Saw me size it up. Done deal after that. Can't let me come back to you. Say, *We got 'em, Dig, let loose the hounds.* 'Stead, he had hisself a good old timey time. Chained me behind one of they's cars, dragged me around circles in a parkin' garage. An some other stuff. Oh, they brought back some memories they did.

Smoke floats into his eyes, he squints through it at me.

—*Geronimo?*

I shrug.

—I scalped him.

—Particular reason?

—You met the man, I need any other reason than he was breathing?

—No. No you did not. Sure as hell, he had it comin'.

Something cracks deep in him, he coughs, bile sprays from his mouth.

—Ah damn.

He curls the one good finger around Digga's thumb.

—He was gonna string you up. Take off the head of the Hood an see if the body would die. How 'bout that. But over now. They got no one up here. Left me all alone in this van. Top of the rock, an no one home but us black folks. Got to read somethin' in that, my liege.

Digga closes his eyes.

—Don't call me that shit.

—Uh-huh, heavy lies the crown. You wanted it, it yours now. I doubted, all these years, but you the man. Luther X left him no heir, but you the man now. Hail an well damn met.

Digga rubs his eyes.

—Shit.

Percy shakes his head.

—Got to run now. Got last things to say. Lissen close.

Digga opens his eyes.

Percy starts to whisper.

—Kill all yo enemies now. An Predo gonna call soon. Lookin' for to bargain an armistice. Promise you stay in your place an he won't cross One Ten. Send gallons of blood. An mean it too. Then he gonna march below Fourteenth. An when he got it sorted there, come back up here for yo head. That what.

Digga nods.

—What's my play?

—You play is you take what he offers. Bargain it some, but take.

Digga shakes his head.

Percy looks at me.

—Pitt.

I nod.

—Take the deal.

Percy nods.

—Uh-huh.

I stop nodding.

—And when Predo turns south you shoot him in the back.

—Uh-huh, that the way.

He looks back at Digga.

—Be a hard-hittin' brutha. Don't take no shit. But cogitate before you act.

—Yes, sir.

Percy's pupils expand like smoke, like the black is leaking into the rest of his eyes.

He turns them on me.

—An look to the young people an they's baby.

I step a little closer.

—Where are they?

He manages to move his head, jerking his chin south.

—Seems they was disillusioned some by what they found up here. Said they needed a proper community for they's child if it was to *blossom.* Talkin' 'bout the lady down south. One with all them big ideas 'bout a cure an integration between infected an uninfected an all that. Seemed to think that was the right place for them an they's *unbounded love.*

Digga squeezes Percy's finger.

—They important, Perce, somethin' I should do? Anything to what they think about that baby?

Percy manages to lift his head a little.

—*Important?* They's kids damnit. Got they heads up they asses maybe, they just a couple of children young an in love. Got to be room for that. Ain't no thing hard to think 'bout.

Eyes on me again.

—Hey there, Joe Pitt. Got to be room left for love in all this, right? Mean, got to be room we go out on a limb, help just because. World where we been drinkin' the blood of children raised in the dark. Got to be room to make somethin' better. Shit. Help the young people is all. An for they's baby, it more than likely just a baby. Shouldn't need more reason than that.

His head drops back.

—An leave me the hell alone. Still Enclave. Gonna die proper from no blood. Die proper. Cut me a few times, let me go, cut me and let me go.

Digga doesn't have a knife. I hand him mine. The Vyrus is almost dead in the old man, bled out too fast to find that place where he'd frenzy, past healing. The fresh cuts open and close like mouths for a moment, then hang gaping, the last little blood seeping out. Digga climbs from the van, closes the doors, hands me the blade, and walks away some. I stand there, listening as Percy thrashes inside, no screams, just dying as quiet as he has it in him to die.

*The young lady with all the big ideas.*

It's not like I didn't see it coming. But still.

Set to look for one runaway, I find myself staring down a path that beats its way to another. The original lost girl. One of the top names on the list of people I'd hoped being underground would keep me away from.

Not that she's ever done me wrong. Just that she radiates danger with a half-life of forever.

Just that she has no fear. Smarter than everyone else put together, but still not sure that I wasn't the one who killed her mom.

I did.

For all the right reasons.

Man, this time out, the crazy barrel is getting emptied entirely. Right on my head.

Digga's rhinos pack the van with stiffs. Not the type to be particular about a man's remains, he leaves Percy where he lies and lets the other dead be piled on top of him.

There is a curious absence of sirens after all the shooting.

I mention it.

Digga gives his take.

—Probably not a good thing. Says to me the cops got a sense there be shit they should best keep clear of. Says they started to map the places that kind of shit goes down of late. Like, back in the day, cops did not roll on any shit in Harlem, yeah? What it was, a death wagon came 'round in the morning, picked the stiffs off the street. Then the cops come and try to sort shit out. Or not.

An every now an again, they draw some circles on a map, 'round those areas they knew shit was most fucked up, an they roll with the paddy wagons an the tear gas an the billys an they crack skulls and drag niggahs out. Like to remind everyone which the muthafuckas in charge of this shit. An such.

Jenks and two other rhinos are what's left of the crew that came up the park. And Jenks looks worse than ever. They close the back doors of the van, and Digga waves them off.

—Drive it up to the Jack. Put 'em in a lye bath.

Jenks croaks, gets in the van with one of the rhinos and they drive off.

Digga checks me out.

—Coulda thanked the man for savin' your life, muthafucka.

I'm rolling a smoke.

—He never thanked me for sparing his.

Digga nods.

—True dat.

We start down the path.

I light up.

—Cops aren't gonna sit pat much longer.

—No. No, they ain't.

—City feels all wrong.

—Yes, yes it do.

We reach the spot where we shot it out. I couldn't find bullets that fit my gun, so I took one off a dead enforcer. Lean gun, sleek, like a fashion accessory. It fits at the base of my spine, but the weight is wrong, lighter than I like.

I kick some pebbles through a puddle of blood.

—It's gonna be a mess.

His hands are deep in the pockets of his coat. He shrugs without pulling them free.

—I try an be philosophical about this shit. Got people depending on my ass to make the right calls, but they's only so much a man can do in this climate of mental instability. I got to try an keep the Hood together, fight for the betterment of my bruthas and sistahs, but, same time, can't afford to live no fantasy about how fucked up shit is.

He nods to himself.

—People gonna die. My people. Lots. Trick from my end is to see more of someone else's people die first. Be sure we can claim what's ours when the smoke clears. If it go that far. Which I ain't sure 'bout as yet. Possibility people could all have a sudden attack of gettin' they's shit together. Never know.

—Don't count on it.

—Oh I don't, I don't.

We're at the bottom.

He looks up at the top.

—Got to do the old man's biddings now. Kill on some folks.

He looks at me.

—Don't suppose?

I'm dropping a butt in the gutter, rolling another.

—Got lost people to find.

—Uh-huh. Young lovers and a baby.

He brings his hands out of his pockets and waves them about a little.

—You find that hole. You light the match, put it to the fuse and set that flame headin' to the powder. Then while we all run around tryin' ta stomp the damn thing out, you just go 'bout your fuckin' bizniz.

I set a match to a fresh smoke.

—That's how I had it figured. Why?

I drop the match.

—It not working for you?

He lowers his hands.

—Pitt, tell you a true thing, you drew down on Lament, for whatever the fuck reason, an that played out right. Maybe kept me from havin' a neck stretch. But still an all, muthafucka, if Percy didn't say he wanted those kids looked to, I'd be killin' yo ass right this fuckin' second. An you ask me, I called Predo and Bird and everyone else together and dropped yo head on the floor, everyone be so damn happy they just get to huggin' and settlin' they's differences. Say to that shit?

I take a drag, consider the prospect that he might be right, and blow some smoke.

—I say that if you think that, you're pretty fucking stupid to be letting me walk off with my head.

He thinks about it, I can see it in the way he's looking at my neck.

Me, I'm thinking how many times I've been told my mouth is gonna get me killed. First time was about the first time I opened it to cry because I was hungry. Seems the last time was less than an hour ago when Digga busted my nose. How a man lives that long without figuring that keeping his mouth shut is an option is beyond me. I've had the point reinforced enough times. Except I don't like doing what people want me to.

Mostly because I don't like them I guess.

People, I mean.

Digga takes his eyes from my neck. I appreciate the restraint. More than I could have mustered in his shoes. I was him, my head would be in the gutter by now.

He shakes his head, turns and points at the cars at the curb.

—The Escalade's mine. I ain't givin' up the Bentley for your ragged ass. That leave the '95 Impala.

He looks at me.

—Percy's favorite ride.

We walk to the car.

—Any tips on crossing One Ten?

He touches the nape of his neck.

—Well, it's night, so that help. An fact is, anybody can only watch for so much. True this car is one they know. Coalition spotters likely got pictures, got the plate number. But unless you get stuck at a light right at One Ten, right where a spotter is lookin', you can squirt through. Border always been porous that way. Trick is how to stay invisible once you across. 'Specially seein' as where you headed. Was me, I'd maximize my potential, take Harlem River Drive, come west once you drop far enough south. After that, could try drivin' up on the doorstep where yo headed, right through the door. Might get in safe that way.

I open the Impala's door.

—Tight?

He puckers.

—We don't get much news from down there, but you size it up. Middle of Coalition turf a crazy little chick thinks she can cure the Vyrus sets up shop, declares she's *Clan Cure,* an invites all the infected losers she can get to come live with her in peace. Shit goes sideways. She guns up and turns her haven into a redoubt. No one in, no one out. Tell me what Predo does 'bout that. No, I'll tell you. Embargoes they's ass. No blood. Let 'em sit in that building with no egress or ingress at all. Eyes all over that street.

He shakes his head.

—What Percy thinkin' lettin' his young people in love run down to that shit is beyond my ken. Wild shit is what it is.

He shakes his head, fiddling with his hair.

—Had to go an die now, he did. Just when I need a haircut.

I look somewhere else.

He makes a soft sound.

I keep looking away.

He drops his hand from the back of his head.

—Muthafucka.

I get in the car and turn the key.

—Thanks for the wheels.

He puts a hand on the open door.

—Percy an shit.

—Yeah. Percy.

I take the wheel.

He pushes the door closed. I put it in drive and pull away. Watch him standing there in the rearview.

King in exile in his own land. Alone. And most cruel.


There's a worm at the heart of the world, eating itself.

Did you know that?

It's true.

And with each bite it does itself injury. Kills itself a little more. Digests another mouthful of its own intestine. Its howls are muffled by its body. But, being as it's at the heart of the world, people still hear it. They get driven mad from listening to the damn thing eat itself. They want to make it stop so they won't have to hear it anymore. And the way you kill what's at the heart of the world is, you kill the world.

Tell me you don't know the people I'm talking about.

Driving down Harlem River Drive, traffic breaking now, the Impala growling to itself about the pace, I let the radio scan the frequencies. A year underground and a man misses out on a lot. Arts and culture. Science and technology. Politics and finance. Most of the music puts my teeth on edge. But it always has. The news doesn't so much put them on edge as make me wish for something bloody to sink them into.

I think in verbs while I listen to the news. Rend. Rip. Tear.

I hear that worm in the news, eating itself, choking on a bite, puking it back up, eating it again. And I wonder where it all starts. This cycle. What I feel on the streets, the tension, does it start with what people like me are doing just around the corner, the almost immediate danger of things that feed on blood going to war? Or does it start with what people completely not like me are doing, far away and out of touch, blood feeders of a different sort, going to war?

The scan hits the Jam, "That's Entertainment." I turn it up and let the subwoofers in the trunk of the Impala pound bass through my spine.

Fuck the worm. I have a gun and a knife and a couple feet of braided wire that can saw through bone. Get that worm between my teeth, eat it before it can eat itself. Like finding it at the bottom of a bottle of mescal.

Mescal.

I need a bar.

I'm not a complicated guy.

What it takes to keep my hackles down is mostly a drink, a smoke, no one fucking with me, and at least a pint of blood a week. Although on one a week I'll be getting pretty cranky by Thursday night. Right now what I need is the drink. A plain drink. Booze. There wasn't much of it to be found the last year. I had a couple guys I could slip a couple bucks to and they'd do my shopping for me up top, but you couldn't much trust those sterno suckers to bring back a bottle for you and expect to find anything in it. Now, once I start thinking about how good a drink would go down, I can't get clear of the thought.

I need a drink. And a place to have it in where I won't get fucked with.

The HRD became the FDR around Gracie Mansion. Like that's a surprise. At Seventy-third I slip off to an exit lane, take it two blocks to Seventy-first, cut west and over to First Avenue and back uptown. I've only been on the Upper East a couple times in my life, but it's a part of Manhattan, so I know there are bars. I go with a pub this time out. Safest choice when you're going in blind. Yeah, they'll likely serve you your drink in a stemmed glass, but they have every flavor of whiskey, at least one good-looking girl with a brogue, and the Pogues on the juke.

There's a guy parked just up the street in an idling car, waiting for someone to come out from a building. I pull in alongside him and beep. He looks, I hand signal, asking if he'll clear the space while he waits so I can park. He turns away, acting like he didn't see.

There's a bunch of change at the bottom of one of the cup holders between the seats. I dig out a handful, roll down my window, and throw it at the guy's door. He jumps and looks at me with that *Oh no, I've upset a crazy person* look that all New Yorkers get once or twice a year. I give him a new hand signal, pointing at him, pointing at the street, hoisting my middle finger. Sign language gets through this time as he begins to pull from the spot, clear on the fact that he's supposed to fuck off now before I hurt him.

I park, lock the Impala, walk into the Banshee Pub, pass the happy-hour cluster of dart-playing ex–frat boys, order a double, and a guy drinking something light blue looks at me and points at my eyepatch.

—Hey, you look like a pirate.

I swallow my drink, put the glass down, look at the bartender, point at the glass, and look back at the guy with the blue drink.

—You look like a punching bag.

I get my second drink, and no one else fucks with me.

Bliss.

• • •

Tick-tick-tick.

I drink.

Tick-tick-tick.

I smoke.

Tick-tick-tick.

I know people in Cure. I know the top ladies. I just don't know where I stand with them these days. Call them, could be they sound all happy to hear from me, *Sure, Joe, come on in, we got a secret passage all set up, just say open sesame.* Come through to the other side and find Sela with her favorite machine gun. Or just her bare hands. Hard to say which would kill me quicker. Figure she'd be happy to see me gone no matter the situation. Her main squeeze is the big question mark.

Amanda Horde. Founder and true believer of Cure.

How she feels about me, it all depends on what she remembers now. And how insane she is these days.

But I got other phone numbers. One of them, it's always been pretty lucky for me. Another woman, for fuck sake. But it's not like that with us.

Lydia.

Good thing about Lydia, you know how she'll play her hand every time.

Straight.

No pun intended.


—Who is this?

—Hey, Lydia.

—Who is this?

—Me.

There's this pause, the kind of pause it's easy to imagine the person on the other end of the line wishing they could reach through the phone and grab you by the throat and shake you up and down until you break.

There's a hiss of held breath being released and pushed through a word.

—Coward.

Could be. Could be. Either way, it's not a word that skins my feeling.

—Good to hear your voice too, Lyd. Hey, I got a joke for you.

—Pitt.

—How do you know a lesbian is on a second date?

—Was it a lie?

—Hang on, this is OK material.

—Was it?

—You know a lesbian is on a second date when she shows up with a pickup truck full of stuff to move in.

—Is it there?

I try to think of another joke.

She doesn't wait.

—Are those kids really out there? Was it a lie, Pitt? Was it an angle you were playing? I don't care about what it's done to everything. It doesn't matter. But the kids, Joe. Are they really in that hole? Is it real? Tell me. Did you make it up? You made it up. Tell me. You made it up.

I can't think of another joke.

All I can think of is the truth.

Damn.

—No. I didn't make it up. It's there.

She's someplace quiet, I can hear her breathing. The breathing stops like she might say something, but she doesn't.

Then she does.

—You left them there.

She's right about that. Isn't she.

—Well. I tell ya, Lydia. If I'd had my Pied Piper gear with me, I'd have played 'em a tune they could have all followed me out to. Just didn't happen that way.

—Fucker.

Again, she's right about that.

—Want to get this all off your chest now, or you gonna keep dragging it out? I only ask 'cause if you're gonna drag it out I might set the phone down while I go to the bar for a drink.

—Hey, Joe?

—Yeah.

—Have you noticed something?

—Tell me.

—I'm not laughing at your jokes. Know why?

—Because you never have?

A plucked-wire tone comes into her voice, making me glad I'm not in the same room with her.

—I'm not laughing because the idea of someone uncovering an underground concentration camp and spreading news of that camp, setting off a war, and then running away from the consequences and responsibilities embodied in his discovery and subsequent actions, I'm not laughing because the idea of that doesn't leave room for anything to be funny anymore. I'm not laughing, Joe, because you're not funny. Sad. Pathetic. Cowardly. But not funny.

—You haven't asked why I called.

I've been making a cigarette while she talks. I light it now.

—I'm calling because I need your help.

I take a drag.

—Now tell me that's not funny.

She doesn't tell me any such thing.

Instead, she says something of her own that's funny.

—We have to go and get them out.

This cigarette, why isn't it a Lucky?

—If they're really down there, we have to go and get them.

I mean, I've been up top how many hours now?

—Everyone is fighting, but they've already forgotten the point of what the fighting is about.

I've got a pocket full of Chubby Freeze's money.

—We need to do what's right. We need to go and get those kids.

Why haven't I walked into a deli and bought a carton of Luckys already?

—I have Fury and the rest of my Bulls. We have some weapons.

Distracted. That's why.

—We have vehicles.

I keep getting distracted.

—But we can't just drive over to Queens and go around in circles.

Every time I think of a Lucky, something distracts me.

—We need to know exactly where it is. How it's set up.

What is she talking about?

—You know where it is. You were inside.

Is she?

—We need you, Joe.

Crazy.

—You're crazy, Lydia.

—Yeah. But tell me it's not funny. Us needing each other.

Give it to her, it's funny.


—What's Terry say to your little plan?

She grunts.

—Terry says there's no point in going over there if we don't know where we're going. He says you're the only one who knows. He says that even if we found you, we couldn't trust anything you say.

—Because I'm me.

—Yes. But if you were with us, we'd know. You'd have to steer us right if you were with us.

—Because you'd kill me otherwise.

—Yes.

—Fuck, Lydia, put it like that, how can I resist. Sign me up, I'll be right there.

—It's the right thing to do.

I don't laugh exactly, but I maybe chuckle.

She doesn't.

—Fuck you, Joe.

—Yeah, yeah.

She inhales.

—You haven't told me what kind of help you need.

I have a little whiskey at the bottom of my glass, and then, suddenly, I make it disappear.

—I'm not gonna make a deal, Lydia.

—What do you need?

More whiskey in my glass.

I signal the bartender.

—I'm looking for Chubby Freeze's daughter.

A sound, like Lydia's tapping her teeth with her thumbnail.

—The baby.

—Comes with the rest of the package from what I hear.

—Who wants her?

—Chubby. You meet her or her boyfriend?

More tapping.

—Terry kept them sequestered. *Shaping the message* was his line. But the message was already shaping. People heard about them and their baby, they started thinking fantasy. Heard some *savior* talk. Like that kind of belief and faith hasn't caused the world enough pain. They had ideas of their own, I guess. Slipped off. Terry was irate. He thinks she's important. Symbolically.

—She's a little more than symbolically important to Chubby.

More tapping,

—Sure, but I don't know where she is.

—I didn't ask.

Tapping stops.

—You know where?

—I have a lead.

Tap. Tap. Tap.

—And?

—You might be able to help me get there.

—And?

I take a hit off my drink.

—Ever talk to Sela these days?

—No.

—Too bad.

—No. I mean, *no*. I mean, *not there*. Is she there? Is that where she? With the baby?

—Could be. Last place she was headed.

—Joe. That place. Joe. It's gone wrong in there.

—Yeah, Predo's trying to starve them out.

—No. It was already going wrong. Joe. Some of our people who joined up, they tried to leave Cure. We got word from them. There are things happening in there. Chubby's daughter. The baby. They can't. Are you sure?

—Lydia.

—Get them out, Joe. Get them out.

—I don't even know how to get in.

—You.

She raises her voice more than just a bit.

—You fucking asshole! You go through the front fucking door, you asshole!

—Coalition.

—It's East Seventy-third between First and Second, you asshole! Take a fucking cab, jump out, run up to the door and start knocking! What the fuck are they going to do, shoot you in the middle of their own fucking turf? Fuck!

She may be onto something.

—Hey, Lydia.

—Fuck. What?

—So I was right, calling you, you did kind of help.

—Fuck you.

—Sure. And something for you too, sweetheart.

She's catching her breath after all the excitement.

—What?

I measure it once, start to measure it again, making sure I want to cut before I do, but hell with that. I just chop the fucker up.

—You want to launch a raid on that hole. You might try asking Terry for directions.

She's all caught up with her breath now.

—Terry.

—Yeah. Him.

—Don't fuck around, Joe.

—Hey, lady, like you said, I was there. I saw it.

I finish my drink.

—Trust me, I'm not fucking around.

—Terry.

—Just saying you should ask.

Tap. Tap. Tap.

—You know, Joe, there's a second half to that joke.

—Don't say.

—Sure. Goes, How do you know when a gay guy is on a second date?

—Tell it.

—What second date?

We don't laugh, either of us, but it doesn't mean we aren't amused.

—See ya around, Lydia.

—What's really funny?

—What?

—I almost hope that's true.

She hangs up.

Lydia Miles.

A sense of humor. The world must truly be coming to an end.

I celebrate with a last drink, pay my tab, roll a cigarette for the walk to the Impala, hit the sidewalk, smell bleach, take a second to wonder why the guy scrubbing the sidewalk with a push broom is wearing such nice shoes with his coveralls, and then another guy in coveralls and nice shoes pops up and points a bright orange toy rocket launcher at me and I just finish reading the words LESS LETHAL printed on the weapon's stock before he pulls the trigger and a 40mm shell loaded with five wood slugs hits my chest, breaks a few ribs, slams me into the wall, puts me on my ass, and keeps me there while he shoots me a couple more times. Not that he needs to.


So, turns out the Coalition doesn't have any problem with shooting it up on their own turf after all. I'll give them points on restraint to the extent they used the riot gun, but it was still quite the spectacle. And it hurt plenty. Generally, a gun like that, you want to be at least twenty or thirty feet from your target, skip the rounds off the ground so they break up and pepper the legs of your average unruly mob. It'll leave a mark, but who can't live with a charley horse? From five feet out, put square in your chest, things get a little intense.

I move, feel the loose ends of ribs grating against each other, and stop moving.

A few of the wood slugs bounced upward off my chest and got me in the face. When I open my eyes I feel dry blood crack, same when I open my lips.

I'm looking at a concrete ceiling, fluorescent lights. Smells like gasoline, exhaust fumes and motor oil. I hear an engine starting somewhere, echoing, squeal of rubber.

Parking garage.

—Asshole.

I turn my head. It hurts. All I get for the trouble is confirmation that I was right, I am in a parking garage. Black SUV nearby. Couple limos farther away. A ramp coming from a lower level. No ramp heading up. We're at the top.

—Asshole.

Oh yeah, and I also get a look at the guy who shot me.

He's out of his coveralls now, stripped down to black suit. Just a little of the bleach smell they used to cover their Vyrus scent clings to him. But he still has the orange riot gun, and he's still pointing it at me.

—Asshole.

I finish casing the situation and look at him.

—Are you talking to yourself?

He nods.

—Funny, asshole.

He shoulders the gun, takes a bead on my face.

—Next round is pepper juice.

—Got it.

—Do anything I don't like, gonna get it in the face.

—Got it.

—Find out what a face full of pepper juice feels like.

—Said, *I got it.*

—One move I don't like, *bang!*

—Yeah, like I said, *I got it.* Clear on the pepper juice in the face. Now will you shut the fuck up so I can lie here and think quietly about how good it's going to feel when I shove the barrel of that thing in your mouth and empty it down your throat.

Bang!

It's a new one on me, shell full of pepper juice in the face. Blinds my good eye. Goes up my nose, gets in my ears, in my mouth, so much of it I swallow some. I vomit and that sure helps my ribs out. It hurts so much I have to move. I crawl in little blind circles, screams echoing, blotting out the sounds of the cars below.

—Asshole! Shut up! Knock that shit off before I hit you with another baton round.

Voice is close. He kicks me in the thigh. I crawl and scream and vomit a little more. He kicks me again. I slump against his leg, screaming, rubbing my face into his leg, trying to get the burning off. He grabs me by the hair to pull me away.

Which is how I know he's not pointing the riot gun at me anymore. So I wrap both arms around his legs, pull them out from under him, hear the crack when his skull hits the concrete, reach up his leg and find where it meets the other leg and grab a fistful of what's there and start squeezing and yanking and twisting, use my other hand to make a fist and start hammering the middle of his stomach, hear a clatter of plastic and metal, see a blur of bright orange next to me, pick it up and swing it like a club, bringing it down over and over on the place where I think I see his face.

By the time my eye has cleared enough for me to get a look at how I did, there's no point in emptying the gun in his mouth, but, like with Lament, I said I'd do it. Laughing when I get another look at that legend printed on the stock.

LESS LETHAL

But just enough.


Anyway, kind of a shame about emptying the thing. Seeing as it means I don't have anything lethal or otherwise when I climb off the enforcer's dead body just as another limo tops the ramp, pulls to a stop, and three more enforcers get out and grab me and hold me down while Dexter Predo exits from the back of the car.

—Pitt.

He takes off his jacket.

—I can't tell you.

He undoes a button on his white shirt, tucks his tie inside.

—Just how pleased I am.

He undoes his cuffs and rolls his sleeves to his elbows.

—How unequivocally delighted.

He takes a pair of calfskin black gloves from a back pocket and snugs them onto his hands.

—Imagine the odds.

He reaches in the open door of the limo, comes out with a small black doctor's bag that looks like a prop from an old movie.

—Meeting like this.

He walks over to where I'm pinned, steps across my body and stands over me with a foot on either side of my torso.

—It could only happen through sheerest luck.

He lowers himself and sits on my chest.

A rib end pokes my lung.

—Or if someone were idiot enough to park a known Hood vehicle in a high-surveillance area of Coalition turf.

He sets the bag next to my head and twists open the brass clasps.

—Leaving it there for nearly an hour.

He takes a pair of green-handled shears from the bag.

—While he slips into a bar for a few drinks.

He opens and closes the shears, testing the action.

—How fortunate for me that you are just such an idiot.

He looks at the enforcer holding my left arm and the guy shifts his grip and puts a knee in my shoulder and lifts my hand from the ground and I ball it into as tight a fist as I can.

Predo shows me the shears.

—Through a long process of elimination, over many years, I have found that the compound action of a good pair of hoof rot clippers allows for the easiest and cleanest severance.

He nods and the enforcer starts to pry at my fist.

—Now, we could start small, work our way up, but I feel we've covered so much ground already in our relationship. So many threats unfulfilled. At this juncture, I think we can do away with the formality of gradualism and move directly to actions that make a distinct impression. Permanency can be difficult to accomplish in this line. You've lost an eye already. And what's another toe, really? A man of your experience, what can I do that has not already been done?

Trying to open my fist, the enforcer has broken my pinkie and ring fingers to get what he's really after. But he has it now.

Predo points.

—Do you know what separates us from the animals, Pitt? Our thumbs.

He fits the open shears around the base of mine.

—Our opposable thumbs are what allowed us to become users of tools. And our use of tools is inextricably linked to the development of our brains.

He looks at me.

—But you, Pitt, with your profound and recurring idiocy, you can undoubtedly spare a thumb.

He squeezes.

—Perhaps even two.

The blades pass through the skin and meat and bone in a single smooth snip that proves Predo was right. They really are the best tool for the job.

My thumb on the ground, he decides to change tack for the moment and snip off my broken little finger next. One knuckle at a time.

I manage to stay with the show for the first two knuckles, by the third I've blacked out.

Not wondering if I'll wake, but if there will be anything left of me when I do.


I'm gonna die.

Not a news flash or anything. We all live under the same headline. But I'm gonna die here and now. Soon, anyway. In however much time it takes Predo to whittle me down to dead.

I know I'm right because I've felt the same thing so many times before. By now, I know exactly how it feels to know that you're about to die. And in all that time, it only ever happened once. And that lasted for less than a minute. I'm not saying it makes me feel optimistic about my chances here, but it does make me feel like there may be a play left in my hand.

All I have to do is sell people out.

• • •

I come to.

Count my fingers.

Still got five on the right hand and three on the left.

That's the good news. Bad news is, Predo's still on my chest, has the shears fitted at the top knuckle of my left ring finger, and seems to have just been waiting for me to open my eyes.

—Ah, there you are, Pitt. Welcome back.

He clips the knuckle, and I lose another fingerprint.

He moves the shears down about an inch.

I sell someone out.

—Digga's going to backstab you on the treaty!

He doesn't take the knuckle, but he doesn't move the shears from the finger either.

His brow furrows.

—I told myself.

He squeezes the shears just enough to break the skin around the knuckle.

—I told myself I'd finish the whole hand first.

A little more pressure and I can feel the blades touch bone, the scrape of steel.

—Before I asked what you could possibly be thinking that would make you do something so monumentally stupid.

He stops squeezing.

—When we both know, truly, that despite your best efforts to prove otherwise, you are not at all stupid. And, Pitt.

He closes his eyes and gives his head a little shake.

—I do not at all appreciate your interjecting here and causing me to rethink my plan of action.

He opens his eyes.

—You understand, yes?

I nod.

—Yes sir, Mr. Predo, I understand.

The corners of his mouth crimp.

—Ah, there it is, that air of sarcastic servility.

He snips away the knuckle.

—I've so missed that.

He lowers the shears from my hand, and rises, standing over me, looking down.

—And it appears you'll get one last chance to employ it, won't you?

He steps away, tilts his chin at the enforcers, and they release me.

I stay where I am, and hold up my mutilated left hand.

Index finger, middle finger, stub of a ring finger.

I show it to Predo.

—Got to thank you, Mr. Predo, you left just enough so I can still tell a guy to read between the lines.

Turns out you need two opposable thumbs to roll a cigarette.

—Are you going to fumble endlessly with your bad habit, Pitt?

I rip another rolling paper and spill more tobacco on the ground.

—I'll take any help I can get right now, Mr. Predo.

He looks at the three enforcers, they all shrug.

He unfolds his arms, comes away from the limo he's leaning against, and takes the pouch from my good hand.

—A lost art, it appears.

He tugs a paper from the folder.

—It has been some time for myself.

He settles tobacco into the crease, rolls the paper back and forth around it, shaping a cylinder, pinches lightly and spins it into a tight bundle.

—Ah, like a bicycle.

He licks the glue, seals the edge, and passes the smoke to me.

—And the match?

I dig the pack from my pocket, fold one down and under until the head touches the sandpaper, and give it a snap that brings it to light.

—I got that covered.

He nods.

—Useful, should you live for any time at all.

He drops the tobacco pouch into the tacky glaze of my blood that I'm sitting in.

—Unlikely as that may be.

He walks back to the limo and resumes his posture, leaning against the front fender, arms folded at his chest, ankles crossed.

—About that treaty you mentioned. It does not exist.

My hand has stopped bleeding. Stumps scabbed over, scabs drying and falling away, revealing fresh pink scar tissue. The fingers will never grow back. Something like a slender wart might sprout where my thumb was, but that's at most. And I'd just as soon it didn't. Cuts in my face feel all healed over. I can brush the dry blood off and find slightly stippled skin. If I don't move around too much, the ends of my ribs will finish knitting back together. Feels like a couple of them may end up crooked. I can still taste the pepper juice, I reek of it, but my throat and stomach have stopped burning, so that's OK.

I wonder what it's gonna be like to punch someone with a fist made out of two and a half fingers.

—Yeah, the treaty, you'll be negotiating it pretty soon.

—Details.

—Lament is dead.

He looks at his shoes.

—How. Unfortunate.

I take a drag.

—Yeah, that was my reaction.

He looks up from his shoes, long bangs in his eyes.

—Not that you had anything to do with it, I assume.

—Oh hell yes, I shot him a bunch and then I scalped him. Good night's work.

He pushes the hair off his forehead.

—I would add the killing of another Coalition officer to your record, but it is more than redundant at this stage.

—I'd hate anyone else to get credit for killing the fucker.

—Noted. I can assure you that when morning comes and you are staked out in the sun it will be included on the list of charges proved against you.

He puts a hand on top of the clippers he set earlier on the hood of the limo.

—And this treaty that does not exist, you foresee it for what reason?

I pick more scab from my finger stumps.

—Lament is dead. All his enforcers are dead. The Hood have cleared out the top of the rock. They got nothing distracting them up there anymore. No threat from inside their own border. Digga's going to clean house. Anyone on opposition. Papa Doc, that mouthpiece you keep up there, I expect Digga already executed him by now. He's done fucking around. By morning he'll have a unified front. And he'll be looking at One Ten, ready to get serious about war. Especially if it will force you to broker an agreement. Official cease-fire, and a resumption of trade.

He touches the tip of one of the shears' blades.

—They are starving.

—Sure. So they can either fight it out with you and try to expand their borders and their hunting ground, or they can settle and start buying your blood again.

He removes his finger from the blade.

—Digga made it clear he is not interested in our blood.

He looks at me.

—Having learned where it comes from.

My smoke is down to a nubbin. Knowing how hard it's going to be to get another one rolled, I pinch it like a roach and try to eke a last couple drags.

—We going to cry over spilt milk?

He picks up the shears.

—No. We are not.

He moves from the limo.

—So, you are telling me that Lament is dead, the top of the rock has fallen, Digga is assassinating his opposition in order to prepare for aggressive action along the border, but he is open to negotiating a treaty that he will then break at the earliest convenience.

One of the enforcers slaps the remains of my cigarette from my hand and the others close and I'm pinned again.

Predo cleans some of my dry blood from the blades of the shears.

—All terribly shocking to me. Indeed, how could it be that I did not already know the single most disputed piece of real estate in Manhattan had changed hands? Being only the head of Coalition intelligence, how could that bit of information have slipped past me? Ah, yes, but of course. Because it did not.

He snaps the shears open and closed.

—Truly, Pitt, is that your bid? As if I would not know. As if I could not surmise the rest. Of course we will negotiate a treaty. Of course Digga will plan to break it. But not before we break it first. There are machinations at play, Pitt. Upon whom would you care to place your bet, D.J. Grave Digga or myself?

He makes certain his tie has not become untucked from his shirt.

—Now, regarding that other thumb.

I wrap the fingers of my right hand around my thumb.

—The girl with the baby is inside the Cure house.

He's at my feet, looking down at the shears in his hand.

—Yes.

He turns away.

—That would give us something of value to talk about.

They keep coming.

SUVs and vans full of them.

Enforcers filling the top level of the garage.

I don't have nearly enough fingers to count them all. Even very recently I didn't have enough fingers to count them. Dozens. Over a hundred maybe. The full force. Fewer of the stylish black suits. More coveralls. Black slacks and windbreakers. Sweats. I see four dressed in police uniforms. A team of six in black tactical outfits including body armor, coiling ropes, snapping open carbon-fiber grappling hooks.

Sitting in the corner where they stuck me when the vehicles started rolling up the ramp, I remember something. I remember from the time I was on the Upper East a year ago, when I first came to the Cure house, I remember the parking garage just a few addresses west on the same block.

Lydia's sense of what the Coalition will or will not shoot up on their own turf appears to be for shit.

I think about that some. Mostly I think about mastering the one-hand cigarette roll, but I think about a shoot-up some as well. There are just too many guns not to think about it a little. Still, the cigarette roll is pretty all consuming. The tobacco I keep spilling isn't that big a deal, I just scoop it up and try again, but I've ripped a lot of papers trying to get this right. Those I'm running low on. Truthfully, it's not a one-hand roll, it's more a seven-finger roll. And after about ten shots at it I end up with something I can stick in my face and light on fire. It looks like a crooked Tootsie Roll more than a cigarette, but I can live with it.

I'm making do with that smoke when Predo comes over. He's still in shirtsleeves, but he's untucked his tie and gotten rid of the gloves. For now. I'm sure he could be ready to get back to work on my digits at a moment's notice.

He takes a second to look at a phone one of his boys holds up for him, taps the screen a couple times, nods, and the guy with the phone and the enforcer who's been watching me back off.

—We will be brief, Pitt.

I take a puff.

—Sure, I can see you have a set piece to coordinate here. Didn't realize you'd gotten into the action movie business.

He's not biting today.

—How do you know the young woman is in there?

—Digga's man, Percy.

—He told you.

—He told me.

—Reliably?

—Dying words.

He ponders that one.

—Quote them.

—Best of my recall, he said they were in the Cure house. Said he sent them there and they sent word back they were inside.

He stops pondering, puts his eyes on me, focusing.

—They sent back word. To the Hood.

—What he said.

He stays on me.

It's uncomfortable.

Those eyes of his, very old, staring out of that baby face, that skin kept taut and glowing by probably a pint a day. Those eyes have always been hard to meet. And with the years he's had in the game, he's seen about every tell any man's lie can give. He's sussed out most of my lies before they got past my lips. Half the lies I've told him, I got the idea to tell them from him in the first place. Because that's what he wanted me to do. Sometimes when I talk to the man, I have to look at his fingers, to make sure I'm not wrapped around one of them. He plays me that well. Always has. Only way I've ever played him back is with a smart mouth and the truth. And they don't stack up to much in the game he plays, not with the chips he's piled on his side of the table.

Those old eyes. That young face. That blood.

Knowing. Knowing where the blood comes from that keeps him so fiddle fit, it does something. 'Cause I scrabble out a living. I don't turn down what comes to me on a plate, but it's not offered too often. Mostly, I hustle or hunt for what I eat. It's not raised in a cage for me. It's not bred for me. It's not slaughtered for me.

I kill for myself.

His eyes, they may or may not know if I'm lying, I just don't fucking care anymore.

So I look right back into them, and let him play it how he wants.

He blinks. Which means fuckall. But he does it.

—I'd be interested in knowing through what channels that message was sent.

—Telephone.

—He told you that?

—He told me they picked up a phone when they were safe inside, called him, so he'd know.

—The girl, her unborn baby, and who?

—The baby daddy.

He turns, waves over the enforcer with the phone, takes it and looks at the screen again, taps, hands it back, looks at me.

—And they've not left?

I'm at the bottom of my skanky little smoke, the last drag burns my lips, but I take it anyway.

—You're the one with the stakeout. You tell me.

He nods.

—Yes, but if they got in without our seeing.

—Yeah, sure, they might get out. But as far as I know? Inside.

His hands go in his pockets.

—And your interest in this?

I push myself off the concrete and stand.

—I know the girl's dad. He asked me to find her.

—So you are a humanitarian.

—He offered me a shitload of money. Enough I thought I could maybe get off this rock and go find someplace new to hide.

He gives a little smile.

—New Jersey, perhaps.

I smile myself.

—Yeah, something like that.

He loses the smile.

—You can get inside?

—If your boys don't shoot me first, I think maybe yeah.

His phone guy shows him the phone again.

—And you can get them out?

—Hell if I know.

—Some confidence would help your case, Pitt.

I'm doing a seven-finger roll.

—Some confidence would be a lie. I haven't seen anyone in there for over a year. And things were tense. Sela could rip my head off on sight.

—But not the Horde girl.

—No. Maybe. Could be. I don't know. Any case, she wouldn't rip my head off herself, she'd have Sela do it.

He sends the phone guy away.

—It does sound very like a win-win for me. Either you come out with the girl and her baby, or Horde and Sela rip your head off.

I light up on another spavined reject from the cigarette family.

—Or I squat in there and you can go fuck off.

He nods.

—Well.

He gestures at the preparations going on around us.

—I wouldn't count on squatting unmolested for very long.


—There are time issues.

—So I gather.

—But there would be advantages to having them out. The girl and the baby. The father I do not care about.

—Sure, I get it. You don't want to see the symbol of the future accidentally shot.

He's unrolling his sleeves.

—*Symbol of the future.* Indeed. I think it might be more apt to say that they are a symbol for the virtues of proper birth control practices. But not everyone is as clear-minded. The Coalition is purely socio-political in nature, but even here there have been whispers of the *significance* of the unborn. Until I can eliminate that whiff of mythology, I'd rather avoid any unfortunate mishaps that Bird might publicize to his advantage.

—Always best to minimize the potential collateral dead bodies before you go crashing through the windows.

—We will be using doors. It is not a spectacle we are performing here. It is an action. One made unavoidable by the untenable presence of the Cure house on Coalition territory. It has become hermetic. Information does not flow out. We cannot have a mystery box full of infected, lorded by a mad girl, in our midst. Not now. Not with tensions as they stand.

—Especially not when you don't know if they're secretly allied with the Society and the Hood.

He buttons his cuffs.

—Irrelevant.

I run a hand under my shirt and over my chest. I can feel a couple knobs of bone where the ribs have healed out of true. They don't hurt, but they'll be weak points that will snap easy the next time they take a shot.

I point at some of the action going on in the garage. Weapons being stripped, blueprints reviewed, a couple laptops set up in the back of one of the SUVs, a tiny mobile communications center.

—Pretty heavy action for irrelevant.

He reclaims his jacket from an enforcer.

—They have been starving for months. They possess no coordination as a military force. But in the absence of any knowledge to the contrary, we must assume they are a threat to expose themselves at any moment. However many of them are left inside, they must emerge sooner or later. When they do, they will not be in control of their appetites.

—So this is a mercy mission.

He slides his arms into the jacket.

—No. This is a tactical operation that will eliminate a threat to the Coalition.

I'm looking at some guns that look big and useful.

—Always thought this kind of action on your turf was verboten.

—Events progress. We must adapt.

I point at the guns.

—Can I have one of those?

He squints.

—One moment while I think. No, you may not.

I point at the ramp.

—Whatever's going on in that place, it's gonna be hairy. I know you won't be shedding tears at my funeral, but the point is for me to save the girl and the baby, yeah? Get them out before you come in with the goon squad. I may need to be armed to make that happen.

He shakes his head.

—No. You are far too spontaneous in how you choose to distribute bullets.

He looks up at a flickering light fixture.

—But yes, you should have something. The knife and the garrote you were carrying.

—I'd rather not have to get so intimate if Sela has a beef with me.

He looks down from the light.

—Truly, Pitt, if Sela is no longer amused by your monkey tricks, do you believe a gun or any number of bullets will keep her at bay?

I think about Sela, six foot plus of weightlifter muscle grafted onto a Vampyre and combined with the particular hormonal imbalance of a pre-op tranny. She is unique and dangerous and I don't understand a thing about her. Except that she's one of the six most dangerous people I've ever met. And she once took on two of the others at the same time and came out on top.

—No, I don't think it would help much. But I do like to have a gun.

An enforcer approaches with my wire saw and amputation blade. He hands them to Predo.

Predo slips a few inches of the blade from its rubber sheath.

—Have you ever seen one employed by a surgeon?

—Can't say I have.

He pulls it the rest of the way free.

—To amputate a leg above the knee, one must wrap their arm around the limb, from underneath, bringing the blade toward oneself, angling the tip downward. The goal is to cut into the flesh deeply, to the bone, while whipping one's arm away, unwinding it from around the leg. When perfected, the maneuver leaves a single incision that circles the femur. A moment's work with a bone saw and the leg is off.

He studies the edge of the knife, slips it back in its sheath, and hands it to me.

—Please do not lose it, Pitt. Should you survive without the girl and the baby I may want to put it to use.

I sling the blade under my arm.

—Sure thing. And thanks for the tip. I'm thinking the same move would work on someone's neck.

He considers me, giving a look like he's trying to figure if an abstract painting has been hung upside down.

—Was that a threat of some kind?

I drop the saw in my pocket.

—Hell no. Just, I like to see the utility in things.

We're walking to the stairwell at the corner of the garage.

—We are alike in that, if nothing else.

He stops.

—Do you have a watch?

—No.

He looks at the phone again.

—No matter. Synchronization is unnecessary. We will begin our operation sometime after midnight. That gives you as little as three hours, but perhaps more.

I'm trying to roll another smoke.

—So this is a precision op then.

He lifts a hand.

—It is quite precise.

He drops the hand to his side.

—I simply have no interest giving you the precise details.

I nod.

—Wise.

—Yes.

He brushes his hair from his forehead again.

—Indeed, we might simply be using you to open the door. You may find us at your heels. Perhaps we have no intention of executing a raid at all. The Coalition owns this garage. This could all be a drill. My only interest may be in sending you to your death inside the Cure house. There might be several tiny listening devices tucked into your clothing. Placed while you were blacked out. I could, at the end of this sentence, break into maniacal laughter and have you dragged back to the floor so that I may complete whittling you to a trunk. But, for the sake of argument, you may as well assume that you have as little as three hours to lead the pregnant girl out. Or secure her within the building.

The new smoke is a little better than the last couple, giving me hope for the future. I light it.

—As long as we have a clear framework for how we're handling this, I'm cool.

He opens the door to the stairs.

—On your way then.

I tilt my head to him.

—The way we always work something out, Predo, you'd never guess how much we're looking forward to killing each other.

I step past him and he puts his hand in the middle of my back.

—Then let us put an end to any misconceptions.

He pushes and I go down a half flight, those two ribs that didn't mend right snapping for the second time in a couple hours.

He waves two enforcers into the stairwell.

—I think someone should be chasing you. Combined with your general state of disarray and mutilation, it will make whatever tale of woe you tell that much more convincing.

I'm still on my ass, holding my ribs.

He brushes his hand at me.

—Best to scamper, Pitt. For the sake of absolute verisimilitude, I've instructed them to kill you if they do in fact catch you.

I get up.

The enforcers start moving their lips, silently.

Predo points down.

—Do hurry, they will only count to fifteen before they begin their pursuit.

Footsteps on the stairs above me.

I save whatever I have left to say and get moving.

The sidewalks outside the parking garage have that same abandoned feel as the ones around Morningside Park. The vibe is clearly in the air. People who don't live here take a look and figure they can walk a little farther and cross east or west a block away. The people who have to get to their front doors do little more than that. Walk quickly from the corner to the stoop, key in hand. Dog owners pull their mutts down the street, dragging them at the ends of their leashes if they pause to piss at the base of a dying tree.

But there are a few people about, heads down, minding their own, marching home or quickly to the corner where the air doesn't feel as threatening, and those few people, they slow the enforcers to a trot when they follow me onto the street. Another time they might just barrel after me, but with the action ready to go down, they're trying to play it cool.

Not me.

I don't know if they'll really kill me if they get their hands on me, but I don't want to find out. So I run as fast as my bad knee, my gimped toe and my broken ribs will let me, right up the steps to the front door of the Cure house where I start by pressing the buzzer and, with the enforcers closing ground, graduate to pounding the door with my fist. The complete one. Because I figure it will be louder.

—Fuck off!

Said through a suddenly opened peep door just big enough for me to see the mouth behind it.

The enforcers are three stoops up the street.

I lean close to the peep.

—You guys got trouble coming.

The peep snaps shut.

I kick the door.

The enforcers are two stoops away.

The peep opens and the barrel of a shotgun pokes out.

—Fuck! Off!

The amputation blade drops from its sheath into my hand and I slip it into the barrel of the gun.

—Pull the trigger, fuckface.

Enforcers are one stoop away.

The guy inside tries to pull the shotgun back and I grab the barrel with what's left of my left hand. Not the best grip, two fingers and a palm, but I put my back into it.

—Let me the fuck in or there's gonna be blood on your doorstep and cops in your ass.

The enforcers are at the bottom of the stoop, hands in jackets.

The door opens, my grip on the shotgun swinging me inside. I whip the blade out and turn toward the door and my view of the enforcers is cut off as it slams shut and someone gets a good shot on the back of my neck with the butt of their shotgun and I hit the deck and the barrel is in my face again, but I've lost my grip on my blade and I don't feel like sticking one of my fingers in the thing because I'm running a little low.

—Don't fucking move!

I don't.

—Who the fuck are you?

It's funny what being chased will do to you. Get you all out of sorts and scrambled. Make you focus just on what's in front of you, just what you see in the tunnel vision of the moment. Like the barrel of a shotgun in your face can plain blot out the sun. Your own heartbeat can drown out thunder. The smell of pepper juice coating your clothes can swamp the odor of a well-known pomade.

But I'm evening out now, with just the shotgun to worry about and no enforcers drooling over the prospect of shooting me in the back.

I'm seeing and I'm hearing and I'm smelling.

The guy with the gauge jams it closer to my face in the dark hallway.

—Who the fuck are you?

I go ahead and put a finger in the barrel.

—What ho, Phil, you don't recognize a friend?

A flinch travels down the length of the barrel.

—Aw, aw, shit. Aw shit. Joe. Aw shit.

I touch the lump at the base of my skull. It swells and starts to recede.

—That smarted, Phil.

—Aw shit.

I take my hand from the lump.

—But you could make it all OK between us with just one thing.

He nods.

—What's that, Joe?

—Got a cigarette?

He deflates.

—Aw shit.

He offers the shotgun to me.

—I quit months ago.

I take the shotgun and stand.

—You're shitting me.

He raises his hands.

—Would I hold out? Given the dynamic that, you know, we follow, I mean, would I hold out on a fucking cigarette?

I take the Bugler from my pocket.

—Can you roll one of these?

He takes it from my hand.

—Asking can I roll? Jesus, Joe, who are you asking can I roll? Can
I roll? Like asking if I can cut a line of coke.

He starts to roll.

I listen to some howls rising from below the floor.

He hands me a hand-rolled smoke that looks like it was run off
an assembly line.

—Nice work, Phil.

He grazes his blond pompadour with the tips of his fingers.

—A man has certain skills, he's got to maximize them.

I nod and light up.

—So, Phil.

He nods.

—Yeah?

I heft the shotgun and wave it at the hallway and front door.

—What the fuck?

He shakes his head.

—I tell ya, man, I barely fucking know myself.

• • •

The howling, it turns out, is the least of it.

Time to time, something bangs against the basement ceiling and vibrates the floorboards. Every time it happens, Phil jumps. And there's the smell. Dead being the basic theme. Vyrus, being the key variation. Feces and rot play into it. Makes me happy I emptied my stomach when the pepper juice hit me. Matter of fact, it makes me pretty damn happy about getting hit with the stuff in the first place. Good chance I'm the best smelling thing in here.

—She said you'd come.

—She says a lot of crazy things.

—Sure, I mean, hell yeah and all, but still, she said it. And, you know, man, here you are.

—She can't see the future, Phil.

He stops at the steel door at the end of the hall and pulls on the chain that's clipped to his belt, drawing a heavy ring of keys from his pocket.

—I know that. Mean, I'm not a total asshole.

He smiles.

—Mean, sure, I'm a total asshole, but I mean, I know she's no psychic, she's just right about a lot of things.

—It's because she's smart.

He unlocks three dead bolts.

—More because she's so fucking weird.

The hall we're leaving has just the two doors, the front stoop and this one. The hall we're entering has four or five lining it, and all are broken down. From the inside, it looks like.

Phil closes the door behind us and does the locks.

I think about submarines. How they dog all the hatches behind themselves so if there's a leak it will only flood one compartment.

He points at the broken doors.

—No one lives down here anymore. Not since the shit storm.

—Evocative.

—If that means effed in the a-bone, Joe, you just hit the nail, man.

Something especially big hits the floor from below and seems to trigger a riot. Howling, screaming, rapid hammering.

Phil skips a couple times, moving ahead of me on his toes.

And I realize that the epicenter of the howling and pounding seems to move with him.

He starts jumping up and down, screaming at the floor.

—Fuck you! Fuck you! Fucking leave me alone, you fucking freaks of whatever the fuck! You can't fucking have it! It's fucking mine! I was born with it and I'm gonna fucking keep it! It's mine! All mine!

The racket from below rises with his screams, crests, and then subsides to moaning and tapping.

Philip Sax, a man who is not at his best without a skinful of speed and a mouthful of booze, slumps against the wall.

—Fuck.

I knock my heel against the floor.

—Friends of yours?

He moves from the wall and starts unlocking the door.

—No.

He opens the door on a stairwell.

—It's just that they can smell blood through the floor and it makes 'em crazy.

The stairwell is fun.

The doors to the second and third floors have been torn off their hinges, and through them I can see large barracks-style rooms. Lots of cots and bunk beds. Signs of hasty construction. Bare plaster, wires dangling from unfinished fixtures. Pipes sticking raw from the walls. More signs of hasty destruction. Broken furniture, scattered personal effects, ragged holes in the drywall. There's also a fair number of bullet holes, dry blood, fingernail claw marks on the wood and in the plaster, some recent cuts in one area of the floor where an axe has been wielded repeatedly. Not in an effort to chop through, but as if someone has been hewing something, the blade cleaving and biting the floor.

I point.

—Someone chopping firewood?

Phil turns his head away.

—Yeah, um, pretty sure that's where Sela was euthanizing.

—Speaking of big words.

—Yeah, well, you know, I could say she was hacking the heads off spastic Vampyres, but that kind of lingo doesn't go over here, man.

—A spade is still a spade.

He mounts the stairs to the next landing.

—That lingo don't fly neither.

There's some more howling, coming from up ahead now.

Phil pauses with his foot between steps.

I usually run these next couple flights, man. You mind?

I raise a hand.

—Settle down and join me on the scenic route. Man doesn't get to see this kind of thing every day.

He hunches his shoulders.

—Not unless he's me.

We climb.


The next couple floors are still inhabited. In deference to this fact massive slide-bolts have been mounted on the door. Some kind of electromagnet freezing them in place. A cluster of wires running from floor to floor, door to door up and down the stairwell.

I knock on one door and get what sounds like a half-dozen giant rats scrabbling at the other side.

—What about the windows?

Phil is at the edge of the landing, itching to move on.

—Sela drilled into the brick at the sides. Bolted two-inch planks over them. Before it got like this. Said it was heightened security because of, you know, Coalition and all. But she just knew what was coming is what I think. Jesus, Joe. That chick is one tough motherfucker. What's a chick do to get that kind of tough? I mean, shit.

I come away from the door and follow him.

—Got me. But she scares me shitless.

—A-fucking-men.

I can see we're approaching the top. Midpoint of the flight, with the howls from the last floor diminishing, I tug the back of Phil's black and white bowling shirt, says *Rick* over the pocket, and he stops.

—Joe?

I hand him the tobacco pouch again.

—Hit me.

He starts to roll.

I point the barrel of the shotgun up and down the stairwell.

—So you still haven't told me what the fuck.

He hands me another perfect smoke.

—Well, fuck, Joe, I thought it was pretty abundantly clear by now. Coalition cut off the blood, and shit got all fucked up.

I light up, take a drag, shake my head and tap the barrel against his chest.

—No, I mean, *what the fuck?*

He nods.

—Oh, right, yeah, well. You know, man, I guess I just kind of wore out my welcome everywhere else.

I blow a cloud over his head.

—Say it ain't so.

He nods.

—Yeah, right? Because what have I ever done but try and help everybody out?

—If by *help out* you mean *sell out,* then I get what you're saying.

—Now is that?

He finds some umbrage somewhere and runs with it.

—I'm saying, Joe, is that? Here we are, you and me, some of the last of the old school, here we are, getting reacquainted, I'm rolling your cigarettes for Jesus sake! Here we are and, come on, here we are like almost having a nice conversation for the first time in forever, and you have to take on like that. Like I've never been on your side. Like I, Joe.

He shakes his head slow.

—It's a discouragement is what it is, Joe. That's what it is.

I raise a hand, the one that's not all there.

—Don't wear it out, Phil. You been on my side like you been on everyone else's.

He lifts both arms over his head.

—Exactly! I've done for everyone! Who doesn't have me to thank for something or other I done to help out? And now when things get tricky out there, when a man was thinking maybe he'd get his chance to really shine, helping out, you know, for whoever needed it, everyone gets all uptight and decides they don't want me around. Mean to say, Joe, they tried to bump me.

—Who was at the front of that line?

—Terry is who. Calls me up, asks me to come see him. Terry Bird, all polite. As opposed to just telling me to do whatever the fuck *or else.* I don't hear *or else* at the end of a service request, I know the jig is up. I was going out the fire escape, someone was kicking in the door. Tried to use my phone drop to Mr. Predo, got a suspiciously warm welcome to Coalition turf. Nuh-uh. *Come in out of the cold.* I seen that fucking movie at Film Forum once. Came to last resorts, this was the place. All my old regulars got no love left, I got to find new love. Sad. What kind of appreciation is that? Trying to cap a useful asset like myself. None. It's none appreciation. It's, I don't know what it is.

—It's expedient.

He drops his arms.

—See, and there you go insulting me and doing it using words that I only sort of know what they mean.

—Means it was the smart play.

He stares at me, shakes his head.

—Well, thank you very much, Joe Pitt.

I lift my shoulders.

—Don't take it hard, Phil. You played the center against the middle and the ends against the top and bottom so well, when the chips were finally down they all decided you were too dangerous to live.

He smiles.

—Yeah, yeah, you know, put like that, almost kind of flattering. *Too dangerous to live.* Make a cool tattoo.

I lean the barrel of the shotgun on my shoulder.

—So it's not all bad.

Howls drift up from below.

I take a drag.

—And you roll a mean smoke besides.

He smiles wide, shows blank spots where he used to have silver caps to replace the teeth I knocked out of his jaw. Pawned, I suppose.

—Thanks, Joe, that means something. Coming from you and all.

He looks down a little.

—Say, Joe?

—Phil.

He looks up a little.

—What happened to your fingers?

I furrow my brow, look at my left hand, shake my head.

—Damn. Where the hell did I put those?

We have a little laugh.

Phil Sax. He's not all bad. Just he's an untrustworthy dirtbag is all.

That's probably why I stick the shotgun in the back of his neck when he starts to unlock the door at the top of the stairs. Why I hiss at him to keep it zipped when someone on the other side asks what's up. Why I kick him in ahead of me and follow only after he stumbles in and no one blows any holes in him. Why I go in barrel first, crouching, at an angle.

Why it goes all sideways at that point is because when Sela jumps from the blind corner at my far left and I turn and try to put one in her gut before she lands on me, I find out that as bad as things have got in here they haven't yet got to the point where anyone is giving Phil a loaded weapon.

Shame on me for not checking that one.

Advantage Sela, on me, grabbing a fistful of hair, lifting my head and slamming it into the floor, raising a fist that will likely collapse my face. Good hand is attached to the arm pinned under her left knee, bad hand is free, clawing at her eyes, just enough fingers to do that. Wonder if I'll feel the second punch, or if the first will do the deal. Fuck, I hope so.

—Sela!

The fist grazes my skull, feels like being grazed by a sledge-hammer, splinters the floor next to my head.

—Baby, come here, baby.

Sela's nostrils open, then her mouth. She leans her face to mine, I'm waiting for her to bite, and she's gone, jumping like a tick, and I can feel an imprint of her hot skin where her legs and thighs and bottom rested against me.

And I smell blood.

Up on an elbow, those two fucking ribs broken yet a-fucking-gain, I take a gander at what it looks like when everything goes completely off the rails.

The room takes up most of the top floor. Large parts of it have been turned into a lab. Steel tables, refrigerators, computer equipment, things that look like they analyze stuff, test tubes, an autoclave. Hell, there's even Bunsen burners. Just missing a Tesla coil to make it a complete mad scientist setup. Another part of the room is devoted to another kind of business. There are a lot of guns scattered around, cases of dehydrated high-energy and high-protein meals. Cases of whiskey and vodka, jugs of water, batteries, a couple small gas-powered generators. A bank of flickering CCTV screens, most dead, with an occasional jump to a picture of the front stoop, the stairwell, one of those empty barracks, and a night vision–green view of a row of steel doors in a basement. In front of the screens, a length of 2x4 with a series of knife switches screwed into it, wires running to a hole in the floor. The office consists of a big wood desk covered in papers and uneaten meals, three computer monitors, a model made out of sticks and little balls and geodesic blocks. Across the room are two open doors: through one I can see a bathroom, through the other it looks like living quarters.

A couple things are especially riveting. Start with a row of glass jars, big-ass jars, along one of those steel tables, each with a head floating inside. But that's not the showstopper. That's the young lady sitting at the desk.

Young, beautiful, brilliant and rich, Amanda Horde always had it all. Including a bonus set of whacked-out parents. Still, long as I've known her, she's been looking for more. Looking to do something special. Cure what ails us. Even though she's not one of us. Girl on the edge of things, special she is.

And at the moment, her half-starved Vampyre lover's mouth is latched over a cut on her forearm.

She runs her fingers across Sela's forehead.

—That's right, baby, it's OK. We're OK.

She looks at me.

—Joe.

I look at her.

—Hey, Amanda.

She gives a flat smile.

—Can you come over here and give me a hand, Joe? I mean, mostly she's *fine,* but sometimes it takes a little extra work to pull her off once she gets started.


It takes a little extra work to pull her off.

She keeps feeding while she swings her fist around, trying to force me back, but I get an arm around her neck and manage to wrench her face from Amanda's arm. She's pretty pissed about that and looks to kill me for it, then her eyes kind of roll up and she goes to all four and crawls away and curls up and goes to sleep.

So I get to live another day.

Or another minute anyway.

Time will tell.


—I'd say, if anyone was asking, I'd say he's working for Predo on this one.

—Shut *up,* Philip.

—Just I'm saying is all, how those enforcers didn't exactly beat down the door to get after him is all.

Amanda stops flicking through the slides that zip across her monitors.

—How about that, Joe, are you working for Predo again?

I pause in my rummaging.

—Yeah, afraid so. He's getting ready to raid the place. I'm supposed to get some quick intel, get out and let him know if there's anything in here to worry about.

She starts flicking through slides again.

—*See,* Philip, nothing to worry about.

Phil rocks back and forth in his chair.

—Man, there are like sooo many things in what he just said that I can worry about.

I hold up a carton of shitty clove cigarettes that smell like candy.

—Is this all you laid up?

She glances over.

—Yeah. Help yourself. I totally gave up on that bad habit.

I think about it. I will admit that much, I do think about it. Then I drop the carton back where I found it and grab a bottle of Scotch instead.

—You give up this bad habit?

She shakes her head.

—No. But I'm a total *lightweight* these days.

Sela is still sleeping, but I cut a path well around her anyway.

—Yeah, wonder why that is.

Amanda fingers the edge of the bandage she put over the fresh cut in her arm. Both arms have several more similar wounds, from well-healed to barely scabbing.

—Don't be an asshole, Joe. I *mean,* don't be that kind of asshole. I mean, *please,* am I going to let her starve?

I twist the cap from the bottle and find a couple dirty glasses in the mess on her desk and pour a couple drinks.

—That would be my plan.

She takes a glass from me.

—No it wouldn't. I mean, say it if you need to, but *no,* that wouldn't be your plan.

Phil looks up when he hears liquid hitting glass and comes over.

—Yeah, Joe's plan would be more like to just shoot her.

We both look at him.

He shrugs.

—I'm just saying, but I don't know anything, so I'm just saying.

He points at the bottle.

—Um?

I drink what's in my glass, refill it, set the bottle down and find a chair.

—Help yourself, Phil.

I take a sip.

—What we got going on tonight, it won't happen again.

That worm, I was waxing poetical about, it's fucking here. Looking at Amanda in her dirty jeans and filthy lab coat as she stares at her monitors, I can just about see it behind her eyes.

Something's eating her. And I don't mean Sela.

—I can barely look at you, Joe.

—What's that mean?

She flicks a couple more slides across her screens.

—I mean, Joe, I mean, come *on.* We've been through *so* much together. I *mean,* would I even be here without you. I don't mean like would I be *alive,* because, yes, yes, I'd have been dead years ago without you. I mean, would I be *here?*

Still looking at those screens, she flips a hand, taking in the circumstances.

I empty another finger from my glass. Ha ha.

—Don't blame me, kid. You got yourself neck deep.

She shakes her head.

—*See,* and that is why I can barely look at you. Because after all *this,* you're still this person I don't even know. This thing I don't even *know.* Gah. I *hate* it.

I'm watching the screen myself. Those slides. Some I can tell are blood cells. I've seen that kind of thing before. White and red. Little blobs and little donuts things. Other stuff she's looking at, I don't know. Could be explosions in space, could be sculpture, could be deep-sea spine creatures, could be mold. Could be anything.

But knowing the girl, they're all viruses. That's her bag.

Viruses and the Vyrus.

I look into my glass.

—What's to know.

She giggles.

—Joe.

Giggles some more.

—Oh, Joe.

Gets ahold of herself.

—If you only knew.

I take a drink.

—Har-dee-har-har.

She spins her chair to face me.

—Spying for Predo.

—Yep.

—Again.

—Yep.

—I *mean*.

—Yep.

She waggles the fingers of her left hand.

—You didn't have to do that, Joe.

I set my glass down, go for my tobacco.

—What's that?

She folds her left pinkie, thumb and most of her ring finger into her palm.

—You didn't have to sit still for Predo doing *that* to you.

I flip the pouch at Phil, quietly shaking, drinking his booze and staring at Sela.

—Make yourself useful, Phil.

He picks up the pouch and starts to roll one.

I look back at Amanda.

—I'm sorry, you were suggesting what craziness now?

She unfolds her fingers.

—I was *suggesting* that you went to some odd length to convince Predo you were desperate and would, I mean, you know, do his *bidding*.

—Lady.

I snap a finger that has a thumb to work with and Phil hands me my smoke.

—You find new ways of being crazy every time I see you.

She turns to her screen.

—Joe Pitt lets himself be *captured* by Predo. Lets himself be *tortured*. All so he can *convince* Predo to send him in here. And make sure I'm *OK*.

She giggles.

—And I'm not even your type.

I light up.

—Know what's funniest about how wrong you are?

—Tell me, Joe, I mean, *tell* me.

I blow smoke.

—It's that the missing fingers are supposed to make *you* believe Predo really tried to kill me and I just barely got away.

She tosses some hair.

—Well *sure,* but I'm talking about subtext.

Phil comes for the bottle and pours himself another.

—You are both, I'm just saying as a casual observer and not like an expert or anything, but you are both in need of some, what I'd call, some serious help.

She flicks to another slide.

—We have some *strange* history, Joe and me.


The bottle is almost empty. Not that it took very long.

Sela's breathing has changed, become less peaceful. I've wandered around the room and looked at most everything I can, but I still can't get a look through the half-open door into the living quarters. Phil's nodding, not quite passed out, but not for lack of trying.

Amanda's getting weirder as she gets drunker.

And she's talking. And talking. And talking.

—So for a while I went on this *other* trip. I mean, OK, the Vyrus, it just won't make sense. It won't behave at all *virusy.* Yes, OK, yes, it lacks the ability to reproduce on its own. Yes it accesses healthy cells so it can get at the machinery it *needs* to reproduce. But there's no, like, modus operandi. Like, take a normal virus, it might do *all kinds* of stuff to get into a cell. It might *pretend* to be another cell. It might just jump out from behind something and *attack* a cell. It might, just, you know, like, anything. But like *just* one thing. OK. And, the Vyrus, it does *everything.* Watch it long enough, take enough *samples* from enough infecteds, you'll see it do everything.

She flicks through a series of slides that look like gunshot wounds, but they aren't.

—So, OK, so it's an RNA virus. Start with that. *I* did. 'Cause an RNA virus is fast. It creates so many copies of itself so fast, it makes just a *ton* of mistakes. More mistakes equals more mutation equals greater variance. And blah and blah and blah. Hardier species, we've all read *Darwin* by now and so *OK*. But so what? Because this thing isn't mutating over eons or centuries or years or, *whatever* periods that normal stuff mutates over. I mean, lasting mutations. Not flukes and sports. Not that a virus can *really* be a sport, but you know, right. So. Radical and lasting mutations that happen like when you *turn* your back and then turn back.

She looks over at me and bugs her eyes.

—Creeepy.

She looks back at her screens.

—Cool. But creepy. So I start thinking *creepy*.

More slides.

I drift closer to the door into the living quarters.

Sela snorts, twitches, settles.

Amanda stops on a trio of slides.

—Really, really creepy. Like, don't laugh, what if, and I hadn't slept in like *six days* when I thought this, but what if it's a space virus?

She taps a key and the slide in the center zooms and it's just a smear on the screen.

—And I don't mean like a drifty space virus that hitches a ride on a *meteor* and crashes into earth and like somehow is adaptable to our environment and stuff. I mean, what if it's like a targeted virus. I mean, Joe, I mean, germ warfare from *outer space,* I mean.

She taps that same key and the smear becomes a blur.

—Not against us. That's stupid. I mean, I hate calling it this but my dad never gave it a name and just *whatever,* but look at the *zombie* bacteria. There's all this, like, *snobbery* in the Vampyre community about this stuff. You all act like, oh, *Zombie scum created by a bacteria must be eliminated while we higher forms created by a virus must live on.* But, ha ha, bacteria are so much more *advanced* than viruses that it isn't even funny. I mean, *bacteria* are alive. Viruses don't even have a *nucleus.* But still, the Vyrus and the zombie thing, they have these weird similarities. Like, one thing the Vyrus does is it sometimes mimics bacteria. To get close to other bacteria. And infect them. It burns out like that, but it happens when you put them together. Which is *weird.* So imagine this scenario where you have, and I already said *don't laugh,* you have these aliens at war. And this war it's on like, a *massive* scale. Galactic in scope. Which means, ipsy-facty, that it's *slooow.* 'Cause of E=MC$^2$, yeah? OK. So what if a big part of this war is about territory. And so they, here, see, they *infect* whole worlds. They, this is *wild,* they design bio-agents for prospective territories, places they may want to colonize in like *millions* of years, and they *shoot* these weapons at the worlds and they infect certain species and their enemies do the same thing and the *idea is* that the infected species will fight it out and the one that *wins* is programmed by the infection, I mean, just in the way it has to exist, what it eats and just the *basics,* what it does to live will help to make the world more hospitable for the aliens in millions of years if they *ever come.*

I laugh.

She doesn't.

I stop.

She looks at me.

—*Who* are you, Joe Pitt? *What* are you, Joe Pitt? I mean, are you secretly trying to backstab me by pretending to backstab Predo?

Or are you secretly fighting for your alien masters and you don't even know it?

I lean against the wall.

—You're not serious.

She tilts her head back and forth.

—Well, not anymore. But I *was*.

She turns to her screens.

—Just that it's unnecessary.

A series of slides that look like railroad ties welded together at odd angles.

—Because we know like, *what*, like one percent of the life on earth. And there are at least ten times as many unknown viruses as there are other life-forms in that remaining ninety-nine percent.

She shrugs.

— I mean, who needs outer space to explain weird stuff with all that right here.

I edge the door open an inch.

On the bed, a foot. But I can't tell if it's attached to anything.


It's all stuff I can't follow, but Amanda keeps talking anyway.

Says stuff about how most of the genetic material on the planet is viral. String it all together and you'd have a line that stretched ten million light-years. Talking about three branches of life, eukaryotes, bacteria and archaea, and how viruses just live off those three. Mentions something called LUCA. Says that's the last universal common Ancestor. The first single life-form before life split into its three categories. Tells me that a virus's strength is its ability to persist. That most of the human genome is viral DNA. How things called retroviruses program RNA to make viral DNA that splices into host cells' DNA and how it gets passed on as the cell does its normal replication.

Mostly it's just words and letters to me.

If I get the sense of one out of ten things she's saying, I'm lucky. But it's kind of always been that way. Between how smart and how crazy she is, there's not much room for a guy like me to understand much of what comes out of her mouth.

I stay busy with whiskey and cigarettes.

And with thinking about that foot on the bed. Wondering if it's attached to a pregnant girl.

I'd go try and get a better look, but I'm trying not to move around too much because one of Sela's eyes is open now and I can't tell if it's just something that happens, or if she's awake.

Talk about creepy.

But there's room for more.

—Want to see something *amazing*?

I go over to the desk and look at the screens. Moving slow, trying to see if Sela's eye follows me.

It does.

—What you got?

What she's got is more blobs on her monitors.

She's pointing at one, harsh pink and green, rods and blobs.

—This is it.

I look.

—It what?

She looks up at me.

—The Vyrus, Joe. That's what it looks like.

I look again, but I don't recognize it. It's not the face of god or anything, just a picture of the flu I caught a long time ago. The one that makes me need blood to survive.

—It's pink and green.

She flicks her fingers and something similar appears, but it's blue and green and the blobs look more geometric.

—This is it too, but a *different* sample. From someone else. And it's like that. I mean, *whoever* it's in, it's different in them. Not just how its traits *manifest,* but its appearance. Which is the weirdest thing about it. And it had me totally *pissed* at it.

Sela grunts.

I point at her.

—Is she gonna try and kill me?

—Um, I don't think so. I mean, I don't know, but mostly she's cool after a little blood. *Mostly* she's like herself. But she's been *hungry* so long now, months, so she's also *mostly* kind of feral. But I think you're cool.

I move toward the gun racks.

Sela growls.

I move away from the gun racks. Remembering how I looked for cigarettes and booze instead of setting myself up with a piece.

Now I'm starting to get itchy about the clock.

Amanda is still going on about the Vyrus.

—But I'm thinking *primal* thoughts now. Earthy. Who needs space? I mean, we all *came* from something. That LUCA thing? That's our slime. The primordial one they're always going on about in PBS specials. But what was it that took the *pre*-nucleus slime and gave it a nucleus? Made it into nuclear cellular stuff.

A slide that looks like an organ that's been pierced from the inside by glass rods.

—Take some pre-LUCA bacteria. No nucleus. A cell without a nucleus. *Perfectly* normal stuff. Lots of it all over the place. And say, I mean, say for fun there's a pre-LUCA virus. Which is *generally* considered primal bullshit because what's a virus living off of back then, but we don't care about that because we all know just how weird stuff *really* is. So we have this thing, this virus, with a strong ability to *mutate* and *persist,* and we have it penetrating some bacterium. And what, I mean, what if it *mutated* into a nucleus? I *mean*. And all.

Been here an hour, I think. Still plenty of time before Predo crashes in, I think. But time to get it together and figure out-

Wait, what did she say?

—What did you say?

—I said.

She spins toward me.

—I said, *Joe,* I said what if we're all, all of us, what if all life is descended from a virus? I *mean.*

—Wait.

—I mean, the *Vyrus,* I mean. What if. Because-

—Wait.

—There's more.

—I didn't finish fucking high school. Wait.

She waits.

I think a little. But it's not like it helps.

So I take a drink instead. And that shakes it loose.

—Why aren't we all infected?

—*HERV.* Human endogenous Retrovirus.

I take another drink. No help.

—I don't think any of this matters.

She spins her chair.

—It's the remains of viral material scattered in the human genome. But it's *not* all the same.

She points one index finger at herself and the other at me.

—My HERV is different from your HERV.

I rub my eye. I have a headache. A bad one. I want to punch someone. It reminds me of how I felt every day at school.

—I was infected.

—Yeah-huh.

—Someone chewed on my neck to get at my blood and some of his blood got into me and I was infected. That happened.

—OK.

She spins again.

—But not *really.*

She flicks another slide. Two shapes. One with a corkscrew of material sprouting from its side, looking like it's stretching toward a hole in the other blob.

—I mean, that *happened* and all, but what you were was *more* like you were triggered.

She points at the screen.

—Like this.

She taps a button.

The corkscrew grows.

—The Vyrus, active, it's got a prong. *Usually.* Some Vyrus doesn't. Active, inactive. No prong.

The tip enters the hole on the other blob and begins to twist, drawing them closer together.

—Inactive, the Vyrus has a, and I *know* it's all very sexual and all, but I didn't make it up so don't blame me, but it has a hole. The inactive Vyrus.

It twists in until the two shapes are snug together.

—Watch, this is the gross part.

The blob with the corkscrew starts pushing into the tiny hole, pulling itself inside.

—*Gah.*

With a final lurch it disappears, as if it were sucked in at the end.

—Aaand now we get an eclipse phase where *everything* looks normal for a while. We can zip past that.

She taps a button, the image vibrates, blurs, stops when she taps the button again.

—Here.

The blob shivers, pulses and turns inside out, erupting from the tiny hole, coalescing, and suddenly still. Warted now, in a violent yellow, and with a prickle of corkscrews clustered where the hole was.

—And that's what happened.

I'm looking at the screen. She's looking at me.

I shake my head.

She nods.

—An active Vyral cell, with a nucleus *stolen* from a cell in its host's body, enters a new host and infects an inactive Vyrus with no nucleus. Gives it the tools to reproduce. And it does.

She taps the screen.

—This little fucker will *screw* just about any cell it can get to. Screw in, mutate, pop out more and more *specialized* components. I *mean*. And now, now, it's not just that it's active and ready to go to work on the host where before it was just this *dormant* scrap of HERV all this time, hitching a ride on the genome, now it's ready to drop into a *new* body and look for another bit of Vyral HERV with the right kind of hole.

She waves a hand.

—It's a *randy* dude, alright.

She twists toward me.

—See, Joe, *that's* what I mean. I mean, it was always there *in* you. Just waiting. Just *waiting* for the right person to come along and wake it up.

She touches my arm.

—What it *is,* is it's *you.* Just on the outside now.

I think of the worm, eating its own tail. The kind of sense that makes, that's the kind of sense what she's saying makes. Follow it around all the way, you come back to the head. Take that last bite, and then what? Where do you go from there?

Some stuff, I can't swallow.

I walk over to Phil and kick him fully awake.

—Get up and roll me a smoke.

He gets up and rolls me a smoke and I light it.

—Predo's gonna be here in a little while.

Amanda is watching the recording play out again.

—Uh-huh.

I look at the door to the living quarters.

—You and Sela the only ones left in here?

—I mean.

—Because it's time to go now. I got a plan for how we get out and past Predo, but we got to start now.

—Really, I *mean*.

—So if anyone else is here we need to get them together and move.

—*Joe*.

On the screen, the active Vyrus cell is infecting the other again.

Amanda watches.

—It's not like I'm going to let you *take* her with you.

—I figured you and Sela would both come.

The new Vyrus explodes out of itself.

—High school diploma or *not*, Joe, you're not stupid. Don't pretend.

Phil's by the exit with his hand on the knob.

—Someone say something about leaving?

I've got a hand on the door to the living quarters.

—For the sake of argument, Amanda, say I am that stupid.

She lets go with a good old-fashioned bored-with-the-world teenager sigh like she used to do when I first met her.

—I'm not going to let you take her with you.

I'm pushing the door open.

Amanda is restarting the Vyral infection.

—You *can't* take Chubby's daughter.

The door is open.

On the bed, legs twisted together, a teenage pregnant girl and a boy, sleeping.

I look at Amanda.

She gets up from her chair.

—I need her here.

She crosses to me, pointing back at her monitors.

—This is, I *mean,* this is just getting started. A cure, that's still what, I mean, all this.

She lifts her arms to the building around us.

—Why? *Because* a cure. And I mean, Predo, what*ever,* because we're not afraid. We have.

She chews the ends of her hair.

—We have stuff, Joe. We're *not* defenseless girls.

She lets the hair fall from the corner of her mouth.

—And I *just* need her. Is it rocket science? It's not.

We both look at Chubby's sleeping daughter.

—Joe, you had, *what* you had, you had a girlfriend? Right. Something *happened.* She was sick. OK. I've *heard* the stories. It's like, Joe, your private life is like *gossip* central. This girl you had hidden all secret. And, bits and pieces, I *hear,* she was sick. And you tried to infect her. But she wasn't Vyrus positive to start with. So when your Vyral cells went into her, they *just* killed what they found. Because there was no socket that *fit* them. She wasn't like *you.* And before that, you were with her for, I *mean,* I hear it was *years,* and the thing is, knowing you and what all, we think, *people* say, you and her, you never *hooked up.* Really. All the way. Because you were afraid it would *infect* her. And you only tried at the end 'cause she was dying. I *mean.*

She lifts her eyebrows.

—Half it's just *impossibly* romantic, and half it's just *impossibly* lame.

I'm thinking about what Predo said about how I'm spontaneous with bullets. I'm thinking he's right. I'm thinking maybe it's better I don't have any to use right now.

Still, I want them.

She must not see it in my eye, because she won't shut up.

—Because it just doesn't *work* that way. I mean, Joe, and I don't want to *hurt* you, but you could have been fucking your *brains* out. But you're not special that way, not knowing. Everything anyone knows about the Vyrus, it's *all* anecdotal. And there's only *so* many people to ask. And a guy like you, I'm guessing that asking about the facts of life *wasn't* what you were comfortable with. Which I *totally* get. I mean, my mom practically gave me a demo when I was nine, and did I need that? *No.* So someone mentioned *something* around you about how no one knew how the Vyrus really transmitted and you went all celibate. But *them.*

She points at the kids on the bed.

—They didn't care. They were just *into* each other. Just hot kids who wanted to *do it.*

She shrugs.

—Fucking won't infect Delilah. But the *baby.* I need to see what happens with the *baby* is all.

She looks up at me.

—And it's *just* too early to take it out.

—Are you here to save us?

We look at the pregnant girl, pushed up on her elbow, rubbing sleep from her eyes.

—Please tell me you're here to save us.

I shake my head.

—No, I'm just here because your dad wants to see you.

She shakes the boy.

—Awake, Benjamin, he's here to save us.

Amanda shakes her head.

—Really, Joe, is it any *wonder* I drugged her. She will *not* stop talking like that.

I take a step toward the kids as the boy starts to rouse.

—Whatever.

Amanda clucks her tongue.

—Sela.

The blade is in my hand, my arm is wrapped around Amanda's neck, the edge is on her throat.

Sela is on the balls of her feet, I can see the flutter of pulse under her jaw. Too fast. She's at zero percent body fat. Her skin is starting to get that stretched look. Everything about her looks stretched to the limit.

—Let her go, Joe.

—Open the door, Phil. Kids, over here.

Phil fiddles with the knob.

—Um, I got this feeling, Uh, like, if I open the door Sela will kill me.

—So stay here, Phil. Be here when Predo comes. Better, Predo doesn't come, be here when Amanda can't let enough blood herself to keep Sela alive. Phil, why the fuck do you think you're still here in the first place?

He hangs his head.

—Maaan. That sucks.

Sela twitches.

—Gonna finally kill Joe Pitt.

—Thought we always got along OK, Sela.

—Till you put a knife at my girl's throat. Till you found those bleeding children in that hole in Queens and did nothing.

—Oh, that.

Chubby's daughter has gotten the boy awake. I step from the door to let them past.

—Phil.

—I don't know, man.

—Just run. Leave the keys. Take the kids and run. She won't come after you.

—Awww, shiiit!

He yanks the door open and runs, not with the kids, but he does drop the keys.

Exceeding expectations.

Delilah is dawdling.

—And you, sir?

I don't look from Sela.

—Start downstairs. Don't stop. Just keep going until they run out.

The boy points at Sela.

—You want help with her? I'm, you know, I'm like you.

—Kid.

Tighten my grip on Amanda.

—Seriously, you're not.

The girl grabs him and pulls him out the door.

—Come, Benjamin, we must flee.

They're gone.

Amanda tilts her head a bit, baring her throat further.

—Come on, Joe.

I start backing toward the door.

—Sela, just get him off me, will you, I *mean*.

She laughs.

—It's Joe. He won't hurt me.

Sela takes a step for each of mine.

—Be quiet, baby.

—Just get him off me and go get the girl and the baby.

We're at the door.

Sela bounces in place.

—Kill you, Joe.

Amanda lifts her chin higher yet.

—Come on, Joe, *slit* it. Sela, he won't. He *can't*. Just come over here and he'll push me at you and run. He won't *even* use me as a shield. He won't risk *hurting* me if you two fight. Just scare him off me, knock him down and, I *mean*, the baby, Sela.

—Be quiet, babe.

I back us through the door into the hall.

—Pull it closed.

Amanda goes limp.

—No.

Sela steps closer.

—Do not play games with him.

I jerk her upright.

—Amanda.

—Joe, *dear*.

—I killed your mom. I murdered her.

She stiffens a little.

—That's a lie.

Sela, getting closer.

—Babe.

I think about Amanda's mom. Her neck breaking. Just after she kissed me. A long time ago.

—I killed her. And if you want to know why, close the fucking door.

Amanda reaches for the door as I let her go.

Sela moves.

It's shut. I have the keys, snap a lock, and run.

Amanda grabs me.

—Joe. Tell me.

The door rattles in its frame. Double cylinder locks, take a key to go in or out. Sela will have to find hers to open it. Seconds. More if she loses it and goes feral.

—Joe.

I look at Amanda.

Worm at the middle of the world.

I sheath the blade.

—Girl, you don't want to know.

I shove her away, vault the banister, hit the next landing down, feel it in my bad knee.

Door being pounded above, Sela screaming. Doors pounded below, howling, increasing floor by floor as Phil and the kids descend.

But all I can hear is her.

—You couldn't do it, Joe. You couldn't hurt me. Not really. You couldn't.

But she's crying while she says it.

So I know it's not true.

I can hurt anyone. Experience counts for something.


We're fucked before we hit the ground floor.

I catch up to Chubby's kid and her boy. She's waddling down the stairs, he's got her arm, helping her. I hit the landing next to them, racket from the door there, whatever's behind it can smell her blood.

I grab the girl and swing her off the floor and turn to the kid.

—Carry her.

He takes a step back.

—She's a little heavy right now.

She's trying to writhe out of my arms.

—No one need carry me.

Door upstairs is hammered. Sela screams.

—She's going to rip off your legs if she catches you.

I shove the girl into the kid's arms and drop her and he takes the weight of her before she hits the ground.

—Run.

He takes off, faster now, but not fast enough. I follow to the next landing, one of the empty floors. Quieter upstairs. Sela's stopped screaming. No smell of blood outside their doors, the good people on the upper floors have settled down.

I hear a jingle of keys at the top.

Because any asshole would know that Amanda has a set of keys.

Shit.

When the door on this floor came down they used a catering table as a battering ram. One of the steel legs is on the ground. I pick it up. It's hollow, the top jagged and bent where it was ripped from the bottom of the table.

I can hear Amanda whispering, jingle of keys, snap of the lock, the bang of the door slamming open and I look up and Sela is over the banister and dropping, flicking her arms, she pushes off the narrow middle of the stairwell, silent now, just the rush of air as she falls at me, little thumps as she controls her plunge, sounds like a giant cat running on a wood floor, headfirst she's coming, gives a hard shove off the opposite rail just above, changing course, sudden angle onto my landing, heedless, fast, she'll break me when she hits. The steel table leg will bend around her when I swing it, thin and feeble, but it might knock her off course long enough for me to run another half flight.

Guns. Why am I always losing guns?

She's in my face.

I jam the jagged end at her, catching the soft flesh above her collarbone, her momentum forcing it deep and she slams into me and we both go down, her blood sprays my face, tastes like acid on my tongue, I can't reach the blade, she screams and wheels off me, table leg jutting from her shoulder, right arm hanging at her side, something inside severed. I push to the edge of the landing and tumble down, crawl, she's making wet coughing noises, the end of the leg in her lung. I tumble down the next flight.

—Joe.

Phil and Chubby's daughter and the boy, standing at the door that opens toward the front of the building.

—Joe! Keys, man!

I stand, bent over goddamn broken ribs, start toward the door under the stairs.

Phil shakes his head.

—Aw shit, no, man. No. This way, man.

I get the keys out.

—Predo will kill us all.

I shake the keys at him.

—And Sela's not dead.

She screams, there's movement up there.

Phil grabs the keys.

—Shitshitshit.

He opens the locks.

The kid moves closer, Chubby's daughter still in his arms.

—I don't think it's safe down there.

A sound like rusty chain scraped over a blackboard.

Chubby's daughter shakes her head.

—There is peril.

I push them both through the door, grab Phil, drag him after, pull the door closed.

—Lock it, Phil.

—What if we want to get out fast?

—Lock the fucking door.

One by one he does the locks, cursing with each one.

—Fucked. Oh, now we're fucked. Double fucked. Fucked for sure.

Light comes from a half-dead exit lamp over the door. No light down below. Howls. Good news seems to be that whatever lives down here hasn't killed us already.

Things are looking up.


We go down.

Concrete steps and walls. Phil and the girl keep a hand on the wall as they go down and the light at the top fails their eyes and they become blind. I lead, still able to pick out the shapes of things. Kid is at the rear. No specialist, but he can see.

Hit bottom after a flight, and I can see something dangling from above. See a squat shape in the corner at the base of the stair, smell gasoline. I go over there, feel around, find a primer, pump it, find a handle, pull it. Takes three yanks and the generator kicks to life, feeding power to the work lamp hanging overhead.

—Sir.

I look at the girl.

—I fear we are not safe here.

She's wearing moccasin boots with a rim of fringe at the top, several lace skirts, a peasant blouse tented over her belly, skinny dreads pulled up on top of her head. No end of bracelets, rings, necklaces and charms. The boy's got the same boots in black, brown cords tucked into the tops, kind of a pirate shirt, black leather jacket with epaulettes, a load of silver amulets dangling from leather straps around his neck or tied to the jacket, and a thin goatee.

I go to the door under the work lamp.

—You don't like it down here, go back up.

She rubs her arms.

—It was supposed to be a haven here. Safe from the rising storm.

Another steel door. More locks. And an iron bar braced across it, ends resting in u-joints bolted to the concrete.

Phil raises a finger.

—Joe.

The girl looks at some trash piled near the wall.

—My father spoke so highly of Percy. Our expectations were overmatched by reality. He seemed more a fool than a wise man. And the Hood itself, more a prison than a paradise for people of color. *Cure.* The very word promised safety. How were we to know?

I think about jamming my fingers in my ears, but keep looking for a way out instead.

There's no ventilation to speak of. Exhaust from the generator flows into a plastic tube that runs duct-taped to the wall until it reaches a tiny vent above the door up top. A bundle of wires comes in through the same duct, snakes down the wall and into a hole drilled in the concrete wall next to the steel door.

Phil edges closer.

—Joe.

The boy steps up.

—I had the number. It gets passed around. Coalition, Society, people in need can find a number to call to talk to someone at Cure house. I think they ran a help desk when they first started. Or a crisis line. But I had to call a few times before anyone answered. Sela. I told her who we were, what we needed. What Delilah is carrying. She told us to come to the building over there.

He points north.

—On Seventy-second. Cure owns it. Buzz the super and it rings upstairs here and they let you in. Go straight back, Sela was in the alley waiting to bring us into here.

The girl shakes her head.

—That was the first sign that all was not well.

Phil clears his throat.

—Joe.

The boy is nodding.

—Yes. Sela didn't look very. Healthy. And as soon as we got inside, we could see the situation was not what we were looking for.

The girl points up the stair.

—The Horde woman seemed all but mad. She spoke to comfort us, encouraging us to stay, but I sensed something.

The kid touched his forehead.

—Delilah can see things sometimes. Like she has the sight.

She raises a palm.

—Just what is given to me. And I sensed she had mad designs on the child. Soon, my fears were confirmed. She gave us drink, but it was drugged. We slept.

I've got my face close to the door, my nose at the crack.

I can hear that chain-scraping sound. Moaning. Can't tell how many. Smell Vyrus. Wrong Vyrus. Something wrong. Smell dying. Smell wet concrete and mold and shit.

—Joe.

I look at him.

—What, Phil?

—Joe. We shouldn't open that door, Joe.

—Why's that, Phil?

—It's bad in there.

I look around the space.

—Well, you can stay here and choke on exhaust fumes until Sela gets it together and Amanda opens that door up there for her.

He's staring at the garbage against the wall.

—She stopped feeding them is all.

I take a closer look at the garbage.

I.V. bags, dry and crusted. No wonder I feel light-headed. Thought it was just the way the girl smells. All that extra blood pumping around inside her.

Phil points up.

—Why Sela is like she is, the blood, what was left, it's been coming down here, to keep them alive. But Horde stopped.

—Not like it's a secret her people are starving, Phil.

He shakes his head.

—Uh, no, that's the thing, I'm not like an expert in the field, but what I'm saying is, on the upstairs floors, those are her people. People who, you know, came here to join, to join Cure and get the, what she promised, get the cure. And yeah, they're starving too. But this?

He points at the door.

—This is where she keeps, and I'm just the messenger here and I tried not to let you take us down here so don't be uncool about this, but this is where she keeps her experiments.

He scratches his head.

—In what she call, um, *cross-splicing*. Which, I don't know what it means, so don't ask, but if I were to guess I would say it means like, *experiments in playing god*. Or something. And what I'm saying is, that these . . . *things* . . . they don't just, this is the scuttlebutt, they don't just get into uninfected blood. Sure, yeah, that's the flavor of choice, but they go any which way.

He points at me.

—If you're following what I'm saying.

He scratches his head.

—Which is, I'm saying, they drink infected blood too.

The door at the top of the stairs rattles.

The girl points at me.

—Can you not fight?

The kid puts an arm around her shoulders.

—I'll stand with you, man.

The girl makes a fist.

—And I. She wants our baby. She wants our baby to experiment on. And I will die to save our child.

I sort keys, find the ones that match the brands stamped on the locks.

—No.

She steps back.

I open the first lock.

—She won't do anything to you or your baby. Not yet.

I open the second lock.

—You'll be safe.

I fit the key to the last lock.

—Until I get back.

I pick up the iron bar that I took away from the door.

She sticks a finger at me.

—You said you knew a way out.

I heft the bar.

—I was probably wrong.

She steps back.

—We are abandoned.

I could tell her again that I'll be back, but who the hell am I? What would it mean to her? And I'd probably be wrong anyway.

I get both hands on the bar.

—Open the door, Phil.

—I don't want to.

—Do it anyway.

He puts his hand on the key.

—Story of my whole life.

He turns the key.

—I don't wanna do it, but I'm doing it anyway.

He pulls on the door.

—Shit.

It sticks.

—Shit I wish I was high.

He's not the only one.

*They drink infected blood too.* Like I don't have enough to worry about, I got to worry about something trying to go for my neck.

Phil gives the door a good yank and it comes unstuck and something whips out of the darkness and there's a mist of blood and Phil is gone. So it looks like it really does prefer uninfected blood, and I'm running after, swinging the iron bar, beating on something that has my friend.

Huh. Phil Sax. My friend. You think the craziest shit when things get all fucked up.


I don't get a look at it.

Not a good one anyway.

It's brittle is what I know. Fast, but brittle. Every time I bring the iron down, bits of it snap off and clatter to the ground. So I keep hammering, breaking it down, beating a hole in it, trying to ignore the thing sticking up from its shoulder that looks like another head, until I hit it and it snaps off too. Stuff is running down the bar and my bad hand keeps slipping off when I make contact. It's come away from Phil to rake its claws at me. Gets my thigh, back of my left arm. Lift the bar over my head and bring it down tip first, jamming it into the wound where the head thing was and there's a sound like when you pull the neck of a balloon and let the air keen out, only loud, and it runs into a wall, bounces off, runs into the wall again, and again, and collapses into a heap stippled with broken spines, looking like one of the slides Amanda showed me.

I'm yelling at the kid to close the door for fuck sake. He starts pushing it closed. I catch a glimpse of Chubby's daughter throwing up behind him. Their names come back to me: Delilah and Ben.

I hope Sela doesn't kill them.

Door closes, locks lock.

I keep still.

—Aw shit.

I move forward a step.

—Aw shit, Joe. I think it ate part of my stomach.

Smells like water ahead. Smells like water and waste and wet rusty metal. Smells like sewer grate.

I know where to go.


Phil's gonna die.

There's a hole in his side I can stick my hand in. And that's what I'm doing, trying to shove his shredded shirt into it to slow the blood. Most of his scalp is gone, an ear. His right foot has been twisted around backward. There are pinholes in his cheek. When he talks, little bubbles of blood pop out of them.

He's gonna die, but there's still a lot of blood in him.

Enough to do me right.

—Joe.

Light is coming from a blue safety lamp up at the junction that takes you out of this access duct and into the tunnel. The Lexington line. Somewhere close to a platform I think. I can smell people.

It all smells like fresh air.

After the Cure house basement, even the sewer smells like fresh air.

I found the grate not far from the door. Found it when my heel caught in it and I dropped Phil. He started screaming and I thought the rest of whatever was in there would be on us, but they just howled and pounded walls. The one I killed, the only one that had gotten free of its cell. Too dark to know how many more. Ran my hand down the wall, felt at least seven doors, dead bolts, felt some kind of jury-rigged motors hooked to them, wires. Seven doors I could feel, but it's a big basement.

I got the sewer grate off and pushed Phil through. He got knocked out when he hit his head. Good for him. Got him shouldered, went against the flow of waste. It spills toward bigger and deeper avenues. Felt some dry cold air and scented it back. Had to use the iron bar to open a hole in rotted masonry.

And here we are.

With him dying.

All that blood just spilling out by the second.

—Joe, you can do it.

Him talking nonsense.

—Infect me.

Why would I do such a thing?

—You can save me. And, hey, OK, we've had some problems in the past, some times when I've been less on the up-and-up than maybe I let on to be, but mostly, mostly you've been able to beat a straight answer out of me when you needed one so. Do you know where my pomade is?

He pats around at his hip pocket.

—Had a can. I. My hair feels like it's messed up. Can you, Joe, you got a mirror or something?

—Hair looks fine.

—Like you know. This, hair like this, it's a constant maintenance issue. It doesn't just, you don't let it be casual or anything. Got to invest in upkeep. Time and effort. And. Joe. Infect me. It'll take, I know it will. And. Hey, here's a happy thought, if I'm, aw shit, I got to try not to laugh, but once I'm infected, and I heal, and, think, think of the beatings you can give me then. Huh? Huh? Pretty good, huh?

He giggles.

—Aw, shit, I laughed. Oh, and, Joe, who's gonna roll you a cigarette? Right? What asshole is gonna line up for that gig? Joe. Bleed a little is all. Just bleed on me a little is all. Come on, saying, I'm just a fucking wound anyway, bleed on me a little. I know it will take.

More of his blood lost, without me drinking it.

His fingers flutter.

—And I know what you're thinking and OK, I get it, because you already can't stand me and why have me around even more, but, Joe, it's what I've been after. Saying, why have I Renfielded around so many years if it wasn't for a shot at this? Know? So, I won't hold it against you either way, but, Joe, come on. I. I. Man, saying, man, I don't want to die, not without trying.

I think about Amanda's slides. I think about what the active Vyral cells do to a person who isn't Vyral positive. I've seen it. There are worse ways to die, I suppose. But it would be a short list.

—Phil.

—Joe. Joe Pitt. My main man, Joe Pitt.

—Phil.

—Come on, Joe.

—If I infect you, I won't be able to drink your blood.

He blinks.

—Aw shit! Jesus, I'm saying, Jesus, I'm saying, is that what we've come to in extremity, Joe? Is that what we, a team we've been, is that what it comes to? You don't want to try and save my life because it will mean you can't eat my corpse? Is that, is that how, and excuse the term because I know I'm on a limb here, but is that how friends behave?

—Who said we were friends, Phil?

He looks away.

—That hurt, Joe.

I reach into my jacket.

—Phil.

—Don't even try to apologize.

—Phil.

—I do not want to hear it.

—Sorry about this, Phil.

—What did I just?

The blade comes out and I pull it across my palm and hold my hand over the hole in his stomach and my blood dribbles into the wound.

He looks at me.

—Hey, Joe, hey.

His eyes go side to side.

—Hey, Joe, thanks.

White mucus starts to well at the edges of his eyes. The blood pumping from his wound blackens. A tremor runs through his bones. And I drop the blade and grab his head and yank it hard to the side and pull up and I don't know for certain, but I think I broke his neck before he felt too much of it. And he lies there dead.

I get up. Pick up the blade. Find my tobacco, but my fingers are too sticky with blood to roll one. Matches are wet anyway. What else I got? I got some keys to the Cure house. Got some car keys. Chubby's money and phone. Got my wire saw.

I toe Phil's corpse.

Asshole. I'm an asshole.

An asshole for wasting all that blood for no good reason at all. No reason at all. Just no damn reason at all.

Start walking. I can't take a train looking like I look. So I start walking down the tunnel. Then I start running.

I don't know why.

I just do.

•   •   •

At Sixty-eighth I stop running.

Platform full of people. No dead tunnel to use to cut around. Coated in blood and stuff that you'd have to call ichor. I plant myself against the wall of the tunnel, pressed into the angle of a beam, and wait. Few minutes pass and I feel the first tickle of a breeze. I wait couple seconds and it turns to wind, pushed ahead of a Six local. And then the train, squealing and sparking, clashing past me and into the station, back of the train about fifteen yards away in the light.

I wait till the doors open, wait as people bump each other out of their way getting on and off, wait for the chimes to sound and the doors to close. Wait for a rush of air from the pneumatics and the lurch of the engine pulling. Then I break cover, run, jump onto the stub of platform at the end of the last car, grab a fistful of chain that dangles from the side, and crouch away from the window in the door so any kids staring out at the tunnel disappearing behind them won't see the blood-covered monster hitching a ride.

Huddled close to the steel, my face turned from the lighted platform, I got no way of knowing if anyone will see me. They do, there's a good chance they'll chalk it up at thrill-seeking kids and not bother telling the station master or Port Authority cop. Got no choice either way. No time to do this on foot.

Evie wants me to find Chubby's kid.

Mission accomplished. But somehow I don't think I'll get a break from her if I show up and tell her where I left the girl.

So, more to do.

Always more to do.

At Fifty-ninth I jump off the train as it eases to a stop. I find a service ladder up an air shaft to the yellow line above. Hopping a line can only help if someone saw me on the Six train. Five minutes' wait gets me an R going downtown. I take another break at

Fifty-seventh, jumping tracks to the express side, and hunker down. Seven minutes and a Q rolls in. Expressed past Forty-ninth, and held up at Times Square. I jump off again, waiting deeper in the tunnel this time. Some kids at the end of the platform are throwing snappers up the track. Little bundles of black powder and sawdust wrapped in white tissue, tiny flat cracks when they hit.

The Q jerks forward, I run, coming out of the dark, the kids jump up and down, peppering me with snappers, screaming almost as loud as the things in the basement of the Cure house, pointing as I jump onto the back of the train and grab hold, people all along the platform turning to stare as I roll past and back into the dark at the far end of the station.

They won't stop between stations, I don't think. They won't want to chase some loon through the tunnels. At Thirty-fourth we roll, slowing just slightly to pass through, and I think I see a couple cops at the end of the platform, craning to get a look at the end of the train, but I've moved to the roof already. Using my seven fingers and a stub to find a grip in the grooved steel, trying not to skid to the edge and over on the curves. Twenty-third and we roll.

Fourteenth Street next. Big station. Trying to figure if they've had time to clear the platform before we pull in. Won't want to try and deal with a guy riding the open back of a train with people around. Guy that crazy could be any kind of trouble.

I don't know. And that's not good enough. So I jump off.

No good way to do it. I just try not to stab myself with my blade as I hit and tumble. And make a point of jumping away from the third rail. Not too bad all in all, but those ribs break one more time. Got a feeling they won't be knitting again. Not soon, anyway. Not unless I get some more blood.

I get up, go through my pockets to make sure I haven't lost anything, and something stabs me in the gut and stirs around. I sit, hold my middle, grit my teeth and wait for it to pass.

It does.

I've felt it before, the jabs the Vyrus gives you, telling you to kill something and drink it. I just wasn't expecting it so soon. Just yesterday I took care of the guy who killed the cripple. Should have lasted. Would have lasted if I hadn't spilled so much of it all over the place. And the healing. Puts a strain on the Vyrus, all that clotting and growing new cells.

I get up and turn around and look back up the tunnel and think about Phil.

Should have never listened to him.

Even dead he's fucked me again.


I know what I'm doing.

It's simple.

I'm trying to stay out of the worm's mouth.

Not forever. The worm always gets you in the end. I'm just trying to stay ahead of its mouth for a little longer. The way you do that is you run up the tail as fast as you can. Real question is how you'll play it when you come back around and find yourself standing on its neck. Jump again and you'll be right where you started, mouth about to snap down on you. Stay where you are, and it'll be there soon enough to do the same.

Jump in its mouth and get it over with.

Stay still and let it get to you in its own time.

Or keep running in circles until it takes that last bite of itself, you included.

The worm gets it all in the end. Lucky man has options about the how and the when, but that's really all that's in your hands. How and when.

I'm playing for *fast* and *in just a little while longer.*

Just long enough.

Truth is, I get that part of it, keep the worm off me just long enough for that last thing I'm gaming for, I'll give ground on the *how* and take it however it comes. Fast, slow, easy, hard. In the worm's mouth is in the worm's mouth.

I feel its teeth in my gut again. Telling me how close it is.

OK. I got moves left. I've run this circle before. Jumping at the last second to clear its open jaws, landing and sprinting. Around and around. I know the route.

I know what I'm doing.

Really.

I do.

Tell myself that as I come out of a storm drain at the end of an alley off Avenue C. Tell myself that as I walk from the alley into the middle of the vomitorium the bar hoppers and college kids have turned my old neighborhood into. Stinking filthy drunk, limping and shuffling, trying to roll a cigarette from a damp paper. Getting plenty of berth on the sidewalk, right till I pull myself up a stoop at the end of the block and find a couple skinheads blocking the door.

They move to shove me back. Then they get a whiff of what's under my stink and hands go inside the vintage peacoats they both wear.

I raise my hands.

—You wouldn't shoot a cripple, would you?

—Ta, an sure dey would, Joe, sure dey would.

I look up at the monolith standing in the open doorway at the top of the stoop.

—Hey, Hurley. You look good. Huge. As usual.

—An you, Joe, you look a little worse fer wear. As usual.

I lower my hands.

—I'm a creature of habit.

He pushes the brim of his hat a little higher on his forehead.

—Well come inside, ya sorry fooker. Force of habit an all, I suppose you'll be wantin' a severe beatin'.

I go up the steps.

—Don't waste it on me, Hurl, it never seems to do any good.

He pats my shoulder as I pass inside.

—Not ta worry, Joe, I got one ta spare fer an old friend like yerself. Not ta worry a'tall.


There was a time I was a very bad person.

If you can imagine.

Funny thing is, that time of my life, I was never so sure I was doing the right thing as those few years.

Soldier in a cause. Society. Soldier in the Society. Front lines, pushing back the dark. Making the world a safe place for infecteds to live openly. A goal like that requires unity first. Everyone has to be pointed in the same direction. Can't have Vampyres going around killing indiscriminately. That kind of thing creates the wrong impression.

You have to have rules. Rules about where and how you feed. Who you feed on. How often you can get away with it. Strict policy of non-infection. Don't want to be perceived as spreading a plague or anything like that. Since you're trying to preach this gospel against the Coalition's dominant philosophy of keeping a lid on all things Vyrus-related at all times forever, you also have borders to secure. The occasional incursion to deal with. Advents of diplomacy.

Fine detail work. But that wasn't my bag. I didn't make policy, I rammed it down throats. More often than not, I simply tore out the throat in question. Anything more complicated would mean

I'd have to understand something. Explain it. Might have required nuance.

Terry did the explaining. Explained to me when he picked me up off the floor in the can at CBGB. Told me what had happened to me. Told me what my choices were. Offered the Society to me.

So let's just say I hadn't been offered too many chances to be a part of anything. Not that I was last picked for softball games, just more that I was likely tied up by my wrists and hanging from a steam pipe in my folks' bedroom closet, somewhere between a good solid belt beating and having some scalding water poured over my feet, when the sides were being chosen up.

And before you get all sobby and sympathetic for my plight and put a hand to your brow and realize how much it all explains, keep in mind that whatever got done to me, I've done worse to others. It don't balance out. Whatever my parents were, at least they kept it in the family. No one out for a walk at night had to worry about them jumping from an alley and thumping them on the head and cutting their neck open.

So they said I was a monster and they were only punishing me for my own evil deeds. So what. Turns out they were right.

So being asked to join someone's club, say that was a new one on me. Had to be a mistake. But I wasn't going to let on. Tell me the Society was going to lead the way to a brighter future? Great. Keep the details to yourself and tell me what to do. Tell me what you want is for me to go see a guy who's been making waves and make sure he doesn't make any more? Great. I'll keep the details to myself and get it done.

Put yourself in some asshole's shoes.

You're just trying to get by. You're living downtown, Society turf, things aren't too well organized. Lots of rules they want you to follow, but they're not exactly helping you to make ends meet. Not like someone drops in once or twice a week with a little blood to ease you through, like the way they do it up on Coalition turf. So say you make a deal here or there. This instance, say you sneak above Fourteenth and trade some Society gossip for a couple pints. Maybe you share one with a buddy who's down on his luck.

Asshole.

That's where you went wrong. Your buddy, he's in the same grind as you. Your handout aside, he's dry more often than he's wet. Smart boy that he is, he slides over to Society HQ in some dingy basement, drops a dime. Exits with tangible appreciation in the form of a pint of his own.

Next things next, you're feeling no pain. Well fed for the first time in weeks or months, hanging at your flop, thinking you'll take a stroll and enjoy this nice little blood high you're riding.

Knock at the door.

Who could it be?

Take a look out the peephole. It's that kid who's always at Terry's side. That punk with the tight plaid pants, calf-high Doc Martens, loose suspenders and surplus flight jacket covered in Sharpied anarchy symbols and Bad Brains stickers.

Joe Pitt.

Two things you can do. Let him in, or pretend you're not home. What you hear is, pretending you're not home pisses him off. So you open the door, let him in, give the big smile, try to play it all off. But before you can start acting all casual and social and put him off the scent like you got planned, he's grabbed your hair and pulled your head down and put his knee in your face three or four times.

See, he's not there to ask questions about what happened and why. He's not there to be coy and put it all together and tease it out. He's there to do what he's been told to do. And he doesn't see any reason to waste time.

Besides, he likes doing it.

He's good at it.

And it feels good to do what one is good at.

And since he's so good at it, he tends to improvise a bit. Where a knife or a gun might get the job done in a hurry, he's inclined to hold your ear against a gas burner. Got a steam pipe in your closet, he knows just how to rig a belt to hang you from it and use you like a punching bag.

All in all, it probably would have been better for you if this guy's parents had finished the job.

But they didn't. So you pay the price. Along with a lot of other people.

That went on for years.

Then somewhere in there I lost my taste for the work. Got bored with the same old thing. And tired of being told what to do. Time goes by, you see how things are done, even someone like me can get the idea that the system is being gamed in someone's favor. Most times, you look at the top of the pile and you'll find where the favor lands. I'm not saying I was shocked, I just didn't like what my slice amounted to. Thought I could do better on my own.

Thought maybe I'd like to walk in a room and not have people scatter like roaches from a light. Maybe have a conversation about something other than war. Know something more than how long it takes a guy to grow back all three layers of his skin before you can peel them off again.

Maybe I got soft.

That was the word. Not to my face, but that was the word.

Anyhow, all this reminiscence, it's by way of saying I have history with some people. Way it works for us, there are only so many who have what it takes to stick. What I found out, the longer you stick, the more history you get. With everyone. But with some people you have more history than with others.

With Terry, I got enough history to choke on.

—It's not like I go in for torture or anything, you know? Counter-productive. What's the point, is what I always ask myself. You get into that game, you always have to, you know, ask more questions of yourself than the person you're torturing. And I'm not just speaking to the inherent unreliability of information received under duress, yeah? That goes without, I hope in this day and age, that goes without saying. What does not go without saying is that torture forces the torturer to ask him or herself more ques-tion than he or she is asking the torturee. Tortured? Whatever, doesn't matter. So, you get into this cycle, because, follow me around here, because if your information is unreliable, how do you make it more reliable. Do you retorture? Ask, *Hey, guy, were you just lying to me? Tell the truth or I'll put you on the rack.* Is that it? I don't think so. And the whole time you, you know, you have to ask yourself, *What am I doing? Am I accomplishing anything here? Am I just becoming, you know, the enemy?* Ends, and yes, this is hard for some people to swallow, but the ends do some-times justify the means. I believe that. Warts and all. But damn, it's a tough call to make. And you got to live with it. Got to own up to it. So that, yeah, while torture is not really my thing, I have to admit that right now, I'm looking at you, and I'm thinking to myself, *Hey, I'm kind of glad Predo left Joe a couple fingers for me to cut off.* If you get me.

Terry looks up from the copy of the *I Ching* he's flipping through.

—The thing is, based on past experience, any answers I'd get would be about as reliable with or without torturing you. And, sorry to say it after all these years, Joe, but, you know, I don't think I'd have too much soul-searching to do over the moral is-sues involved.

I look at Hurley, waiting by the door.

—Old friends. How we kick around old times, huh, Hurl?

He shakes his head.

—Don't fook aboot, Joe, tis not da time fer it.

I look at Terry.

—When'd Hurley get so serious? Used to be such a light-hearted fella.

Terry picks up the three coins next to his book.

—Serious times, man, require serious thoughts. An attitude like yours, it's counter to everything that's going on these days. Hang on now, I need to frame a thought.

He starts tossing the three coins, picking them up, tossing again, until he's done it six times.

—Oh, man. I know this.

He flips through the book.

—You'll like this, Joe. Listen.

He finds the page, adjusts his wire rim glasses.

—Hexagram thirty-six. *Warmth and light are swallowed by deep darkness.*

He looks at me over the tops of his glasses.

—This is one of those modern versions that offers analysis. Seriously, you'll like this.

He looks back at the page.

—*You have been deliberately injured. Going blow for blow will only escalate the war. Abstain from vengeance. Sidestep your aggressor's headlong charge, giving him the opportunity to fall on his face.*

I hold up my hand.

—So I get to keep my fingers?

He looks at Hurley.

—Hurl, how hard can you hit Joe without killing him?

Hurley rubs his chin.

—Well now, Joe, he's a purty tuff nut an all. An I've some experience hittin' him. That helps. I'd say, if pressed, I'd say I could hit him damn hard an not do more than break several bones an rupture an organ or two. At most, I'd say.

Terry looks at me.

I lower my hand.

—Yeah, sure, I'll shut the fuck up.

And I do.

Terry sets one of the coins on edge and gives it a flick, setting it to spin.

—What I asked the *Book of Changes* here is, I asked it how I should respond to a new threat that has recently entered an already complex situation.

The coin starts to slow a bit.

—Here we are, at war for the first time in decades. All quiet on the northern front for now, but still, you know, it's a hot war, shots have been fired. We're facing all the past issues we could never resolve with the Coalition. Thanks to, you know, thanks to you telling everyone about the blood farm.

Hurley makes a *tsk* sound and shakes his head.

Terry ignores him, watching the coin begin to list.

—Which, yeah, I'll agree, that was information that wanted to be free. Sure, yeah, OK. But still, bad timing there. So we're people, we can adapt, and we do. Diplomacy, it wasn't an option. No one was in much of a mood to talk. Converse. Work it all out.

I cough.

—Lydia wouldn't shut up, would she?

The coin falls and Terry slaps it flat before it can wobble down.

—Hurley.

He doesn't hit me hard enough to kill me, as promised, but I cross the room and put a good dent in some drywall and spend a second being grateful that he didn't punch me in the ribs and that the wall isn't brick.

Hurley comes over and offers me a hand.

—An did I break anything?

—No.

—An will ya shut it fer a bit?

I have to think about that one, but I get it right.

—Yeah.

He pulls me up, rights my chair and drops me in it.

—Be good.

Terry spins his coin again.

—Yeah, man, Lydia. You told her about the blood, she opened her mouth and kept it that way. Which, you know, it's her prerogative to speak her mind and all, but, in a situation where restraint can really reward the restrained, she could have been a little less, I don't know, strident, maybe. That would have helped. Still, I was able to convince her that a full frontal assault on the Coalition was not a viable option.

The coin slows again.

—We're no match militarily, that's not like a secret or anything. We're getting constantly harassed by the Wall Streeters and Chinatown crews in the south. Christian and his Dusters are clinging to some kind of neutrality. We'd like them to skirmish down there, but they refuse.

Hurley nods.

—Well an dem, dey do have dere own problems just now an all. Not dat I don't say it's time fer 'em to stand up and pick a side, but dey do have dere hands full wit dat udder stuff.

I raise my eyebrows.

Terry flicks eyes from Hurley to me to the coin.

—Something out in Brooklyn is causing problems. The Chosen, they're having internal conflicts. Seems that when you were there, you did serious damage to their power structure. Left a vacuum. And, you know, I don't know, nature may abhor a vacuum, but chaos loves one. Infighting. Someone, we get very little information from that quarter, but from what I gather, someone over there, one side or the other, has used a nuclear option.

The coin goes to its side, he watches it wind down this time.

—Making golems.

I can't help myself.

—What the fuck?

Terry shakes his head.

—I said the same thing. I don't know, all that East European mythology, mixed with all that biblical mythology. Mixed with, you know, us. Anyway, seems the confusion is just a matter of semantics. What they call a *golem*, we call a zombie is all.

Hurley pulls down the corners of his mouth.

—Nasty creatures. Imagine, usin' such a ting 'gainst yer fella types. Be a special punishment waitin' fer dem when the final horn blows an all dat. Zombies. Detestable is what it is.

Terry spins the coin, stops it, looks at Hurley.

—No telling what pressures they were under. Not for us to judge a course of action. Right and wrong, absolutes, that gets us nowhere. Some liberality of mind, some flexibility of spirit, it all helps to keep us out of outmoded practices. Thinking forward, that's where we need to be. Condemnation is a losing proposition.

Hurley shrugs.

—Say what ya will, Terry, an ya know I know ya know an all. But still, *zombies*. Dere's a limit ta what civilized folks should be willin' lay hands to. Dat, I'd have ta say, dat would be my own.

Terry looks at the coin, rubs his thumb over it.

I tilt my head Hurley's way.

—Got to say I'm with you on this one, Hurl. Making shamblers, that's a scummy business to be in. Let alone sicking them on anyone. Open the door to brain-eaters, it's all downhill from there. How you figure that, Terry, someone *making* zombies?

Terry raises his eyes to me, looks back at the coin between his fingers, nods, gives it a spin.

—It's all theory, anyway. I think, and this is the theory, I think someone caught a zombie and stuck it in a basement and kept it alive. A process that, I don't know, I don't want to think about. And they used it like a deterrent. Like, *Don't fuck with me or I'll start making more golems and sending them onto your turf.* So, again the biblical thing, they did it. Now they got them over there, golems in Brooklyn, started in Gravesend, but, these things, now a couple have wandered over the Manhattan Bridge. Duster turf.

Hurley raises a finger.

—It'll end poorly fer dem dat done it. Mark me. Bound ta pay against 'em. An it should if dere's any justice a'tall.

Terry puts a finger in the spinning path of the coin and it bounces off and falls.

—Anyway, as if we didn't have enough complications. I don't know, you know, our visibility factor now, we're just below the skin of things, one pinprick away from a gigantic pop that blows it wide open and just this chaotic mess with no sense of control, no order, and I am a big fan of things taking their course, but I'm trying to forge, you've heard this, trying to make a dialectic here. That's what we're about. We're a counter-argument to the Coalition. We're antithesis. For this to work, for us to achieve a synthesis, there has to be a degree of control in the conflict. Otherwise everything is destroyed. No synthesis, just a fucking mess. So. Here I am, consulting the *I Ching*, looking for clarity of thought, trying to illuminate my consciousness and see a way out of the fog, what they call the *fog of war*, and, as if you've been summoned to add darkness, you come and knock at the door.

He taps the edge of the coin on the tabletop.

—And what is especially, I don't know, *ironic*, about your timing is, I'm, in my search for clarity, in this time of multiple crises for all Vyrally infected, I'm asking the book a question about how to deal with this new threat, like I said, yeah, and, the threat is, I'm asking the book, I'm asking it, this leads back to something you mentioned, about Lydia and her unwillingness to think before she speaks, part of what I'm asking the book is, *How the fuck did Lydia get the idea that I know the location of the blood farm?*

He stops tapping the coin.

—And you walk through the door. As if.

He taps once.

—As if, man, as if there was any doubt about it in the first place, man.

He drops the coin.

—As if.

He takes off his glasses, rubs the lenses with a tail of his faded madras button-down.

—Hurley, will you get Lydia in here, please?

Hurley *tsks* again, walks to a closet door at the far end of the basement apartment, opens it, reaches in, and drags Lydia out. Wrapped in twenty yards of coaxial cable, a racquet ball stuffed in her mouth, dried blood from her ears and nose.

Terry rises and points at her.

—We're all responsible for our own actions, Joe, I do believe that, but I have to say, I don't know, but I have to say, in my opinion, and this is regressive, in my own opinion, this is your fault.

He sits.

—Though Lydia may disagree with me on that interpretation.


I can only assume that Lydia won't be saving my life this go-around.

Shame.

Especially seeing as I'd been kind of banking on setting her and Terry against each other and using the fireworks as cover to get what I wanted. Old dog needs new tricks. I'd put an ad in the paper, but I don't have time.

Time.

Shit.

Time.

—Remember that time, Joe, when I asked you to, this is many years in the wayback machine I'm talking about, I asked you to take care of Selby Lovelorn? Do you remember Selby?

I shrug.

—His name was Lovelorn, Terry, how's a man forget something like that?

—Sure, yeah, yeah, right. So, I asked you to deal with him because, and memory is subjective, but I remember it was because he'd been warned a few times to stop mooning around that Goth club on Houston, stop hanging out there with the blood-letting crowd. He was getting too cocky about it is what I remember. Dropping too many hints to those kids that he was the real thing. *Der Vampir,* and all that crap. Do you remember?

—Yeah, I got it.

—And you, I don't know, took it lightly because, I don't know, because you did. Things were, this was right before you left the Society is what I remember, and you and me, we were having, communication was not at its clearest for us. Lots of information flying over each other's heads. Missed cues about the disrepair of the relationship. So what I'd intended was, I'd hoped what was clear was that Selby was a terminal. And you, Joe, you gave me, you were sullen at the time. It was, I felt like I had a teenager, I mean a real teenager on my hands. You still looked like a kid, but you were old enough to, age does not always bring wisdom, but you were old enough to have grown up a little. At least. And I got all that, *yeah, no, yeah, no* stuff from you all the time. So you go out to visit Selby. To fulfill your roll within the Society, use your natural skill at the best of your ability for the betterment of all. And what did you do? Do you remember this part?

I remember. But I keep it to myself.

Terry illuminates everyone else.

—You, he, Joe there, what he did was, he went and *talked* to Selby Lovelorn. He told him he was on, what you told me was, you said to him he was *on thin ice* and he needed to lay low.

He shakes his head.

—Joe Pitt *talked* to someone. Explained they had a problem. Cautioned him to be mellow.

He rubs his nose.

—Do you, do you remember what happened next, Joe? So what happened next was that Selby Lovelorn, prince of the Goth scene, he went right back out that night and, I don't know, figuring that the heat was on, he went for broke. This girl, this blood-letter, she nicked herself with a razor, offered a little dribble to him, thinking, I don't know, thinking it would lead to some kind of transcendent sexual experience. And Selby, he latched on. And he wouldn't let go. And he started chewing into her arm. And she started screaming. And this was all happening in the lounge at that damn club.

He presses his palms together.

—And I had to deal with it. Which, in and of itself, that should be no big deal. I've never been above getting my hands dirty. But at the time this was happening, I was establishing my face in the uninfected community, trying to integrate with the local activist culture. Very subtle moves were happening. So to break cover, to step out and deal with a major publicity fiasco like that, it upset the tone of what I'd been saying elsewhere. It was. Joe.

He splits his palms and shows them to me.

—It was a real fuckup.

He closes his hands into fists.

—And what I come back around to when I reflect on that incident, what I come back around to, and generally I avoid this kind of self-recrimination because, you know, what's the point, but what I came back around to is asking myself why *I* didn't do what I'd expected *you* to do?

He holds up one fist.

—And I don't mean Selby Lovelorn. I handled him with a great amount of discretion and permanence. What I mean is. It's this.

He holds up the other fist.

—You, Joe. What I mean is, if Selby had crossed a line and needed to be let out of his obligations to this world, well, man, then hadn't you done the same? Didn't I owe it to the Society to remove a man who'd chosen to disregard the greater good for the sake of his own sensibilities? A man who, with every day it became increasingly clear, a man who was turning his back on our philosophy. Didn't I have a responsibility to, I don't know, to put that man out of the sphere where he could do us the most harm? With what you knew about the Society, I think, from where I am now, I think I lost an opportunity there. Blew a chance to make things run smoother. If I'd just fucking killed you then.

I nod.

—We all have regrets.

He unballs his fists.

—Yes, we do.

He looks at Lydia, still bundled on the floor, her eyes trying to find a way to burn holes in his face.

—Speaking of regrets.

He rubs his forehead.

—I seem to have been rash. Letting my anger get the better of me. I should have, like the book says, I should have stepped aside when Lydia charged in here and accused me of withholding, what was it, *withholding knowledge of crimes against humanity*. But that kind of thing gets under my skin. Always has. If I'd waited a moment before telling Hurley to, you know, calm her down, Lydia might have mentioned that her Bulls were nearby and waiting for her to come back out.

He taps a finger on the book.

—A little too late, I threw the coins on that one.

He gets up from his thrift store bargain table.

—They had recognized you, Joe, they would have probably grabbed you off the sidewalk. Just for, you know, being you. I'm guessing they made some socioeconomic assumptions based on your appearance and didn't think to move till you were already on the doorstep. But you'll be the last one in.

He points up.

—We have, I don't know, we have a few dozen partisans in here. Some clerical staff. A couple members in hospice, dealing with the shock of recent infection. And the old school. Us. Lydia's Bulls have the front covered. We have the alley, but they have the rooftop behind us. It's a stalemate scenario.

He circles the table and leans his hip against it.

—How long, if you were to make a guess, how long would this kind of dissent take to travel uptown? I'm talking about the awareness of it, not the dissent itself. Which would make no sense at all.

I scratch my knee.

—Things were normal, maybe a day before word got out. Way things are now, word is already on its way.

—Yeah, that's my thought.

He looks down at Lydia again.

—And when Predo hears we're all tied up here, and that's not meant at your expense, Lydia, he'll jump. Move his people down. You know, the Coalition owns property here. They hold leases. So, while we're fighting with ourselves, he'll literally bus his people down and put them in those properties. By the time we can, if we can, come to terms, we'll have at least two hundred Coalition members housed on our turf. That's if he doesn't just come at us here. Attack Lydia's Bulls from the rear while they're focused on us, and then. It's all so. Things just. I'm.

He takes off his glasses and covers his eyes.

—I'm at something of a loss.

Eyes still covered, he raises a finger.

—Even if we avoid Predo's involvement, a division like this is, I don't know, has the potential to be mortal. Man, it's like, how do you restore confidence in your leadership when they've just gone toe-to-toe in a power struggle? Because, our people, they're out there, watching how this resolves. If we can't, if Predo knows, all the Society knows, and that just. That just.

He takes his hands from his eyes.

—Cripples us, man.

My stuff is on a shelf across the room. Keys, wet matches, knife, saw, tobacco. I stare at the tobacco. I'm getting crawling claws in my belly again and a smoke sounds better and better.

—You need a symbol. Something you can rally around, show unity with. Something that gives people hope that you can move forward. That kind of thing.

Terry raises his eyebrows.

—That's some interesting thinking, Joe. Did you have something in mind?

I point at my tobacco.

—I might think more clearly with a smoke.

He shakes his head.

—Should have picked Camel as your last name instead of Pitt.

I get up and go for the Bugler.

—Sure, except I'm a Luckys man.

—And Joe Lucky wouldn't have fit at all.

I flick out a paper and wave it back and forth. It crinkles enough to let me know it can be rolled.

—Doesn't seem so.

He rotates a finger.

—Your thought, Joe.

I get another of my crippled jobs rolled, but the match heads are just smearing on the striker. I cross to the little propane stove in the corner, turn on the gas, hit the sparker, wait for a flame, and light up.

All is right in the world.

—My thought is, Predo's not worried about you right now. What he's worried about is the hit he's about to lay on the Cure house. Got a heavy contingent ready to go in sometime after midnight. His back is the one that's turned. You kids can settle your differences, you can slide up there and put a hurt on him while he's trying to clean up Horde's mess. As a bonus.

I suck smoke, let it go to work on my lungs, and kick it back out.

—Chubby's daughter and her beau are sitting tight up there too. Complete with their handy little symbol of unity right in her stomach. All you got to do is stop sweating out past scores with me and go get it.

I get some more of that smoke inside me.

—You can keep from killing me too soon, I'll even show how to get up there without anyone seeing you at all.

Terry runs a hand down his ponytail, purses his lips, walks over to the shelf where my stuff is and picks up the amputation blade. Taking it from the rubber sheath, he steps to Lydia, squats, places the tip of the blade against the racquet ball in her mouth, and stabs an inch of the blade into the ball. Putting the knife aside, he pokes his finger into the slit he's made, hooks it, and gives a hard pull, popping the saliva-covered ball past her teeth and dropping it on the floor.

—Can I interest you in a negotiated settlement, Lydia?

She spits.

—You can fuck off and die, Terry. You and your hypocritical dialectic bullshit can fuck off and die.

He picks up the blade.

—My options are limited here, Lydia, and in deference to our working relationship, I'd like to avoid doing anything that I can't, you know, maneuver around. Anything with irreparable consequences. So if you've got your knee-jerk anger reaction out of your system, do we have room to talk here?

Through her teeth.

—After Predo and the Cure house, we go to Queens. The hole. The kids. No discussion. No compromise. We save them. The right fucking thing, Terry. With no gray.

He shrugs.

—Hey, man, that's the kind of opportunity I'm looking for every day of my life.

He starts to untie the twists of coaxial binding her, looking over his shoulder at me.

—Joe?

—Old buddy.

—Why'd you let Selby go?

I drop my butt and crush it.

—To see if I could get away with it.

He yanks a loop of cable free and rises.

—Yeah. I was right. Should have killed you then.

I start pocketing my keys and such.

—Think of all the fun you'd have missed out on over the years, Terry, without me around. Like a king without a court jester.

Nobody will give me a gun.

—Wasn't for me, Lydia, you'd still be hog-tied on the floor.

—I don't see the connection.

I fumble with the buttons of the clean shirt Terry had someone dig up for me.

—Just saying you might have one of your Bulls lend me a piece for this gig. Seeing as how I'm the one talked Terry around to not killing you.

She shrugs her chiseled shoulders into her Carhartt jacket.

—Last time I saw you with a gun, Joe, you were shooting me in the stomach with it.

—Well, if you're gonna dwell on the past like that, we'll never have nothing to build a relationship on.

She shakes her head.

—You need help with those?

Buttons with one thumb, think about it. I'm gonna be a T-shirt and zipper guy for the rest of my life. Should I have a chance to worry about a change of wardrobe.

I look down at the three I got fastened, all in the wrong holes.

—Rather have the gun, but I'll take what you're giving.

She comes over, undoes the button on the old black corduroy, starts to do them up straight.

She's looking at the buttons, focused.

—I'm wondering.

She pops another button into its hole.

—Do you think you have a plan? Because I look at you some-times, and that's the feeling I get. *Joe, he's got this all worked out.*

But when I see you like this, carved up like this, like you're trading body parts for time, I think, *Joe, he's just thrashing in the water, drawing the sharks.*

She does the top button.

—But as if maybe you're drawing them away from someone else.

I take a step back, use my good hand to undo that top button.

—Trying to choke me, Lydia?

She's not looking at the buttons anymore, she's looking at my eye.

—Whatever you're after, Joe, it doesn't have to be just the one thing.

I pull out my tobacco.

—Don't suppose your charity extends so far as to roll me one?

—What I'm saying, I think I know you have something you want, something you care about.

I pull out a paper.

—I care about getting a smoke rolled.

—And if that's true, if I'm right about that, you caring about something, then there could be room for more.

I shake out some tobacco.

—Sure, I care about maybe having a drink too.

—Chubby's daughter.

I roll it up.

—She's running on Anne Rice and crystal power. You won't like her.

—That baby she's carrying.

I put it in the corner of my mouth.

—Kid will probably take after her mom, pop out with fairy wings, stardust on its eyelids.

—Those kids in Queens. That hole.

I bend to the propane stove and light up.

—Funny.

—Another joke?

—No. Just funny how I'm the one went down that hole and everyone else is always trying to tell me what has to be done about it. Like maybe I had my hands over my eyes down there. Just peeked through a crack between my fingers, and ran. Like somehow I missed something. You think I missed something, Lydia? Something you can fill me in on?

She draws a line in the air with the edge of her hand.

—There's a chance here, Joe, to do something that tells people who you really are. A chance to do more than just thrash around. You can do better than make it up as you go along and hope you land on your feet. You can fight for something more than just what *you* want. You can save people who deserve saving. You can show what you're made of. For once.

I'm looking under the table, in the corners of the room, under a couple chairs.

—Lydia.

—Joe.

I take a drag.

—Lydia, you see what Terry did with that ball he took from your mouth?

I blow it out.

—'Cause I'd really like to stick it back in there.

She doesn't move.

—It'll come down to making a choice. Whether you want it or not. You'll have to show what you are.

I sit on one of the chairs, pick up my boots, the worst of the blood and crud scraped off them.

—Interesting you should put it that way. Earlier tonight, had a little chat with Amanda Horde. Crazy twist that she is, she's finally got the thing nailed down. Sounds like it anyway.

She folds her arms.

—What thing?

I put on one of the boots, start to do the laces.

—The Vyrus. The thing. You know.

She stands there.

I put on the other boot.

—So she had quite a lot to tell me about what I am. What we all are.

Lace up.

—According to her, what I am is what I've always been. According to her, I wasn't infected, I was activated. What was already inside me was just switched on. I wasn't turned into a blood-drinker, I was one all along.

I rise.

—Which, if I follow her right, means the same for all of us.

I step to my jacket, hung on a nail next to the radiator, just about dry from the sponging I gave it.

—No one made us Vampyres, we were Vampyres all along.

I slip it on.

—What I'm doing, Lydia, is just what comes naturally for what I am.

I step to her.

—And what I am is the same thing as you.

Past her.

—You want to fight it, be my guest.

I open the door.

—I got better things to take a swing at than myself.


The corridors are full of Terry's partisans and Lydia's Bulls. They give one another the hairy eyeball as they put edges on machetes, load battered sawed-offs, work the actions on a few Tech 9s, and put the finishing touches on a satchel full of Molotovs.

I think about the black-market military ordnance the enforcers were prepping in the uptown garage. I think about a few of those guys getting a drop on us as we come through a door. I think about how high the bodies would have to pile before they'd stop the bullets and let me and whoever else might be hanging at the rear make a run for it.

Ugly things is what I'm thinking.

I find Terry in a second-floor room. Smells like cedar incense and mimeo ink. Posters of Lennon and Lenin staring at each other from across the room. Frameless mattress on the floor with a sleeping bag on top. Camp stool at an old school desk in the corner. Turntable playing a track from *Exile on Main St.* "Ventilator Blues."

Terry's sitting in the chair, changed into combat boots, faded Levis, and a Vietnam-era U.S. Army field jacket with an American flag peace sign on the back, worn open over a Che Guevara T-shirt.

He's cleaning a vintage AK-47.

I give him a nod.

—Time to free the people?

He hefts the assault rifle.

—That's the idea, Joe. Always has been.

I walk over to the turntable and pick up the album jacket, listen to the song.

—Mood music.

He withdraws a cleaning rod from the barrel, dragging out a scrap of cotton.

—There are times when aggression is sadly in order. This is a song that has always helped me to psychologically prepare for the onset of violence.

I put the jacket down.

—Makes you feel like killing.

He shoulders the gun.

—Nothing in this world, Joe, nothing at all.

He dry fires, listening to the snap of the pin.

—Nothing makes me feel like killing.

—Not even me?

He fits a banana clip to the receiver, slaps it home.

—You've tempted my weakness on more than one occasion, but I'm, I don't know, I'm not a man who contemplates killing, even in anger, who contemplates it with pleasure.

I walk to the window, lean against the plywood nailed over it.

—Who said anything about contemplation. I'm talking about doing it.

He lays the gun across his lap.

—What can I tell you, man, it's just not my thing.

I nod.

—Still, you got moves, Ter. May not use them much anymore, but you got 'em.

He takes a black watch cap from the desktop, puts it on, tucks his ponytail up inside.

—Some skills, you just acquire them. Doesn't mean you revel in them or anything. The times taught me what I had to do.

—Funny, I got the idea old lady Vandewater taught you what to do back when you trained to be an enforcer.

He rests the butt of the gun on the floor, barrel against his knee.

—History makes us, forges us, we hone the edge. I was shaped to be a weapon for the Coalition, but I chose to cut the other way. You take what is given you, and you use it. Chubby's daughter and her baby.

—Yeah, how'd you get along with her?

He rubs his forehead.

—I'll admit she, you know, taxed the limits of my sense of humor.

—Relentless with that shit.

—Totally relentless.

—But you talked it right back at her, didn't you?

He smiles.

—*Dear lady, urgency is on the wind. We must act.*

—Nice.

—It didn't help. She, I don't know, got it in her head that she'd be better off somewhere else. I think running is just in her, you know, her personal script. Part of her drama. A shame. Infected and uninfected. That baby. There is real potential in that kind of narrative. I'm sure she'll see it.

—Or maybe she's already sensed you're a two-faced asshole.

He pings a fingernail off the barrel of his gun, but doesn't say anything.

I find my tobacco.

—Me, I'm not worried about you selling us out, Terry. I figure you've done that at least a half-dozen times over the years. Made some backdoor deal with Predo. That's the way of the world. Like presidents and prime ministers, right? In the end, they all went to the same schools, speak the same lingo. Us peons, we just don't understand how it's done. So they do it for our own good. Screwing us, I mean. You and Predo, studying together with Vandewater, once I had that figured, I knew where you stood. Mean, I knew from way back you're full of shit, but it was only the last couple years I knew you're just another player.

He pokes his index finger in the barrel, pulls it out with a little pop.

—If there's a point here, Joe, I have a ton of details to take care of. You know.

I got a cigarette rolled. Lighting it with a punk of incense makes the first drag taste foul, but it improves after that.

—Just that things seem to be closing out is all. And, like you said a while back, I'm a curious type. Things left unanswered, they make me itchy. Speaking of which.

I pick a flake of tobacco from my tongue.

—I was thinking how the Horde kid's crazy dad isolated the zombie bacteria.

He purses his lips, makes the gun barrel pop again.

I smoke.

—That whole deal where he made those nutty dentures that injected the goop into someone and infected them. You know, to start a zombie plague. Bonkers, that guy. No wonder his daughter is short a few cards.

Pop goes the barrel.

I raise a finger, one of the few.

—Come to think of it, after I got my hands on those chompers, didn't I lay them off on you?

I push off from the plywood and stroll toward the door.

—Tell ya, those teeth, in the wrong hands, they could start some serious trouble.

I stop at the door and look back at him.

He looks up, no movement in his face.

Dead face.

I smile.

—Hey, Terry, I didn't know any better, I'd say for sure you were in the mood to kill someone.

Pop.

I wave as I make my way to the stairs at the end of the hall.

—Thanks for the answers on that one, Terry. That itch, been driving me nuts.


*Thrashing.*

Where'd Lydia get an idea like that?

Me, I'm miles from land, clinging to a scrap of wood, hoping to see a sail on the horizon. Someone at the rail to throw me a rope. Get me on deck, I can kill the crew and take the helm and point the damn thing where I want to go.

Meantime, I hold fast, pick a direction, and kick.

Headway.

Because didn't you know, the worm can swim?

—What do ya hear, Hurl?

He rolls his pant leg a little higher.

—I hear tis a brutal an a unfair world out dere, Joe. One not fit fer da likes a me an you. Gentlemen as we are.

I'm not bothering with my own pants, not being a delicate soul like Hurley.

—Mean, how's it stacking up out there? I'm back just a few hours. Lost at sea.

He rises, pants rolled to above his knees, brown socks peeking out of the tops of his thick-sole leather boots.

—Well, an is it any surprise at all you'd be lost in it? Ya hardly spend any time around us a'tall anymore.

Terry comes up from the rear of the line, edging in and around the partisans and Bulls, patting shoulders, lending words of encouragement. Bucking up the troops before a slaughter.

—Joe.

—Terry.

He looks at his watch.

—You said Predo would hit sometime after midnight.

—What he said.

—It's midnight.

—Guess we better get up there.

The basements of the Lower East Side are a warren of code violations that date back to the days of the Whyos and Tammany Hall. Excavated, hollowed-out, chopped, extended, dug deeper than safe, pushed far beyond property lines. A little time spent poking at a flaking brick wall with a crowbar will usually reward you with passage into someone else's labyrinth. Poke at a sweaty wall and you'll either find yourself peeking in at an old drainage or cut in half by a knife of water set loose from a pipe pressurized to lift thousands of gallons six stories up. Best way to avoid that second fate is to put your ear to the wall. Listen for the thrum of water in a pipe. Don't hear it, you can start swinging.

This wall here, seems like I don't hear anything but maybe a soft gurgle on the other side. Then again, I don't feel my best. That uncertainty being what it is, I step aside and gesture to Hurley.

—After you, Hurl.

He pats the head of his sledgehammer.

—Not dat I'm shy, Joe, but the first blow is all yer own.

Terry moves back.

—Your show, Joe.

I look at the wall I picked out for this after breaking us into a basement adjoining the Society safe house and following an eastward read on the compass Terry loaned me.

—My show. And me without a curtain to raise on it.

I use my lame hand as a guide, right arm swinging the crowbar at the wall, stepping into it, like breaking the rack for a game of eight ball.

And come up dry.

I point at the spot.

—Give it a bash.

Hurl spins the sledgehammer, a delicate thing in his hands, winds up, and lets loose. Bricks fly, we all get peppered with chips and dry mortar, and there's a jagged hole the size of a trash can lid.

Hurley points at the water pipe on the right-hand edge of the hole.

—An dat was a close one weren't it?

I look at a dent in the side of the pipe.

—Almost a quick trip.

—Are you masters of engineering ready yet?

We look at Lydia, come to join the fun.

I hook a thumb at the hole.

—Just measuring how close we came to dying.

She shakes her head, kicks a few bricks from the bottom of the hole, and steps through into the ankle-deep sludge in the spillway beyond.

—Make a habit of that and you won't get out of bed.

I look at Hurley, he looks at me, we both look at Terry.

He nods.

—Destined to rule the world.

He follows her.

Hurley shakes his head.

—An more's the pity fer us all if it should come ta be.

He follows.

I think about turning the other way and getting myself lost. But the girl and her baby are north, so I hit the spillway.

—Did ya ever hear of Montaigne?

—Don't think I knew him.

—Well ya wouldn't have, would ya, him bein' dead so long before yer own time wit us. But did ya ever hear of him?

—Nope.

I stop at a sluice. The sludge washed out a ways back and we've been in water to our calves the last half mile or so. Terry and Lydia drifted back to their troops. Neither one much comfortable around the other without a passel of guns at their beck just now. Hurley's stayed on point with me. Not so much for the company, more to be on hand to kill me fast if I make a crooked play. A powerful deterrent Hurley is.

I take a look at the compass, light from a couple dozen flashlights scattered between the crew behind me. The north read lies with the sluice. A six-foot drop to water that could be over a tall man's head.

I'm a tall man.

I look at Hurley.

—Hold that story.

I jump.

I'm under, water up my nose, in my empty eye socket, feet kicking, they find something solid and I put it under me, stand, water to my waist.

I look up.

—Gonna have to roll your pants a bit higher, Hurl.


—Montaigne, he was a torpedo wit one a da cannonball gangs back when.

I check the Ziploc I put my tobacco in before this jaunt. Still dry. There is a god.

—Like you're speaking French, Hurl.

He frowns.

—Don't know a word of da lingo.

I tuck the tobacco away, push on through the water. Cold. It actually makes the Vyrus-burn in my belly feel a little better.

—*Torpedo* I follow, but never heard that *cannonball gang* before.

He nods, hikes a leg and sloshes after me.

—Righto, righto. Cannonball gangs were a bit o ruff back when me an Terry were first settin' shop. Back den, before all dis *mass media* an da like, tings were a bit looser. What we could get away wit, it was murder it was. Cannonballs. Did ya ever do one?

I search my memory.

—I haven't got a clue, Hurl.

He wraps his arms around himself, awkward as he still has the sledgehammer, and jumps up, coming down with a splash.

—You know, cannonball.

—Like the dive?

He waves the hammer.

—Like da dive. Just a clumsy ting ya do ta make a splash. Just fer da fun. Ta make a, well, a spectacle of yerself. An dat's what da cannonball gangs were up ta. Making spectacles of demselves. Go inta a place, say a speakeasy, someplace off da cops' usual beat. Places were mostly soundproofed purty good. Underground an such. So no one would be bothered by all da drinkin' an da music an da like. Ya missed out on New York ya did, Joe, not bein' around in da old days.

I'm draggin' my bad leg along through the water. Now the cold's in my stomach deep and it doesn't feel better at all. Feels like ice water and acid in my bowels.

—You're making it come alive for me, Hurl.

—Well, an it was a time. So an all. Montaigne. He ran one o dese gangs. Run 'em inta a place, come in wit maybe just a little rabble rouse ta start it off. Just loud. Boisterous like. Ya know what da word means?

—Heard it before, yeah.

—Lovely word. Remember da nun who taught it to me. Cracked my knuckles a hundred times wit a ruler before I had it right. An I never did get it spelled proper.

He sighs.

—A true bitch of a woman she was. I killed her, I did. Fer her sins of cruelty on children.

He shoots an elbow at my ribs. Doesn't break any new ones, but leaves me gasping.

—Yeah, an ain't dat a laugh, Joe.

He laughs.

—Killed her *fer her sins*. Oh, if dere's a god, he's gonna be upset wit me over dat bit o humor.

His laugh winds down.

—So, boisterous and all, Montaigne and his fellas would come in, draw a little ire perhaps, an tings would get a little messy from dere. What stared as a tussle would soon become a brawl, and den a riot.

He shakes his head.

—An den a slaughter.

With the butt of the hammer he pushes up the brim of his fedora.

—Ah da yella press in dem days, dey went fer it so. *Gangland Slayings in Den of Sin*. Oh an dey loved it. Had dey just but known the headlines dey mighta had wit just a wee little diggin'. But no, dey were happy wit da obvious, da low-hangin' fruit o dat vile profession. Montaigne had naught ta fear from dem or da police. Worse dey could come cross would be a couple o real gangsters in one o dem places. Couple fellas wit dere .45s in dere pants an maybe a violin case under da table. If ya follow me.

He holds the sledgehammer like a machine gun and waves it back and forth.

—Rat-a-tat-tat-tat-tat.

He rubs his stomach.

—Serious stuff, a belly full of lead. Such a ting had happened, would have saved Montaigne some weepin'.

He frowns.

—Instead of which it came down ta me an Terry lookin' him up at a place he kept off Mott Street. Little lay-by he had wit a fluff I recall was named Eileen.

He winks.

—I always remember da purdy ones, Joe. No matter how far back.

He lifts his shoulders and drops them.

—Shame we had ta put her in da ground wit Montaigne an all. As part of makin' it look right.

He drapes the hammer over his shoulder, trudging along with me.

—He'd just made one splash too many is what he'd done. Could have moderated himself a bit, he might still be about. Not likely, but possible. But even if no one sussed to what he an his fellas was really about, still they were makin' far too much of a ruckus. Too many o dem yella press stories. Too many o dem gangland headlines. Coppers had to make a move sooner or later. Dey started pokin' 'bout, it wasn't gonna do no good fer no one. Me an Terry, we had our own business concerns to worry on. Montaigne, he just served no purpose a'tall. Good ting 'bout dem times, ya just put a few bullets in a fella, dropped him in a gutter. Yella press had dem another headline, an da story came to a close.

He kicks a few gallons of water out of his way.

—Now, Joe, da story ain't never come to an end.

He points the hammer at me.

—Ya ask what I hear? Well I tell ya, I hear tell on da TV dat dere's maybe a serial killer on da loose in Manhattan. Not no normal serial killer, but like a team o dem. A gang o serial killers. Dat's what da story is dey like to tell. In da absence of any sense comin' from the police on da matter. I won't tell ya what da headlines in da *Post* look like.

He waves the hammer at the arched roof of the tunnel.

—All dis conflict and bad feelins, it's makin' fer more dan a man's fair share o sloppiness in tings. Not all bodies get hid, not all witnesses get taken care of. Just makes fer a mess. An a story today, it never dies, not till dere's a better one. An tell me, Joe.

He bumps my shoulder with the hammer.

—Where are dey gonna find a better story den *Serial Killer Gangs*? Unless it's us, Joe, I don't tink dat's a story dat's like to die soon. Not o natural causes anyhow.

He swats the air with his hand.

—An dat's what I hear. Trouble an woe. Maybe, Joe.

He nods to himself.

—Maybe an so dere's nothin' better to do now but to make a big cannonball and go out wit a splash.

He wags a finger at me.

—Not dat I'm one fer despair, mind. Not, leastways, not while Terry is still about ta mind the store fer us all.

I grab a fistful of my stomach and squeeze, trying to distract myself with a different kind of pain.

—Yeah, Hurley, I hear you. Be a terrible thing to find out Terry wasn't in there doing it like it should be done.

—Shake a man's faith to lose Terry.

—Yeah.

I give another squeeze to my gut.

—What else you hear, Hurl?

—How so, Joe?

He chuckles at the rhyme.

I glance at the compass, still bearing north, still on the path.

—What's the word on how it splits up? Coalition's got the Bulls and the Bears, the Wall, the Family. Society and the Hood together. Any word on how the others jump?

—Others, Joe? An who would dose be? Dat rabble in Brooklyn, we don't make truck wit dem no more.

I look into the dark water ahead.

—Any word on Enclave picking a side?

He holds up a second.

—Enclave, Joe.

He carries on with me.

—Dey don't have no side but dere own mad selves.

—Sure, I know that, but what do you hear?

I sidle close, drop my voice.

—Come on, Hurl, you catch a little of everything. Must be rumors.

He looks both ways over his shoulders.

—Well, I don't like to talk on what I'm no expert 'bout, but a man hears a ting or two.

He drops his own voice.

—Generally, dough, tis a sore spot for Terry. What wit how you took da Count over dere, him an all his money an all. Dat was a dissatisfaction. A real blow. Terry now, he always had a patience wit da Enclave dat I could never muster myself. Dem religious types, remind me too much o da nuns. But Terry, he likes ta say dat what a man believes is his own damn business. An I can't argue. Dough I find it hard to ignore dat dem Enclave believe dat anyone what ain't wit dem is just due to be laid low when da time comes. Makes a man tink he'd be better off if dey was done wit.

—Ever fight one, Hurl?

He shakes his head.

—Much to my consternation, no. I hear dey are fierce in battle. An dat fires my imagination, it does. Course, I've fought some udders who was starvin' like, in dat old Vyrus madness. I'd show you da scars, but dey healed.

He laughs again.

—*Healed.* Anyhow, I've tussled my fair bit wit da starved and savage, but I hear tis not da same wit Enclave. Hear dey can control it like. Not just berserk, but remember who dey is and what dey's about.

He smacks the hammer into his palm.

—To a brawler like myself, Joe, dat sounds a challenge.

He shrugs.

—Someday perhaps.

He hooks a thumbs in his suspenders.

—But you were askin' what I heard. An' I'll tell ya, I hear it's no good over dere. Da rumor is, da rumor is dey got some kind of troubles o dere own. Sign o da times it is. Squabbles inside. Da Count, we knew he took da reigns over dere when Daniel croaked it, but we hear he got himself competition. What it is, I hear, is.

He looks back at some of the Bulls trailing us, leans closer, whispers in my ear.

—I hear tis a girl.

I look at him.

He nods.

—A girl is what I hear. Puttin' up a challenge to head Enclave. Not.

He looks behind us again and raises his voice a bit.

—Not dat dere's naught wrong wit it. But.

He shakes his head and lowers his voice.

—A girl still.

He sighs.

—Always a madness in dat place, Joe. No tellin' which a way dey might come out on any issue, but always seemed to me dey were traditional types. Den again, long as I knew, it was Daniel over dere callin' da shots. Never had no goings on wit da man myself, but I heard how he was reliable like. In da way of his kind dat is. Crazy, but reliable like. Fer da time bein', I'm just happy ta have dem off on dere own while we finally settle accounts. Tell ya, Joe.

He slaps my back and I go to my knees in the water and he hauls me up.

—Sometin' like dis? A troop o hard hitters makin' tru da sewers ta lay a hurt on da competition? Well, it may not be good fer business in da short, but tis good fer da soul. A bit o da old days come ta life is what it is.

He comes in close again.

—It's all up in da air it is now. Sideways like. Confusin' even, an I don't like ta utter da taught, but even Terry steps outside hisself frum time ta time. Some o da plays we made of late, dey just don't make no sense. I don't expect ta understand every little ting, but I don't grasp how it does us good when Terry an Lydia are forever at each other's troats.

He rubs his chin.

—An while I know it's not how Terry'd a had it, I have ta say dat fer meself, tis more dan a relief ta be getting' over wit da inevitable. I follow Terry's lead, an everyone knows dat, but it is a ting dat warms my heart ta be getting' dis out o da way once an fer all. Direct like. An maybe get all back ta normal like. Terry his old self again.

He straightens.

—Whaddya say ta a song?

He opens his pipes, belts his tenor, echoes in the tunnel making him a chorus.

> —*Ye haven't an arm, ye haven't a leg, hurroo, hurroo*
> *Ye haven't an arm, ye haven't a leg, hurroo, hurroo*
> *Ye haven't an arm, ye haven't a leg, Ye're an armless, boneless,*
>    *chickenless egg,*
> *Ye'll have to be put with a bowl to beg,*
> *Oh Johnny I hardly knew ye.*


After midnight is what Predo said.

And at his disposal: four enforcers in cop uniforms, those action-movie types with their body armor and grappling hooks, the others in coveralls, sweat suits, business casual. One big Vampyre costume party.

Figure he can play it a couple ways. Lead with the fake cops. Put them up on the stoop to knock on the door, force their way in, make way for whichever masqueraders have been planted on the street. Commandos will be on the roof already. They can come straight down, or just sit up there to pick off anyone who tries to get out through the fire exit up top. Plenty of extra bodies to spread around the streets in case something sloppy happens and they have runners that need to be snatched away. Biggest problem with that play is the cop uniforms. Neighbors see them out their windows, they're gonna pull up a chair to see what it's all about. As long as the action stays inside the Cure house, it's not all bad. But can you count on that? No. Best to count on shit getting all fucked up in this kind of scenario. Not that there's ever been this kind of scenario. So figure he might play it straight paramilitary.

Commandos blow a hole in the roof, pour inside, start flushing everything to the bottom. Fake cops are outside, ready to do "crowd control" on anything that comes out. Some of those coveralls had ConEd logos. Guys might be set to cut power to the house, maybe the whole block.

How good are Predo and his enforcers?

One-on-one, they're good as it gets in terms of being fit and well trained and inclined to want to hurt a person, but not big on independent thought. Rote fighters. Counterpunchers most of them. Fight dirty enough and you have a good shot. Pretty good in small group, but the same weaknesses apply.

But this?

Who the hell knows.

Mean, they haven't done it before. And hard to figure where they'd practice. Chances are, once they pull the trigger and start this thing, it'll all be theory they're trying to make work the way they want it to. Counting on Horde's people being disorganized, starving, poorly armed.

Predo had any idea how far gone things really are in there, he'd probably not be bothering. Just keep his embargo in place and wait a little longer.

Heat. He's feeling it.

What Hurley had to say about the news. That stuff has always stung the Coalition more than it has the downtown types. Psycho-killer headlines, that tension on the streets, the feeling out there that something's not right. Predo doesn't like it. And if he doesn't like it, his bosses on the Coalition Secretariat like it less.

Old schoolest of the old school. Bunch of top hat and evening cape boys sitting on the top floor of Coalition HQ. Fancy Upper East town house just around the corner from the Guggenheim. Calling shots that knock balls over the whole Island.

Used to be, I pictured them smoking big cigars and drinking port. Like from a nineteenth-century political cartoon. Red noses, round bellies, resting their feet on the backs of the slobs. Nothing wrong with it if you can get a seat at the table, I suppose. Not my style, but I get why people want to be on top. Means there's no one overhead to drop a load on you when their bowels get loose.

Got a different picture of them now.

Lean. Burnished. Dipping fingers into bowls of something that looks like looped purple licorice ropes. Putting them at their lips and sucking.

Sucking cord blood from harvested umbilicals.

Hole-raised kids with chains on their necks scattered around the room.

Not a picture from satire, but something literal. Like I'm thinking that's what it's really like up there on that top floor. Very much just like that.

Types living that way, you might figure they have a vested interest in avoiding the kind of headlines Hurley mentioned. So yeah, figure again that Predo's feeling heat, needs to get the situation under control. Minimize risks and exposures. Start with what's right there in the middle of their turf. The Cure house.

A quiet play. Clandestine. That's what he'll be going for. The fake cops, they won't lead, they'll hold back for an emergency. Whole thing will be invisible if Predo has his way. Commandos first, dead of night, figure between three and four. Time for us to make the scene before it goes down. Get inside, make a deal with Horde and Sela, and be waiting for Predo's enforcers when they come in.

And once they're in and the bullets fly, I grab the girl with her baby, try and take the boyfriend if I can, and get the hell out.

Who's thrashing?

Not me.

I have a plan.


You said you knew the way.

—I do.

—It's almost three in the morning.

—Just be quiet, I'm trying to smell something.

—Oh, I'm sorry, is my voice interfering with your sense of smell? Is it getting in your nose and distracting you?

—Lydia.

—Joe.

—If you'd had given me that gun, I'd be shooting you again right now.

She turns to Terry.

—He's lost. He's cracking wiseass now because he's lost and it's what he does when he knows he's fucked up.

Terry sloshes closer.

—Joe?

I hold up a hand.

—Just shut up for a minute and back off.

A cramp hits my gut and I fold over it.

Terry presses the heel of his hand into his forehead.

—How long since you had anything?

I unfold.

—Too long what with the ass-kicking I've been taking. So I'm maybe not at my sharpest. So I need maybe a little space and quiet here.

He turns to Lydia.

She looks at me, jabs a finger.

—Time's almost up.

And works her way through the water back to her Bulls.

Terry tugs the edge of his watch cap.

—Getting late. Another thirty minutes and the risk and reward elements on this will have seriously eroded. We'll have to turn back and, I don't know, negotiate some kind of settlement. Me and Lydia, I mean. You.

He looks at the water.

—To be honest, Joe, you'll be staying down here. Metaphors aside, saying it like it needs to be said, get us the fuck up into the Cure house or Hurley is going to beat you to death with his hammer.

A few yards away, Hurley turns. Shows me his hammer.

—If it must be, Joe, so it will. An nothin' personal.

I nod.

—Yeah, sure, I'll play the nail. No problem. Just give me a shot at this with no one on my back.

Terry raises his hands and backs away.

—Hey, I'm the last one to want to get on anyone's back, man. That's not my thing. Just that we have a timeline. Structure is tough, but once you get into it, you have to stay there.

Another moment when it might be better I don't have a gun, but I'd still be happy to see one come floating by on a raft of shit. Nothing pops up, so I close my eyes, try to ignore the ache that's creeping into my marrow, try and find a scent of dry air.

Something sears my cheek.

I open my eyes.

A flicker of white at the edge of my vision, down the tunnel.

I look back at Hurley, leaning against the far wall, hammer cradled in his arms, whistling Irish war ballads to himself.

The heat wavers in the air. I touch it, feel it dissipating, but know the course.

I raise my arm and point.

—This way.

Seven minutes later we're in the Second Avenue line above Sixty-eighth. Minutes after that we're in the access shaft, making our way past Phil's corpse.

Terry looks at the mangled body.

—Sela did that?

I walk away.

—I did that. Finally had enough of his double crosses.

Could be I hear a chuckle in the dark. Crazy old man chuckle. Laughing at what I said, or at what he's leading me back to. Or could be I hear nothing at all. Nothing but me laughing at myself.

Hurley widens the hole I made when I came this way before. Hunched to make our way up the sewer line, we straighten when we reach the storm vault, looking up at the drain hole I shoved Phil through.

We study it, picked out in crossed flashlight beams.

Grate I removed is still off. Still dark as hell up there.

Quiet.

Terry stands directly under the hole, sniffs, pulls a face, steps back and waves us to him.

—What is that?

I shake my head.

—What's what?

He points at the hole.

—Smell.

I step under the hole, make a show of raising my face and scenting, come back to Terry, Lydia and Hurley.

—Smells like a lot of dead people to me.

He frowns.

—Joe, without this meaning to sound like a brag, because I wish it wasn't the truth, but I've smelled piles of dead in my life.

He points at the hole again.

—That's not what they smell like.

I find my tobacco, unseal it and start to roll.

—And when was the last time you smelled over a hundred Vyrus infected who all died of starvation?

I seal up my smoke.

—'Cause that's what's been going on in there.

I pat my pockets, looking for a light, and realize I never grabbed a dry pack of matches before we set out.

—Shit.

Lydia goes to the hole herself, gets a whiff, comes back.

—It's Vyrus. Dead. Something else.

I fiddle with the unlit smoke, holding it between my fingers like it might make me feel a little better.

—Could be the shit-smeared walls you're smelling. The bile they puked up when they died. Could be the wood rot in the walls. Wait a little longer and all you're gonna smell is Predo's boys coming through the front door.

Hurley is under the hole now. He inhales, flinches, pinches his nostrils closed.

—A proper reek it tis, whatever it may be.

He unpinches his nose, takes another whiff.

—Hard to say an all, but could be a hint o gun powder as well.

Terry pulls a whisker from his soul patch.

—I don't like to be overly suspicious in a team endeavor like this, but, I don't know, I just don't like climbing into a dark basement when I can't really smell what's in it.

He points at me.

—You first, Joe.

I look up at the hole.

—As if there were any doubt.


The ache is in my fingernails now.

Cramps haven't hit the point where I'd rather die than feel the next one, but I can sense them stacking one after the other like waves ready to pound the shore. Bones alternate between freezing and scorching.

I shiver, sweat, stand under the hole rubbing my stomach.

Lydia kneels a few feet away, an old wood-stocked carbine in her hands, aimed at the hole.

—Sooner you go up, sooner you might eat.

I wipe sweat.

—Feel like I'm gonna puke. Cramps. Hot flashes. Cold flashes.

I point at myself.

—Sure I'm the guy you want on point?

She jerks her gun at the hole.

—Jump on up there and stop whining, Joe. Doesn't sound like there's anything wrong with you that most women don't deal with once a month.

—Calling me a pussy?

She drops her aim till it's on my legs.

—Need some motivation here, Joe?

I hold up my half a hand.

—Leave a little for the vultures, lady.

She tilts her chin at the hole.

—Show us how safe it is.

I rub my chin.

—Sure. Safe as houses. Nobody up there but the chickens.

I jump.

Full fed, I'd just about be able to hop straight up and land straddling the hole. Like I am, I get as good a grip on the edge as I can with one thumb, and haul myself up and through.

Nothing kills me.

Light from below shows me the corpse of the thing I did in a couple hours ago. Seeing it twists my stomach in another direction. Looks like someone crossbred a cactus with a manatee and turned it inside out. Only worse.

Amanda. Crazy little girl. What the hell are you doing?

I can't see much more, my eyes not cutting the dark all that well. But it does smell thick with Vyrus. Thicker than I remember. And might be Hurley was right about that gun powder. Did the girl and her boy have a piece? Did they maybe use it on Sela out in that stairwell?

Hell. She'd have killed them both. Might explain the extra Vyrus smell if she killed the boy. Especially if she tossed his body in here.

From below, Terry.

—You dead, Joe?

I stick my head in the hole, shade my eyes from the flashlight beam, look at Lydia and Terry, their guns trained on me.

—That a trick question?

Terry circles his finger at me.

I look over my shoulder at the basement, look back down.

—Let me finish checking it out. And throw me up a flashlight.

One of them tosses the light, I miss it and it sails up through the hole, hits the floor, goes dark and skitters away, a little tinkle of sound trailing it.

I use the light from below as best I can, crawl out of it, into dark, feeling the floor. Put my hand in something wet and knobby-soft, feels like a handful of warm pig fat. I pull my hand back and fingertips skim something on the ground and it makes that tinkle sound as I scatter it.

Broken glass from the flashlight.

Fucking thing better work.

The beams from below are still shooting up through the hole, dancing on the cobwebs overhead. Just ten feet away, but they do me no good. A cramp grabs my guts. Yank, yank, yank. I put my hands down, scatter more glass, hear more tinkles. Feel more warm wet under my knees, soaking through the cold wet clinging to my jeans.

Man, that thing I killed was full of blood.

Wait.

*Warm wet.*

How many hours ago did I kill that thing? Yeah. No. I put my hand down. Smell my hand. Vyrus. No. Doesn't look good for Chubby's little girl's boyfriend.

My hand closes on the flashlight.

Fucking finally.

I turn it on. See my hand covered in blood and something

green, streaks of pink running through it. See the thing I killed, close up this time. Only. Except wait. It looks more like an inside-out lobster mashed with a porcupine. Wait.

Look over my shoulder at the beams coming from the hole. Re-orient myself to the basement. Flash the beam of my own light to the opposite wall. And *there's* the thing I killed.

Cold.

Beam on the thing in front of me.

Warm.

Scuttle back on my heels.

Tinkle, tinkle, tinkle.

Look down. Floor is covered in shell casings.

What are all those black lumps?

Raise the beam, run it over the far end of the basement near the door, pile of bodies, some in black coveralls and body armor, some in police uniforms, coveralls, tracksuits, blood in runnels, a mass under the pile, still twitching, looks like a ball of flesh whips.

I can see those doors I felt in the dark a few hours back. They go farther than I thought. A row of them. Six, seven maybe. Half of them open. The basement takes a turn, there could be more doors around the bend. It's quiet, but I can smell that mystery stink, Vyrus gone wrong, slipping from each of those doors.

They quiet because there's no uninfected blood for them to smell?

Fed and sleeping?

Dead?

I'd like to get that lucky. Once in my life, I'd like to get that lucky. But I'm not counting on it.

I stand, take a few steps toward the hole and something takes me from behind, wraps around my throat, pinning my arms, covering my eyes, my mouth. I'm dragged backward, picturing tentacles, flesh whips, some other madness from Amanda's lab, the Vyrus stretched to a perverse conclusion.

—Quiet, Pitt.

A hand is taken from my eyes.

Not in the grips of a mutated land squid, simply pinned by another trio of enforcers.

Predo, his suit clinging to him where it's been soaked in blood, a crust of something yellow-gray dried along his jawline, a crosshatch of wounds closing on his forehead.

He puts his mouth close to my ear.

—They will hear you.

I nod.

The hand is taken from my mouth.

I look around.

Predo, a couple of his commandos, another two dozen or so enforcers in various costumes, all jammed into the dead end of the basement, backs against the wall that faces another row of doors. Six. Three are open. Bits and pieces of enforcers are scattered and smeared about. Something that I hope is dead, skin the texture of third-degree burns, underside coated in limp cilia, a row of tiny limbs jutting from its back, lying outside one of the open doors.

From inside one of the open cells comes the sound of flesh ripping, bone breaking, tendons snapping, a giant chicken being dismembered. Grate of teeth on bone.

Predo opens and closes his hands and one of the enforcers gives him a snubbed assault rifle.

He puts his mouth to my ear again.

—She opened the doors when we were driven down here. It appears that not all of the bolts withdrew. It could be malfunction.

I hold up a finger.

—It's not. She's fucking with you.

He nods.

—My thought. Yes.

He points at the corner that leads to the central basement, the rest of the cells, the hole, the door.

—Power junction. Cut the lines before she can open any more.

I'm looking at that corner, right in the angle of it, up where the wall meets the ceiling, a tiny dot of red light.

Predo points at the open door that doesn't have a dead monster in front of it, or a live one beyond it eating enforcer corpses.

—Not all of them are dangerous. Immobile, it seems.

I tap his ear, he puts it close.

—Or not awake yet.

He shows me the assault rifle.

—Do you still want one of these, Pitt?

I nod.

He nods.

The hands release me and he gives me the gun.

—Mind where you point it.

I point it down the basement to the corner.

—How many down there?

He shakes his head.

—In the midst of chaos, I am afraid I did not bother to count. Three. Perhaps.

I point at the open cells across from us.

—Plus one dining and one sleeping.

—It appears.

A cramp grabs me, shakes my innards back and forth, let's go.

Predo whispers.

—Are you unwell?

—Starving. But I'll live.

He smiles.

—I'd not have taken you for an optimist, Pitt.

—We have to get out of here.

He nods.

—That would seem wise. Have you any ideas?

I point down.

—Sewer.

A Klaxon sounds and several of the enforcers jerk their triggers, sending a volley of ricochets off the walls. A few of them scream without being struck by bullets. There's the sudden *thunk* of a heavy bolt being sucked back by an electromagnet.

One of the closed doors swings open.

Piercing scream, like two voices in one throat, and a low beast, fat and fast, out of the open cell, head prickled with spines, runs into the heart of a fusillade, rams into an enforcer, impales her in twenty places, back into the dark cell, trailing screams.

And fingers ease from triggers, bathed in the relief that it wasn't them.

I haven't moved. My mouth is still at Predo's ear.

He pulls back, blinks, puts his mouth to my ear.

—The sewer. Yes. That had occurred to us. Until we had to retreat to this dead end.

I look up at the tiny red light.

Little girl, punching buttons. Feeding time at her zoo.

I ball my good hand into a fist, show it to Predo.

Group up, guns out, start moving, shoot the hell out of everything and get down the hole.

Predo looks at his sweating, big-eyed mass of the formerly most dangerous men and women on the planet.

—Yes, I suppose a few might get out. Those at the middle. More if we had cover fire.

I point down again.

—Terry and Lydia and a few dozen partisans and Bulls.

He draws his brows close.

—Pitt?

I shrug.

—Am I supposed to not be trying to betray and kill you at this point?

—Yes. No. Of course. Terry and Lydia and a few poorly armed, ill-equipped rebels. A shame that cannon fodder is not what the occasion demands.

—Hurley's down there.

His eyebrows go up.

—Yes. That might turn the tide.

His eyebrows drop again.

—Now you simply need to crawl to that drain and tell them to pop up here, lay down some cover fire, and not kill us as we come around the corner.

I make the fist again, show it to him.

—All or nothing.

He thinks.

I point at the cells that are still issuing chewing noises.

—Monsters, Predo. Real monsters.

He nods.

—How silly of me not to notice.

He frowns, nods again, circles a finger in the air to draw the eyes of his people. A few sharp hand gestures later and we're balled up like a porcupine, guns facing out, tight. Two ranks deep on each side. Front rank squatting and scuttling, second rank on their feet, hunched. Give Predo credit, he's not at the middle. We're both frontline, far end, where the mass will round the corner first.

Into the teeth of battle.

Or maybe the teeth of the worm.

Predo holds a hand in the air, counts down one finger at a time. Must be nice, being able to do that kind of thing with both hands.

First finger and I'm thinking about when I came to after I was infected. Terry trying to explain things to me. How I was checking the angles of the room, looking to see where I could dodge past this psycho. He never used the words Vampyre or monster. I did. A joke. *So you're telling me I'm a vampire? Yeah? Fucking cool, man. Monster. Fucking cool.* Looking for something to hit him with. He offered me a suck off a loose pint he had. Thought it was Karo Syrup and red food dye. Trying to humor him. But once I had that suck, I knew it was no sick joke. *Cool,* I thought, *I really am a fucking monster.*

Second finger and I'm remembering when I heard about zombies the first time. Terry again, explaining these *poor unfortunates.* Thought it was a turn of phrase. Like he was describing one of the underclasses he always went on about. Like it was a metaphor. Didn't get it till one showed on Avenue D. Back then, it was like Digga's Harlem, death wagons rolled in the morning to pick the corpses out of the gutters. Some had split skulls, no one looked too hard to see if all the brains were still in there. No one but Terry. We did dead patrol. Looking at the corpses before they got hauled away. Looking for signs of rogue feeding. Found a guy with teeth marks all over his face, neck, what was left of his scalp. Head split with a tire iron, not much inside. Terry took the scent and led us to one of the abandoned tenements that made up the better part of the neighborhood in those days. Found the shambler drifting up and down a staircase, just enough of his own brain left to keep him moving and feeding. Terry got him down and taught me how to break the neck and cut the brain signals running to the autonomic systems of the body. Stepped back and watched it die slow as it stopped breathing and its blood stopped circulating. Thinking to myself, *OK, man, now that is a fucking monster.*

Third finger and I'm thinking about the Wraith. Squirming

mass of black and cold. Servant to Enclave. Nightmare Vampyres use to scare each other. Saying, *Don't fuck with Enclave or they'll send a Wraith on your ass.* Something to laugh at, till you find yourself half-mad in a basement, about to die, and something so black you could fall into it whips across the room and kills the man about to kill you. Tell yourself, *I don't know what I saw. I saw nothing, I was dreaming bad.* Awake in the middle of the day, can't sleep, sun outside, beating at the walls, trying to get in through the cracks and kill you, the brightest hour, most fearsome, and tell yourself then, *Monster. I saw a fucking monster.* Come the night again, you don't know what to believe.

Fourth finger and I'm thinking about the hole in Queens. Standing at the top, looking down a shaft that dropped away under my feet, down, down, down, work lights at every level, burning at every level, smaller and smaller, until they disappeared in the depth of the thing. The wax skin on a naked girl with an I.V. needle riveted to her arm. Cooler full of cords. Nursery. The men I killed and wished I had the bullets back out of their bodies, so I could kill them again, slow and proper. 'Cause dead is dead and anything they had coming to them I wasted when I did them quick. Standing at the top of that hole and hearing from down deep, breathing, gasping, one breath taken between each bite. The worm down there at the bottom of that hole, eating itself, spreading its sick madness. Thinking, *No monsters in this world. Just us people.*

Fifth finger and I'm thinking about being up in Amanda's office looking at her slide show. Her explaining to me the origins of life. Vyrus mates with bacteria. How long an idea like that needs to circle around and around in my head before it makes any kind of sense to me. What they call the *implications.* That HERV thing she talked about. All of us with viral scraps in our DNA, just not all of us have Vyral material as well. That idea finally catching up to me. If it all really started with the Vyrus, then it's not just in us, in people, it could be in anything. Inactive Vyrus cells in any DNA. Waiting to be activated. And then who knows what the hell you end up with. Phil saying to me, *experiments*. Little Amanda in her lab, seeing what happens when you activate the Vyrus in all god's creatures. Thinking now, *She's making monsters*.

And no more fingers to think with.

We move around the corner, facing that long arm of the L-shaped basement, row of doors, a few of them open. The thing I killed against one wall, just outside an open cell door, another dead monster by the opposite wall, that thing under the pile of dead enforcers still quivering. Light from the Mini Maglites some of the crew have clipped under the barrels of their weapons. Quiet except for our shuffling feet and rapid breathing. Clear shot to the hole in the floor where we can trickle down into the sewer one at a time. No one wanting to be the short straw, last man on top. Edging closer, waiting for that Klaxon to sound, all the doors to slam wide. Feels like the vibration of the bell is hammering the air already, but it's just heartbeats. Closer to the hole. Ready to go flat and stick my head down there and tell Terry something that will keep him from opening fire on Predo's crew. *No time to be picky about joining up with anyone who has a gun, Ter. The more the merrier.* Few more steps and I'll just start talking, hope the right thing comes out. Something like, *Don't shoot! Monsters!*

Meanwhile, my own personal monster, my Vyrus, goes at my intestines with its teeth. I stutter-step, trip up the guy behind me. Predo yanks me along.

—Pitt!

I try to keep moving my feet, but it feels like I've been bit in half at the waist, no legs to move, innards dragging on the ground.

Then they're back, teeth pull out, feet are under me, and I'm moving for the hole, ready to make my play when something explodes underneath. Stone and mortar and shards of rusty iron blasted into the air as Hurley erupts from the hole, sledgehammer in one hand, .45 in the other, landing on his feet next to the widened hole, screaming to the troops now visible below.

—Tis da double cross i'tis!

And the vibrations that have been hanging in the air waiting to break, the Klaxon sounding, the doors opening, the yellow blur that bursts from one of them zeroing in on Hurley's chest. Size of a large dog, it will chew a hole through his lungs when it hits him, but it never gets there, hammer snapping mid-shaft as Hurley smashes it from the air, a blow so hard the thing splits in half, each part whirling across the basement spewing yellow blood that smells of rotted Vyrus, smacking against the wall and falling to the floor.

Hurley brandishes the broken handle of his hammer.

—Holy shite!

And then more monsters.

And then everyone shoots at everything.

The tiny red dot overhead, the camera watching, Amanda Horde upstairs. *We're not defenseless,* was what she said.

I shoot at something that tries to kill me. What it is, someone with a name I know, or a thing that isn't supposed to be, I can't say. I just start killing my way toward the pile of bodies blocking the door.

It would have been good to know what Predo meant when he said him and his enforcers had been *driven* to the basement. It was a heady time when that word passed his lips and I didn't bother to notice it. Or its implications.

In the basement, I have one thin slice of something resembling an advantage. That being that I don't care about killing Coalition or Society. I don't much like anyone down there, but I haven't been trained to hate the other side. Or anyway, it's a long time since I stopped believing there were *sides*. Monsters or no, most of these grunts finally have a clear target and a piece in their hands and they want to run up a body count. Once the first one uses the distraction of Amanda's experiments to take a potshot at the other team, any idea of sticking it to the mutual enemy evaporates and it's a free-for-all.

When you're used to going it alone, a free-for-all is just your natural environment. If the people around me weren't at one another's throats most of the time, I'd never have survived, starting with my mom and dad.

People may hate me, they just sometimes hate one another even more, but the monsters don't care one way or the other. That's why first thing I do when it all goes sideways is I turn around and shoot the guy behind me in the stomach a couple times and drag him toward the door. He catches a couple more bullets as we pass the hole, but he's still alive enough for a good scream when something broadsides us and plows us to the ground, him on top. Feels like the thing that took us down is trying to dig through him to get to me, but it's just as likely trying to get inside so it can lay a clutch of eggs in his liver. I worm out from under and belly-crawl into a thicket of legs, shell casings raining down, getting stomped.

When a taloned limb appears in the mix, I unload the clip in my gun, bullets severing it from whatever it's attached to, bullets gone astray taking out the legs of a few of the enforcers.

Claws reach into my back, grab my spine, and try to rip it out.

In the time I think it's really happening that way, I've rolled to my back, screaming. But it's just the Vyrus again. Inopportune timing.

Someone steps on my stomach. Someone else steps on my bad knee. The claws let go of my spine and I roll again and move, realizing that the person who stepped on my knee was one of Terry's partisans.

The stupid fuckers are coming up.

There's a pile of bodies in front of me. Can't tell anymore which way I'm pointed. Could be the pile of enforcers that was blocking the door, could be a brand-new pile. My cheek is lashed open by a whip. I look and see that mass of quivering tentacles. So at least I have the right pile of dead people. I start digging into the pile and something has my ankle. I look back, expecting to see one of those tentacles has me, but it's a partisan, one of those shaved-head semi-anarchist fucks that all look alike. Some son of a bitch I don't even know his fucking name, he's missing half his left arm and his jaw, but he's using his last breath on this earth to fuck with me, when he could be looking for someone's dropped gun to shoot himself and die quicker.

Me, I dropped my empty gun a few seconds ago, haven't found a replacement yet. So I swing the wire saw at his wrist, snag the free end as it wraps around, yank back and forth, and he's got no hands to pick up anything anymore.

I'm digging into the pile of dead people again, going under, feeling the weight of them on top, hoping the door is ahead of me, hoping I don't pop out the wrong side of the pile and have my head snatched off. The pile thrums around me as it's raked by bullets. I dig deeper, my hand feels steel plate, I reach down, find a crack at the bottom of the door and start to yank and push, but it's either locked or the dead are too heavy to move. I get the two fingers of my left hand in there and pull and push, looking for something to give.

Just a little.

I'm just looking for a little room. A little room to move. Someplace I can use to make more time. Looking for a little crack to edge through and slip away. One more time. If I can get away one more time I might have a chance. Even if it's a chance I don't deserve, I want it anyway.

The door moves, a tiny bit of give, and I take it. Jerk the fucker back and forth, pushing myself up out of the cover of the dead, bodies tumbling off me as I rise for leverage, grabbing the edge of the door as it clears the jamb. Pull, push, pull.

—Fooker, ya are!

I know who it is, so I don't waste time looking.

I just pull harder, pull and jam myself into the gap I've opened, skinning my face trying to push through.

—Ya backstabber, ya are!

He hasn't shot me. Either for lack of bullets or because he wants his hands on me.

Someone on the other side shoves the door, pushing it an inch farther open against the bodies, I heave myself, the slightly jutting ends of those two broken ribs snagged by the edge of the door, cracking, and I don't care because I'm through and the monsters are back there and I've got a step on Hurley and I just need to get my feet under me and start up the stairs and all I need to do is run.

And I'm on my feet.

And I remember someone just got me through the door.

And I look up and see one of the starving infecteds of Cure. One of the howlers trapped behind the doors along the stairwell. One of the Vyrus-mad Vampyres Amanda released and set on the enforcers when they breached the building.

An explanation of how they were *driven* down here.

I'm trying to bring the amputation blade up, get it in the starved fucker's eye, hoping it will cut something in the brain that will instantly sever communications with the body before it can start ripping me limb from limb, but it's all happening too fast. Man or woman, I can't tell what it is, how it was born. Mommy's little boy, daddy's little girl. Perfect angel or shitty little brat. The years between. Bum or banker. Loved or hated. Ruthless feeder and killer, or helpless infected who lived off Coalition dole. Whatever humanity is worth, this thing is far beyond it. It is hunger and the pain of being hungry, and anything that can't give relief is either a hated foe or invisible, depending on whether it gets in its way. Maddened not by any hunger for my infected blood, but purely by the sight of something that moves and sounds like prey, it's on top of me, feet in my stomach, hunched, hands on my neck, howling at the scent of my undrinkable blood.

And I go limp. Arms at my sides, blade cradled in my good hand.

It crushes my throat, I feel cartilage crack. Its toes dig into my belly, like the claws of the Vyrus. Shriveled, sexless face in mine, sniffing, sniffing. The stink out of its mouth making me gag, but there's nothing to come up, and nowhere for it to go while I'm being choked to death. Speckles at the edge of my vision, spreading. Blackening. My hand opens and closes on the taped hilt of the blade, wanting to stab of its own will.

That darkness irising down the scope of my vision, swallowing the stairwell from the outside in, is there something in it? Something moving in the dark.

Is there something cold coming for me?

God I hope not.

It lets go of my neck and climbs off me. My windpipe uncrinkles a bit, but there's a definite rasp in my breath. Darkness recedes.

The starving infected paws at the bodies of dead enforcers. Jumps up and down on one. Looks at me. I don't move.

I can smell something. I can smell *it*. Its smell clinging to me.

But no, that's wrong. It's me I smell. My own dying. Not as potent, but it's only a matter of time. The smell that comes out of *its* gullet is in my *own* now. Rotting inside.

To emphasize the point, the Vyrus pours hot lead down the middle of my bones and sets me shaking. The starving jumps up and down higher, points at me, opens its mouth, and I'd swear it fucking laughs. Delighted to see someone else in pain.

Then the screams and gunfire beyond the door raise in volume as it is pushed open again and I'm no longer the center of attention.

—Joe, ya fooker!

I'm off the floor.

—Hurley, watch out.

Half through the door, struggling to pull it wide enough to fit his massive frame, the starving is on him. And Hurley, not close to starving himself, his smell is all wrong, and he puts up a fight. A sudden obstacle, the starving tries to kill him. I'm crawling up the stairs, watching, unable not to watch. Hurley's arm reaching through the blur of the starving's whirling limbs as it tries to rend him. Like a man reaching slow into a barrel of thrashing eels. Until Hurley has its neck, and squeezes, and slams the head against the door that still has him pinned between monsters. The head is dented, crushed, spilling down the door. Its arms and legs still windmill. Hurley jerks it back and forth, harder, harder, and the head comes off and he tosses the body aside and it flops and gets to its feet, runs into a wall, falls down, legs churning the air.

Through the blood congealed on his face and in his eyes, Hurley looks up at me, where I'm almost at the door at the top of the stairs.

—A word wit ya, Joe, when ya got a sec.

He looks back into the shit storm in the basement.

—Terry! Here an now, Terry boy!

The heat has run out of my bones and I'm out the door at the top and making for the main stairwell. More dead enforcers about. A second to spare, I pick up a gun. It feels useless in my hand, but I keep it anyway.

Bottom of the stairs, I look up.

Starvings on the stairs.

Misery trying to die.

Turning their heads to look at me as I come into view.

Down the hall is the front door. A short walk out of madness. More enforcers out there? Probably. Ordered to snatch anyone who comes out of the building? Probably. And so what. Them I might kill with a couple well-placed bullets. Here in the asylum, Hurley is the only safe bet to get out alive. And he's trying to kill me.

—C'mon, Joe, tis just a little chat I'm looking fer! An Terry would like a word as well I tink!

I push the door closed. Look for something to block it with, but there are no trucks handy that I can park in front of it.

The starving closest to me on the stairs pulls itself onto the banister and scuttles down it a half flight closer.

I take a step toward the front of the building.

Hurley will be up here in a second. I should leave. No one can tell me I shouldn't be gone from here and taking my shots on the street. Everything is dead here anyway.

Except Amanda. And Chubby's daughter. And her baby.

Maybe.

I close my eye for one heartbeat. Picture Evie. Telling her I was too late. The kids were dead, them and their baby. I tried but I was too late. I really tried.

I open my eye.

My girl, I've lied to her too many times. She knows what it looks like when I pull that shit.

So I start slow up the stairs.

The time I died, I starved to death. Went one step further than these sad pieces of work. Went to the place the Enclave go. Differences. Enclave go there willfully, exercise some kind of discipline, do it in a warehouse of like-minded crazies. All of them holding one another's hands as they go through it. When I went, I just went. Starved and beat, I tilted, heart stopped, air froze in my lungs, brain blacked. And the Vyrus brought me back. Like a built-in heart shock and a stab of adrenaline between the eyes. These, they've been dragged to this stage. Amanda feeding them what she could, until she realized she didn't have enough to really keep them alive. Until they crossed over in her brain and became more valuable like this than like people. Until the idea of someone being better off dead didn't make sense to her work.

Long-starved like Enclave, but without the training to cope. Not quite as far gone as I was when I slipped, but just as unhappy to be there. They know they can't eat me. But that doesn't mean that killing me wouldn't make them feel better. Or just make them feel something other than their own bodies eating themselves.

Half-up the first flight, the one squatting on the banister huffs. Tongue stuck out like it's testing the air for humidity. Or for the taste of blood that isn't infected.

Coated in a thick layer of sewer sludge, enforcer blood, monster slime and the dead Vyrus stink starting to rise from my pores, I set its teeth to chattering. A high tone in its throat, crying alley cat. It shifts up the banister, staying with me. Not sure what the fuck to do at all. Looking tempted to go at me just to resolve the confusion.

The others above are starting to rock back and forth, one rising and walking down and up the same three steps, flickering. Another, higher up, poking its head over the third-floor landing, keeps slapping its own face. Regular sharp smacks that are like a metronome set against irregular bursts of gunfire fading below me.

The one pacing me pulls up, lifts it face, croaks, shakes its head into a blur, freezes, and huddles into itself, eyes closing, seeming to fall asleep clutching its perch on the banister.

New gunfire breaks out in the basement stairwell behind the closed door, and its eyes open and it looks down and even as the door is opening and Hurley comes through with one arm wrapped around Terry, it has let go of the banister and dropped itself at them. The others suddenly flee, swarming down the stairs, focused on something loud and fast and violent and much warmer than me. Something that at least appears to be food. Something to at least satiate a hunger for hunting.

Hurley's curses echo up the stairwell behind my running heels, his precise choice of words drowned out by the crack of his .45, punctuated by the occasional meaty whap of a dumdum round mushrooming as it hits flesh, underscored by the chatter of Terry's AK-47.

I'm not looking down to see who will come out on top. I'm too busy looking at the steps in front of me, trying to find each one at the far end of the tunnel that my eye has retreated into. I'm at a distance to my own body, operating it by remote control, but feeling every thrum of pain that vibrates the string tied to the pain knotted in my forehead.

I'm trying to climb without falling.

I'm trying to remember this pain from years back. Did I feel this then? How long before dying did I feel this? Will I die soon? If I do, will I stay dead this time?

*Please*, asks a part of me that I instantly disown, *please can I stay dead this time?*

No, I answer. Evie wouldn't like that. Or maybe she would. I don't really know. But if she wants me dead she can tell me herself. If I'm there to hear it, I might just oblige her.

I want to look up and see how many more stairs to the top, but I think I'd fall back down to the bottom where the sound of Hurley and Terry's guns has stopped. Out of bullets or out of things to shoot at? Not my problem. Stairs are my problem.

Climb.

Climb, motherfucker.

And don't die.

If you die, it will come and take you away. If you die, the black cold will come and suck you into its heart and you'll be ice forever. If you die, the Wraith inside will come out and be you.

I don't believe it's true, but I fear it all the same.

I don't want to be a monster. Not for real. I want to know what I do in this world. I want to know who I hurt. I want my dead to have faces I remember. I want to know what I've done and the price of it all. I know I'll never have what I want. I know I'll never be where I want. I know I'll never hold who I want to hold. Just that when all doubt is gone and there's no trick left I can play on myself to make me believe that maybe I'll get her in the end, I want to remember everything I did along the way, and know that there had to be an accounting. And her saying *no* is the price.

I just want to be there to remember it's my own fucking fault.

I can live with that.

Someone takes my hand.

I look up.

At the top of the stairs. Amanda has me by my wounded hand, holding it in both of hers. Frowning at me.

—You never told me before that you killed my mom.

I open my mouth, words crack as they come out of my twisted throat.

—Long story.

She pulls me down the hall.

—All we have is time, Joe.

Feet are pounding up the stairs. One set? Two sets? Yes. At least. Maybe more. Maybe more than Hurley and Terry got out of the basement alive.

We're at the door of Amanda's penthouse. I'm coming back to my body. Vision coming to the mouth of the tunnel, opening up.

—Sela.

Amanda doesn't look back at me.

—What about her?

—We need her. Hurley. Terry. More.

She shakes her head as she leads me in.

—Oh them. Never mind them. And Sela.

Inside, she tugs my hand, pulls me to her side, points at the sheet covering a body in the middle of the floor, stains soaked through, drenched.

—Sela can't really help anymore.

She gives my hand a squeeze.

—What a gift you have, Joe.

She pushes the door closed and fastens the locks.

—For hurting the most important people in my life.


—You returned for us as you promised.

—Technically, I *mean*, yes, technically, you didn't kill her.

—And Benjamin and I and our child, we are ready to depart.

—If we want to get specific here, and seeing as she's dead and all *that*, I suppose we can get as specific as we want.

—Whenever you urge.

—So, *specifically* speaking.

—Shall we leave now?

—Deli-*lah*.

Amanda squeezes her forehead.

—Could you *please* let me talk to Joe without interruptions, please.

Standing near the locked door with Ben, hands on her belly, Delilah raises a finger.

—You may have imprisoned us, but no longer.

—Delilah. Dear.

Amanda pulls out the very large pistol that's been weighing one of the pockets of her lab coat.

—I have some *issues* with you right now. So if you don't, I *mean*, please be quiet for a few minutes, I'm going to shoot Ben.

Ben raises his hands to his shoulders.

—Hey, whoa.

Delilah shakes her finger back and forth.

—Mere bullets will not slay him.

Eyes still on the covered corpse of her lover, Amanda raises the gun and points it at Ben.

—Dear, I know *more* about the Vyrus and Vampyres than anyone else on the planet. I *mean*. Trust me, I know where to shoot him to kill him.

She bites the tip of her tongue.

—Or were you *not* paying attention to what happened with Sela?

Delilah opens her mouth and Ben drops a hand on her shoulder.

—Baby, be cool.

She pulls back.

—*Benjamin?*

He raises his hands in higher surrender than when Amanda pointed the gun at him.

—Hey, hey, I'm just saying, Mr. Pitt said he'd come back. And here he is. So let's just sort it out calmly now.

Out in the hall Terry pounds on the door again.

—Time to open up, Joe!

Ben points at the door.

—Because just walking out there right now may not be the best thing as far as we know.

He looks at me.

—Right, Mr. Pitt?

In a chair, bottle of whiskey in my hand, I lift it as far as my mouth and spill a little inside.

—Having a hard time seeing where to go right now myself.

I lift the bottle toward the door.

—I got Chubby's daughter tied up in front of the door, Terry! Knock it down or shoot through it and you'll kill your symbolic baby of the future!

It gets quiet in the hall.

Amanda is shaking her head.

—*Mr. Pitt. As if.*

She looks at the gun in her hand, shakes her head.

—You got her good, Joe. I mean. I mean. She'd been on rations for. I don't *know.* I kept telling her to feed. There was enough for her. But she kept reducing her own so she could spread it around with the membership. As if. I *mean,* this was way past when we knew where things were going. I'd shown her the *math.* She couldn't argue with it. You know. And she just. She wouldn't accept that most of them were going to starve. *Period.* She handled the discipline. The *euthanizing* when someone went over. But she wouldn't let go and let what was going to happen just, I *mean,* just let it happen. I gave her everything I could. I would have given her more. But she wouldn't take it.

She lifts her arms from her sides, lets them drop.

—And then you, I mean, *speared* her.

Another pound on the door.

Lydia this time.

—I don't believe you about the girl, Joe. You wouldn't.

—So come on in guns blazing. Already told you I don't like the girl, Lyd. Do your worst.

Low conversation in the hall.

Amanda stands over Sela's body, rocking gently on her own tide.

—She lost a lot of blood. We have *nothing* left in the reserves. I tried to get her to take a *little* more from me, but it was just a few hours ago. She just. *Hunkered* in the corner, growled at me when I came over. At *me*.

She laughs.

—Like she could *scare* me. *Not*.

She wipes at the corner of her mouth with the back of her hand.

—But then she just. I mean. It had to happen right? She just *lost* it.

She looks at Delilah.

—All that *blood*. Just across the room. She just.

Delilah points at Sela's covered body.

—The lioness maddened.

Amanda rubs her face.

—Sela.

She looks at the gun in her hand.

—I *just*.

She looks at me.

—You knew her, Joe. I *mean*. Joe. *Right?*

I nod.

—Baby, you did right. She'd never have been able to live with herself.

Amanda looks at Delilah.

—I mean.

She drops the gun in her pocket and turns away.

—*Gah*.

A door-rattling knock.

—Miss Horde?

I turn in my chair.

—Hurley?

—It's Miss Horde I'll be wantin' ta talk to, Joe, not yer backstab-bin' self.

—It wasn't a backstab. Predo and his guys, they were just there.

—Indeed. Most like.

I close my eye.

Terry, Lydia and Hurley. Only the survivors survive. Way of the world. That it should come to this. And is it any wonder?

I open my eye and see Amanda slipping a key into the top lock on the door.

I rise.

—Hey! Hey!

Delilah steps forward.

—Yes, it is time we departed.

Amanda twists the second lock open.

I try to walk to her and cramp up all over.

—Don't.

She turns the third lock and steps back and the door swings open.

Terry stands on the threshold, worse for wear, but, heavy feeder that he is, the burns covering the right side of his body are healing fast.

—OK, yeah, Ms. Horde, finally we get to meet in person. We can, you know, we can make some progress here now.

Lydia behind him, aiming her carbine down the stairs.

—Shut up and get in there, Terry, something's coming out of the basement.

He steps into the room.

—Yeah, if we could claim a little sanctuary maybe while we. Some complicated issues have arisen and a real opportunity. I don't know. Hurley.

Hurley steps into the doorway, dragging Predo by the scruff of his neck.

—Yeah, an I guess ya might call it opportunity. Still I don't know why ya just won't let me kill da bastard.

He sees me.

—An Joe in da bargain, if I may.

Lydia squeezes off a few rounds down the stairwell and backs into the room, kicking the door shut.

—Damn, damn, damn. Where's the? Keys for this? It's. What the fuck are? I can't.

She's leaning her forehead against the door, eyes closed.

—I had this nightmare when I was little. This. My mom was always talking about the inherent threat of patriarchy. But she never explained what it. And I saw, when I was about five, my dad took me to see some horror movie. Something I was way too young for. And. My mom, all I understood about patriarchy was that it was something to do with men. And the horror movie, my dad took me and it was all guys in the audience. And I was so scared by the movie. And these nightmares I had after, this creature I would dream about. It wasn't, it's not Freudian, it wasn't like it was covered in penises or anything. It was just all fangs and scales and gross and just a movie monster. And I thought, I told my mom I had nightmares about the patriarchy and it almost ate me, and she told me, she said, *Yes, that's what it will try to do.*

She starts to laugh, keeps talking through it.

—And down there that's all, when they came out and were, I saw them and all I could think was, *the patriarchy is going to eat me!*

She stops laughing.

—What the hell? What the hell?

—And now we are assembled, can we not leave this tower of horrors?

Lydia looks at Delilah.

—Chubby's daughter.

I take a drink.

—Told you.

Lydia steps toward her.

—How's the baby?

—The child is well. But I feel it is not safe here. We must be away. Is there no one here who can escort us to safety?

—Excuse me, if I may.

Predo manages to give the impression that he just happens to be wearing his coat after asking Hurley to hold it by the collar for him.

—Several of my people are still outside. I believe it is safe to assume that no one will be leaving without my complicity.

Terry raises a hand high over his head, as if he knows the right answer and wants to be called first.

—Don't listen to, I don't know, to that propaganda. Even if, even if he still has troops outside, which I think there is room for doubt on that one, it doesn't change the fact that we have him. So, you know, a man like, a man who I've known a lot of years, a man who has a powerful desire for self-preservation, he won't be ordering his storm troopers to open fire when he's going to be the first one out the door.

Predo coughs into his gloved hand.

—Do you think, Bird, do you think it is a matter of what I tell them at this point? The orders regarding hostage situations are long-standing and come directly from the Secretariat. There will be no negotiating. Any arrangements will be made in this room. And I will be dictating terms.

Hurley gives him a shake.

—Terry boy, must we listen ta dis shite?

Terry slings his AK over his shoulder and raises a finger.

—Well, he's full of shit, Hurl, but there is room to maybe settle a few things before we lose, I don't know, all perspective.

—This is full of a, *um,* Vyrally activated bacillus.

We all look at Amanda, at her desk, a small vial made of spun aluminum in her hand, tiny hand-lettered label on its side.

—I mean, like a microscopic version of the stuff in the *basement.* And it's a *sanguivore.* Which means it likes to eat blood, like the Vyrus. But because it can live without a host it doesn't care about keeping you alive. It just wants to eat and replicate. And really fast. And it can survive in any environment I've stuck it in. And. Oh, and um, I just had to *shoot* my lover. So. *Yeah.* I am totally in a fucking mood right now and everyone should put their guns down and maybe you, Lydia, because I know you sort of, you can put them outside the door and use these keys to lock it. OK. So. And, I *mean,* I totally don't expect *everyone* to leave this room alive. Because, come *on,* how could we? I, for one, I think, I *mean.* I think I'm going to kill myself. But I'm gonna talk a little first, and if anyone *interrupts* me I'm going to open this can and I don't *know* if anything can kill this stuff before it kills everything everywhere. So *OK?*

Everyone does as she says, so it must be OK.


She starts by recapping the lecture she gave me, and then moves on to advanced topics in how everything is going to change now.

—This is proof.

She pulls on a beaded chain that hangs from her neck, tugging it from her collar until we can see the fat little rectangle of plastic dangling from it.

—I mean, real scientific proof that you.

She waves her hand at all of us.

—Exist. Or whatever.

She pulls the chain over her head and drops it on her desk.

—Images of all the known mutations of the Vyrus that *I've* cata-logued. Including the ones that I.

She points at the floor.

—The ones that I, *cooked up* myself. Which, I mean, I may have gotten carried away and played a little *god*. Sorry for that. Or not. I could do it. So I did it. Because. I don't *know.* I just did it. And you.

She points at Predo.

—You pissed me off *just* enough to set them loose. Because the idea was just to destroy them. *Experiments.* But you had to starve us. You couldn't *just.* What was so hard to accept? A cure? What was so hard to? It's not like anyone would have *made* you take it if you didn't want to. I. *Gah.* Any*way.*

She fingers the chain.

—This USB drive has my simulations. It has the locations of known Vyral HERV fragments in the human genome. Just a *few* that I've been able to find. But, I mean, *compelling* stuff. If you like that kind of thing. There are the complete records of my ex-periments. All of them *repeatable* for similar results. Procedure for a Vyrus test.

She giggles.

—Can you see the *posters* on the bus shelters? Some Goth with a serious look on her face. *Have you been tested?*

She stops giggling.

—Like the only test you need is to ask yourself, *Does blood sound like what I want for dinner?*

She lifts a hand.

—Yeah, I know, I'm being stupid. But I *mean*. Right? You know that would be the attitude for some people. Testing for the *inactive* Vyrus. People found guilty for having the *potential* to be dangerous. Any*way.*

She counts off a few fingers.

—The images, the HERV map, the procedures, the test, oh, different environments hostile to the Vyrus. All of which kill the host as well, but, well, *there* it is. Methods for killing the infected. There *that* is. And the details of my theory that the Vyrus was the primary building block for *all* life on the planet and that Vyrally active life is the most pure and essentially earthy thing around.

She pokes at one of the old cuts near her wrist.

—I tested negative. *No* Vyral fragments in my HERV. A strand of random breeding that lost it. But that makes me like most people. *Most* people are Vyrally negative. Otherwise you guys would have spread.

She looks up.

—It has a smell, the Vyrus. Even inactive. Not strong like the way you smell one another. Like *subtle*. Pheromone almost. I *mean,* to someone who was sensitive to it, they could pick out Vyrally inactive subjects and infect them at *will*. That idea is in there too. What's not.

She taps the USB.

—What's not in there is a sample. *Obviously.* Runaway replicators like this, they just burn out a host. I have dead *matter,* but no live samples. So what is in here is an *address* book. Me and Sela, we interviewed all the Cure applicants, and, I *mean,* this wasn't the plan, but there's a list in here of every safe house, Clan headquarters, bolt-hole, residence, pretty much every place someone who *wanted* to find Vampyres could start looking and have a pretty good shot at getting a live one.

She shrugs.

—Not like it's a *threat* I'm making, because I totally don't care anymore, but it's in there.

She closes her eyes.

—But no cure.

She covers the USB with her hand.

—No cure.

She opens her eyes.

—No cure at all.

She looks at Sela's body.

—I'm sorry, baby.

She looks at me.

—Joe. You killed my *mom?*

I nod.

—She asked me to.

She crinkles the corners of her mouth.

—Is that what it takes?

I shake my head.

—No.

She raises a hand.

—*Joe.*

I shake my head again.

—I'd like to help, kid. I get it and all. I just.

I look into the whiskey bottle in my hand.

—I just don't got it in me for that.

She bites her upper lip.

—It's OK, Joe. Caring is hard.

She looks at Sela again.

—I *mean.*

She looks at me.

—We've known each other a long time.

She sets the vial on her desk next to the USB drive.

—And I don't think I could kill you either.

She takes the gun from her lab coat pocket.

—Just do me a *favor*?

—Sure.

She waves the gun at everyone in the room.

—These assholes.

She picks up the vial.

—Don't let any of them have this.

She tosses it to me and I juggle it with my lame hand and only keep it from hitting the floor by cradling it against my chest.

She nods.

—That's only for you.

She looks at Sela.

—And don't let them have any of my blood.

She puts the barrel of the gun under her chin.

—That's for you too.


I've wondered from time to time if there's a limit to what you can take. Is there a little gauge somewhere in your brain that slowly rises toward the red, measuring when you've gone beyond your capacity to endure? Blood and madness and death and cruelty. Pouring into you. And at some point, does it just overflow and flood the whole system and everything shuts down?

I've wondered.

It's no lie, I killed Amanda's mom because she asked me to. She asked me to because she was sick and she was about to kill Amanda if someone didn't kill her first. Follow it back around that way and you could say that I killed Amanda's mom to save Amanda's life.

Which strikes me like something close to irony.

As I sit there.

Having refused to kill Amanda so she can exit the misery of all the things she's seen and done in her short life. I watch her do it herself.

Clearly having reached her limit.

Born into so much of that blood and madness, it took quite a bit to push her to overload. But there it was, in the bullet she used to kill her woman, the limit of what she could take and still keep her eyes open.

I'd have liked to help her. Make it a little easier at the end to step out and get all this over with. But I'm still not sure of my own limit. If it exists, where it might be if it's out there. With more left to do, I couldn't take the chance that doing for her what I did for her mom would be as far as I could go.

But I keep my eye open for her. And she looks into it. And there's maybe a smile that passes back and forth between us.

When she pulls the trigger that I can't, I don't blink.

What I owe her.

Looking at her dead body, I wonder if I owe her more.

A pyre made of the dead.

A fire to burn them.

Yes, she'd like that.

And I know how to build such a thing.


Because I don't blink, I see most of what happens when her gun goes off.

Predo raking Hurley's eyes as he twists from his jacket and spins loose.

Terry sliding to the middle of the room, countering Predo, both of them taking an angle on me.

Lydia backing Delilah and Ben into a corner and standing in front of them.

Hurley, wiping the blood from his eyes as he drops Predo's jacket and takes a step toward the gun racks at the other end of the room.

And me, lifting my whiskey bottle, two-finger hand wrapped around its neck, and asking the room at large.

—So am I the only one with a gun at this point?

The question draws a little extra of everyone's attention, and they all take a quick look at the gun I snatched off one of the dead enforcers on my way up here, brandished in my good hand.

—I'm pretty sure I'm the only one who hung onto his when Amanda made the rest of you toss yours out the door. But someone be sure to pipe up if I'm wrong.

Predo combs a lock of hair coated in dry blood from his eyes.

—Shoot Hurley.

Hurley looks at him.

—I beg yer?

—He is by far the most dangerous of us and most likely to kill you. Shoot him now.

Hurley looks at me.

—Ya backstabbin'! I knew it!

I shake the bottle back and forth.

—Easy, Hurl. He's just trying to start a melee.

—A?

—A brawl. So he can make a move.

—Well if it's a brawl he wants, den, he can have it. An you, ya. I never figure ya fer a Coalition sap, Joe.

I take a drink.

—Hurley, my lad, you never figured two plus two is four.

—Is it insults den, is it?

I press the cool glass of the bottle to my forehead.

—Hurley, man, I didn't sell you out. They were just in there. We were trying to join with you guys when you barged in and broke all hell loose.

He scratches his head.

—An I want ta believe ya, but I don't know.

Terry fiddles his glasses up the bridge of his nose.

—I think we can, Hurl. I think, I don't know, but I think there was just a little too much chaos down there for it to have been anything that was meant to have a pattern.

I nod.

—That's right.

I take another drink.

—But it doesn't mean that shooting you first wouldn't be the best play.

Hurley waves it off with the back of his hand.

—Truly, den, open fire.

He grins.

—I tink I can just about take yer best shot, make ya eat da gun, an still have somethin' left over fer Mr. Predo if it comes ta dat.

I look at Predo.

—So much for that. But here's a thought.

I aim the barrel of the gun against the vial I've set on the arm of the chair.

—You can all make a move on me, try and snag this thing, and I'll pull the trigger and we can all find out just how crazy the little girl was.

—You're all crazy! You're all fucking crazy!

Delilah is trying to get out of the corner, but Lydia keeps her pinned there, covering the pregnant girl's body with her own, doing her best to protect Ben as well.

But Delilah wants none of it.

—Who are you people and what the fuck are you fighting over? Can you just live? Can you just all live and let us be? Let me and my boy and our baby go. We just. What are you thinking, mister? Crazy bitch said that shit would kill *everything everywhere*. You think that was a euphemism for killing just who you want it to kill? She meant it. You know she meant it. You people don't want to live, is that it? We do! We do! We! Damn. Damn and fuck. Daddy. Daddy, you made this shit sound so cool.

She runs out of gas about there and Ben wraps her up.

—I told you it's not like the books, baby. I.

He looks at us.

—I told her there was nothing romantic about this life, but she just got ideas in her head.

I thumb the hammer back on my gun.

—You should stop moving, Terry.

He stops.

—You too, Mr. Predo.

He stops.

Both of them having shifted just a little closer to me.

I settle my aim back on the vial.

—I'm thinking about how this might end.

—If you shoot that, Joe, you'll never see Evie again.

I didn't blink when Amanda shot herself, but I blink when that name comes out of Terry's mouth.

He shakes his head.

—Joe, you had to. Joe, I know who she is. I mean, we met. She. I never made a thing out of it. But she was around the neighborhood, with you. And. I don't know what you thought or thought you thought or remembered, but she came to me for help when you went missing that time. When I had to send Christian and the Dusters above Fourteenth to scrape you off that sidewalk when you'd been doped. This is like, I know it's like excavating ancient history, but I did know. So, like, it doesn't take a psychic, Joe, when you had girl trouble, to know who it was. And I have resources. And patterns are my thing. Intuition is my thing. You played it like you killed her, but things emerged. Changes in the social dynamic. Indications about where you were lurking for a while. In the Meatpacking District. Then we get these rumors out of Enclave. The Count in some kind of power dynamic with a recently infected woman. It's not math, not my thing, numbers, but it is poetry, vibes, I can make sense of that. And I know, I know from way back what moves you, how you flow. Your play is cold, but your real moves are hot. From the heart. Little Amanda Horde there, you can barely look at her. Joe, that's not a bad thing, that's a sign. Yeah. Because, come on, man, you couldn't kill her yourself. Because you have that strength in you, that humanity in you. And if you couldn't do that, you won't be cracking open Pandora's box and releasing a plague of who knows what. Not, at least, while the world still has Evie in it.

I'm not feeling too good.

Predo is frowning.

—A girl.

I'm feeling tiny cracks appearing in my skin.

—All for a girl.

Splitting in hairlines, fracturing.

—The trouble you have caused for me. All over a girl.

Like the meat inside is overcooked and bursting out.

—The damage you have done to everything. Over a girl.

My muscles are seared.

—How grateful I feel to know.

Cooked by the fire in my bones.

—This girl of yours, Joe Pitt.

Flames I cannot contain.

—How grateful I am to know her name.

I must let them out.

—And to know also where she is to be found.

Or I will burn.

—I am unbearably curious to see this woman whose face has launched a thousand fiascos.

I will burn.

—And to give her my compliments in person.

I burn.

And I start shooting. Wasting a bullet when I pull the trigger too fast as I draw my aim from the vial to Predo, the round going wide left, thinking it's all over now, that I've messed it up, here in the final showdown, with one chance to get it right, I missed the first shot and he moves too fast and I'll never hit him once he starts moving full speed, an erratic pattern of jumps, impossible to regain my aim, but he comes straight at me, whether herded by Terry and Hurley closing on him from the sides, or driven by the madness of the thought of why I've done everything I have, he comes straight at me, and I pull the trigger over and over, and he runs into the bullets, runs through the bullets, or they through him, still coming, too fast to be caught by Terry or even Hurley, only the twitches of my finger are faster, only the bullets themselves are faster, only those are faster than his hate.

And then he's on me, his hands full of my shirtfront, his forehead pressed to mine. Not immortal at all, his chest and stomach are open wide, his insides are spilling out his back, dragged by the bullets. He still looks young and full of life, the bloom on his check undiminished by the speckle of fresh blood drops.

He's saying something.

—A girl. A girl, Pitt. A girl.

I've dropped the empty gun, replaced it in my hand with the amputation blade.

—A girl, Mr. Predo.

I wrap my arm around his neck and do it as he described, one long cut, deep and to the bone.

—But she's a hell of a girl.

And like he told me, after that, it's just quick work with a saw and the limb is off.

I burn.

But I don't die yet.

Sitting in my chair with the whiskey bottle that didn't quite empty itself when I dropped it. The head of my enemy in my lap.

A body for the pyre, at my feet.

—Hey, Terry. You were saying something about me and how I make my moves. Was that a thought you wanted to finish up?

He's looking at the floor.

—Tell you, Joe.

I look where he's looking, at the vial that was knocked from the arm of the chair while I killed Predo, where it rolled to just a few inches from Terry's toes.

—I'm having very different thoughts right now.

He bends, picks up the vial, and weighs it in his palm.

—Will you get me that gun, Hurl.

—Sure ting, Ter.

Hurley uncurls Amanda's stiff fingers, gentles her gun loose, and passes it to Terry.

He holds both weapons. Dead girl's gun. Bottle of apocalypse.

—Without meaning to be flip about the whole thing, I think it's fair to say that there's been a redistribution of power here.


—Stop being cute, Terry.

Lydia moves away from Delilah and Ben.

—It's time to get serious now.

He shows her the vial.

—Is there something more serious than this, I don't know, something more immediate than pressing this advantage right now?

—Advantage?

He looks up at the ceiling, shakes his head, looks back at her.

—Lydia, I know you have a streak of idealism that is, man, just plain impenetrable, but I didn't think, and forgive me for the bluntness, but I didn't think it extended to the thickness of your skull.

I'm patting my pockets.

—Think he just said you're stupid, Lyd.

She thrusts her palm at me, like delivering a stiff arm on the field of play.

—Shut it, Joe.

Terry makes a rolling motion with the barrel of the pistol.

—Do I need to map this? Is there, I don't know, *confusion,* regarding what just happened here?

He points the gun at the head in my lap.

—Dexter Predo is dead. Dozens, several dozen enforcers have been massacred here. Out of just more than a hundred in the whole Coalition. Lydia, I know I said math isn't my thing, but come on. Add and subtract. They are exposed. Their front line of defense is rotting in the basement here. We, this is, everything has changed.

She's shaking her head.

—What has? Changed? What do you want to? We have nothing to put on the street. How do we? No. And anyway. We have something we have to do.

He holds up the vial.

—We don't need to go to the street. Is nobody, is there a lack of vision in the room? The Secretariat, what are they going to do against this?

He holds the vial higher.

—They're, all they care about is status quo. We threaten everything. We can threaten *everything.* All we have to do is let them keep living and they'll do what we want.

Lydia has her hands on her hips.

—Are you? Terry, even if, if we were the kind of people who would use, are we even talking? The kind who would use *geno-cide* as a threat. What then? How long does it take then to shut it down? And the kids? What about?

Terry squints.

—Shut down what?

She points east.

—The hole. The damn hole. That was the deal. We come here and then we go to Queens and save those kids. Now. It's time now. We do it now.

He lowers the hand holding the vial over his head.

—I can't, I don't know, the lack of. Is it just too much for every-one to see? This vacuum is going to have to be filled, and we're set up to fill it. But look what happened here in this place. The starving. Look at how unbalanced the island is right now. Well, come on, we have to, things have to be mellowed out. We have to assert control. We do that two ways. We, has no one read history but me?

He curls his fist around the vial.

—We use force or the threat thereof.

He tilts his head east.

—And we use bread.

—And yeah, sure, we're gonna shut it down, but it has to be grad-ual. We can't just turn off the spigot. We scale back. The breed-ing, OK, yes, the breeding we can stop that. But the ones who are already there, well, it's not like we're equipped to deal with them anyway. So. Sometimes it's all about expedience.

I find what I'm looking for in my pocket and start fiddling it around.

Lydia's fists are white, balled at her sides.

—I want you to repeat that.

Terry licks his lips.

—*Sometimes it's all about expedience.*

Lydia's fists come up to the points of her hips.

—That had best not have been meant the way it sounded, Terry.

He sighs.

—Don't let your naiveté get the best of you here. Try to remember, if you can take a second away from all your self-righteousness, try to remember how recently you were tied up in a closet. Try to remember that the only reason you were let out was because it was, yeah, *expedient*. Because, I don't know, because the universe is mysterious and just a few hours ago it looked like the Society was on the verge of collapse and your cooperation was needed to save it. Well now, I don't know, but things look like they have changed. Some new balance has cycled in and you don't have any Bulls outside backing you and the Society needs cohesion right now, not your exclusive sexual orientation–based politicking that always gums up the fucking works.

—I have a bomb in my hand.

They look at me.

Hurley shakes his head.

—Tis a cell phone.

I shake my head.

—It's a bomb. And it's ringing.

I put Chubby's phone to my ear.

—Digga. It's Joe. I just killed Predo. Yeah. And his enforcers were just slaughtered at the Cure house. Yeah. The Secretariat is exposed. Run a fleet of Escalades down there with your rhinos and the whole turf will be yours. Yeah. Kill the fuckers now. Sure. My pleasure. I owe ya for not killing me.

I snap the phone closed.

—See, it's a bomb. It just blew up Terry's new balance of power.

Terry points the gun that killed Amanda at me.

—If I didn't think, I don't know, that it would be easier for you if I shot you right now, Joe.

He lowers the gun.

—But I think I'd rather, and I believe I've earned this over the years, I think I'd rather have you starve to death. Just because it will hurt more.

He shakes his head.

—That's the kind of emotion you've brought me to.

—Yeah, I know the feeling.

He keeps shaking his head.

—And it's all so, what a waste of, all so useless, the gesture. It's not like, what Digga, you think Digga won't see sense? You think?

I think it's getting pretty hard to think. I think about the only thing I can think about right now is my hunger and how much it hurts. I think the smell of Amanda's blood is making us all a little feverish in here. But I try not to think about it too much because it's making me dizzy and I don't want that. I want to stay in this chair. Stay here for just the few minutes more that it will take for her blood to spoil in her dead veins, for it to become useless to the Vyrus. I want the stab of that temptation gone. Before I lose out to it.

I rub my eye.

—Sorry. I think? Right. Yeah. What I think. Yeah. Well, what I think is Digga declared war as soon as he heard about the hole. So, expedience, that's not really his gig. That other.

I point at the vial.

—Yeah, sure, you make him believe it is what it is, and yeah, he may dance your steps. But you'll never get a chance to make that threat.

He shoots Lydia, one round, stomach, it pushes her back two steps, she sits heavy, both hands over the hole, dragging her heels back and forth over the floor.

—Fuck. Fuck. Fuck.

He looks at me.

—OK, I don't know, but if we can all agree now that Lydia isn't going to be stopping me, and that you, controversial turn of phrase coming up here, that you are effectively *crippled* right now, then I think we can also agree that I can make whatever threats I deem necessary, whatever means to the end, because I don't see who, unless you mean Ben over there, and, Ben, if you make any move I'll shoot you and your woman because at this point your collective symbolic value is about zero and I'm not the superstitious type so I don't, you know, have high hopes that she's carrying the savior. So, in the absence of I don't know what, Joe, I don't see where anyone here is going to complicate this re-arrangement of power and social values within our community.

I point.

—Hurley is.

Hurley draws his head back.

—An it's mad ya are at da end, Joe.

Terry's lips go thin.

—Your brain is boiling, Joe.

It is. My brain is boiling. I have a fever. I'm not sure I'm sweating anymore. Moisture all used up. Skin feels like ash. Touch me and I'll flake and float away.

I drink whiskey for lubrication.

—Just that Hurley's of the old school. Germ warfare, extermination of the species, that's not his thing.

Hurley hooks his thumbs in his suspenders.

—An of course it ain't. Now, I'm all fer a war, on an intimate scale, mind, a straightaway settlin' of differences when diplomacy has failed, but every man has his limit, don't ya know.

I almost laugh, but my throat's too dry.

—Funny choice of words. I was just thinking along those lines.

He flips his fingers.

—An what worry o mine is it anyway? None. Terry boy, he sees fit ta shake his saber and bug his eyes at Mister DJ Grave Digga an treaten him a bit wit a fate worse dan death, well, so be it an all. Fer goodness sake.

He snaps his suspenders.

—Tis not like he would *do it*.

Lydia kicks her heels against the floor.

—Hurley.

She loses the words, coughing, but nods her head up and down.

Hurley waves the nods off.

—An yer just feelin' sore, Lydia, because ya didn't have yer way. An I know yer worried 'bout dem kids in Queens an all, but we'll take car o dat. Dis *expedience* Terry is talkin' about, dat word, dat word means we'll do it quickly is all. Yer just makin' tings more complicated dan dey is.

—Terry sold zombies to the Chosen in Brooklyn, Hurley.

He frowns, brows drawing down so low they almost cover his eyes.

—Be careful now, Joe. Terry may want ya ta die slow, but if I lose my temper listenin' ta foul rumor, I won't be responsible.

My head, it feels like my scalp is a blister. More whiskey for that.

—So maybe I'm provoking you, Hurl. To make it quick. All the same, I gave Terry the zombie juice years ago. It was in these dentures the Horde kid's dad made. Crazy, huh? Remember that time you saved me from Predo and his goon? Think hard. All that shambler trouble at the time? Doctor Horde was behind that. Terry used the teeth to make a few shamblers, sold them in Brooklyn. That's where the new ones came from.

Hurley's frown deepens, eyes hidden in shadow, a cloud over

the man that could only be darker if it was spitting rain and lightning bolts.

—Strivin' ta confuse me with memories o the distant past is a poor course of action.

—Hurl, move a little away from those guns, would you?

Hurley, standing near the gun racks where he's been gradually drifting for the last minute, born on a tide of uncertainty toward a comfortable shoreline, stops and looks at Terry, and the gun Terry is pointing at him.

—Aw now, Terry boy.

Terry looks at the gun in his own hand.

—Just until your mind clears, Hurley.

Hurley shakes his head. Shakes it again.

—Aw hell, Terry.

—These are complex issues, Hurl, not one of your, I don't know, strengths, man.

—Sure, and but.

He gives his head a final snapping shake.

—Aw, now that's done it but good an shaked everythin' inta place.

He points a sausage finger.

—*Zombies*, Terry. Of all da tings in da world.

Terry inhales deep, exhales.

—Take a deep one, just draw a deep one in and let it go, just to get some oxygen flowing, clear the cobwebs there. Shine a light on what you believe.

Hurley draws in a deep breath and lets it go in a rush, and shakes his head.

—Naw, dat didn't shake da taught loose. It's in dere good.

He takes a step toward Terry.

—Ya did it, didn't ya? Supplyin' dem wit zombies? Ya did it. An I mean ta say, *zombies*. It just goes ta prove what I been tinkin' fer some time now. *Yer not clear in da head yerself, Terry.*

Terry raises his shoulders high, drops them.

—Just flex those muscles and relax, go easy on this, old friend.

Hurley raises his shoulders, drops them.

—Still I feel tense as before.

He stops walking toward Terry and rubs his forehead.

—An I do not feel unsure a'tall. An I know it. Yes, I do.

He takes his hand from his forehead.

—Ya did it, Terry, ya did it an it ain't just a story Joe is tellin'. Ya did it.

—It's a complicated world, Hurl, like I've always said, and some things you do, they have to be done.

—An don't I know it, havin' done so many of dose tings? An don't I know it? But I say it again, *zombies*. Shame, shame on ya, Terry Bird. Shame.

Terry plants his feet.

—Hurley, man, if you suddenly, if you think you can guide things, if you think you can make the choices that will lead us to a better world then, hey, I don't know, say so and we'll change our whole dynamic.

Hurley clucks his tongue.

—It ain't about dat an ya know it well. An I hardly know anymore what it tis we're leadin' to. Dis *better world*. A world wit zombies in it? No. Somehow, an I can't say where it was, but somewhere, ya jumped a track, Terry boy, an tis up ta me, yer true friend, ta get ya back on it. Zombies an shootin' Lydia outta hand like dat, and all dese last few years an da mess we've become.

He rubs at the corner of his eye.

—I long fer da old days, I tell ya. An I don't see nuttin' in what yer talkin' 'bout dat will bring 'em back. So, trust me on dis, trust yer oldest friend, dat gook what ya got in yer hand, I tink ya should give it ta me. If ya can step over da line ta usin' zombies, ya might do about anytin'. An I'll lie an I'll cheat an I'll kill till the graveyards are full up, but always wit me own brain an mouth an hands I'll do it. Openin' a bottle an lettin' out a genie ta kill everyting, dat's not fer us, Terry boy.

He puts out his hand.

—Yer like a souse on da bottle an tis time ta take da cure. Get clear. So hand it over.

Terry nods.

—Yeah, Hurl. Rough times these.

He shoots.

Hurley keeps walking at him, brushing at the spreading blood on his chest.

—Now, *Terry*. We're not children surely? Was dat called fer?

Terry shoots again.

Hurley pats his hip where the second bullet went in.

—An it's not like I'm suggestin' ya step down or anytin'. I'm just sayin' ya need ta remember da limits of, well, human decency here.

Terry shoots again.

Hurley flexes his left arm below the bullet hole in his shoulder.

—It's a tough ting ta admit ya got a problem. An if da fact *yer* shootin' *me* doesn't spell it out ta ya, I don't know what will. Give me da bottle, Ter. Ya dan't trust yerself just now.

Terry shoots again, his arm fully extended, Hurley just in front of him, the barrel almost touching Hurley's neck when it goes off, blowing off a chunk.

Hurley coughs, spits a mouthful of blood on the floor, takes another step, another, and grabs Terry by the shoulders, gun pinned between them.

—Before ya do somethin' ye'll regret, Terry, why don't ya hand me dat bottle o nasty? Just fer me ta put away someplace safe. Where ya won't tink on it an get confused. We'd not want to overstep da bounds of our friendship here, now would we?

Terry tries to pull back, twists, but Hurley's lost one man from his paws tonight. He doesn't ever lose two.

—Hurley.

—Terry now.

—Hurley, this is just, I don't know, man.

—Isn't it now? Isn't it just that.

The gun goes off five more times, two of the bullets come out of Hurley's back, the others trapped inside the mass of him.

He grunts, wraps his arms around Terry, and squeezes.

When he stops squeezing he drops what's left of Terry.

He looks down at the mess. Plucks the gun from it. Pops the clip.

—Empty now. Shame.

He drops both.

Bends and picks up the vial, and walks to me and offers it.

—Joe, would ya mind?

I take it from his hand.

He keeps it out.

—An if I might?

I hand him the whiskey and he walks to Terry's body and lowers himself slowly to the floor and takes a drink that finishes the last three inches of bourbon.

—Damn it all.

He looks at the empty bottle and flips it away to roll across the floor.

—Damn it all.

He folds himself over Terry's body.

—An I never expected to live forever.

He closes his eyes, head resting on his folded arms.

—But damn it all da same.

His barrel chest pumps a few more times, but that's all he has left in him.

. . .

Time was, you'd have told me I was gonna be in the room when Terry died, and I'd have told you that would never happen on my watch. Now here it is, and most I feel is maybe that I wish I'd had a chance to get a crack at him myself. Figure, as unwell as I am, Vyrus going all haywire, dying already started, I got about a thousand reasons why I should feel this bad. None of them having anything to do with Terry Bird being dead and gone.

But that don't mean I'm gloating.

I look at Predo's head, still in my lap, and roll it to the floor.

No, I'm not gloating. Things got to die sometimes. That's all.

So I wipe the smile off my face.


—Did it go through?

Lydia feels at her back.

—No. Shit.

She lost her fair share of blood in the basement and on the stairs. That big old gun put a hell of a hole in her gut. Wound has closed over, no more blood leaking, but she's having trouble finding her feet. We could start a stumble club her and me.

—Someone's gonna have to dig it out.

—I have people for that.

—Lose more blood when it happens.

She stops trying to rise and lowers herself until she's lying on the floor.

—Need to get up.

Footsteps.

—I can help.

We're both looking at her, Delilah, gazing down at Lydia, over the rim of her belly.

—I can help.

—Now, baby.

Ben comes over.

—I'm not sure.

She doesn't look at him.

—Benjamin, I want to get out of here. You know how to do that?

He points at the door, scratches his head.

—I'm not sure what's out there.

She nods.

Lydia is shaking her head.

—No, no, no, no. No way. Never.

I lever myself out of my chair, the cramps keeping me bent, and find a few things to lean on till I get to Lydia.

—Here.

I get a hand in her armpit and pull.

—No, I won't, I won't.

Even with the bullet in her, she's in better shape than me.

I look at Ben.

—Kid.

He gets her by her other arm and we pull her off the floor and start hauling her across the room.

—No, Joe. I won't take a mother's blood. I won't, given or not. I won't.

I get her where we're going.

—Here.

She looks at Amanda.

—Joe. No.

I point at the lab.

—Girl wanted to find a cure, wanted to help. Think she'd care? She wouldn't. Go on, before it goes bad.

Her nostrils are flaring, just *this* close to all that spilled blood, smelling that it's still fresh inside.

—She said not to.

—She was being pissy and temperamental. She wanted to help. Whatever. Stop talking about it. Do it.

It takes her another second to get over her qualm, and she gets to it.

I leave her there, walk away from the desk, find my chair and sit back down, and try not to look at what she's doing, or drown in my own saliva.

Delilah comes over.

—What about you? You'll be more help if you can fight.

The Vyrus rages at the nearness of all that blood.

I wave her off.

—Look who's the realist all of a sudden. None for me. Dilutes my bodily fluids. Need my strength for later. But I tell you.

I take out my tobacco.

—If one of you kids could roll one of these and find a light somewhere, I think I'd be OK.

Ben takes the packet, unseals the bag, looks inside.

—You're out of rolling papers.

I wave a hand at some books in the lab.

—Improvise.

He goes looking for a book.

I grunt.

—Hey, see if she's got a Bible over there. Those onionskin pages at the front work best.

—Classy, Joe.

Lydia is on her feet. Still with a wobble, but shiny-eyed and loose-shouldered.

She wipes her mouth.

—Ready to go to Queens?

Ben comes back with a smoke rolled in a bit of printed paper, and a butane igniter.

—Mister Pitt.

—Yeah, hit me.

I stick the double wide smoke in my face and he burns the end off it and I cough up a chunk of my lung on that first paper hit, but it's worth it.

I look at Lydia.

—Why the hell would I want to go to Queens?

She's at the gun rack, pauses in her inventory and points at Terry.

—Know what that is?

I squint at the body.

—Dead people?

—Karma.

She returns to looking for a gun that will suit her mood.

—That was Terry's bullshit karma finally catching up to him because he delayed and deferred doing the right thing for too long.

—Uh-huh.

—I'm not saying there's anything mystical about it, just that he sowed and he reaped. Being a selfish asshole gets you nowhere.

—Uh-huh.

She turns to look at me, hefting something that looks designed to efficiently kill people in large numbers.

—Are you on the phone?

I hold up a finger.

—Hang on, this will be fast.

—Who are you calling now? Digga has his hands full. Joe? Who are you?

I get my connection, my voice sounding so strangled through the pain in my gut and my half-crushed windpipe that I don't even have to act to make myself sound freaked out.

—Yeah, I want to report a shooting. A murder. A cop, a cop was just shot over here. Where they make cement. Queens, I'm in

Queens. English Kill. Next to the bus depot, where they make cement. I work. Oh my god. There's a, some kind of sex slave thing. In the factory, the main building. Chains and. Please, please, they killed a cop and they know I'm here.

I hang up the phone, drop it, stomp it into shards.

—Really, Lydia.

I take a drag.

—If you wanted to change the world.

I blow smoke.

—That was all you had to do.


Lydia kills the thing on the stairs.

Opens the door, starts shooting, keeps shooting, empties a clip into it, pops a fresh one in the gun and empties that one too. Whatever it was, it had finished off the last of the starvings. Monsters out of the way, we spend more time than reasonable getting down the stairs. Mostly that's my fault. Ben tries to carry me to make things go faster, but I go into a fit of convulsions and the arm wrapped around his neck almost throttles him and he decides he'll just let me lean on him so he can drop me if it happens again.

Delilah walks just ahead of us, one step at a time, waddling with care.

Lydia is leading the way, gun first, poking it into every open door on every landing.

—Insane. I should. Insane.

I trip down a couple steps, grab the banister.

—You were the one that wanted to be public.

She takes the turn on the second floor landing.

—We always thought it would be an announcement. A press conference. Not a SWAT van driving on an officer-down call and finding a Vampyre concentration camp. It was. We wanted it to be organized. Controlled.

—Sure, a civilized declaration that Dracula is real and there are a lot of him and, oh yeah, it's communicable.

She leads us down to the ground floor, stepping carefully through the bodies.

—It's information. We needed to shape it, control the definitions. Why shouldn't the signified define the signifiers?

—You sound like Terry.

Her head snaps around, gun barrel in parallel.

—Don't.

—It was never gonna happen like that. No one was ever gonna buy that. It was always going to happen, and it was always going to be a mess.

I step away from Ben, use the wall, start for the back of the building.

—At least this way we blew it up ourselves.

I find the back door, find the ring of Cure house keys still in my pocket.

—Could have been someone else blowing it up under us.

I start trying keys in locks.

Lydia puts a hand on the door.

—How was this better? How is it better we blow ourselves up?

I grin.

—I don't know. I guess it just feels better than letting someone else do it.

She starts to frown, but it turns to a grin of her own.

—Yeah. Alright. So let's go deal with the rubble.

I find the right keys and pop the locks.

She pulls her hand away from the door.

—So those enforcers don't know about the back way?

I shrug.

—Probably they do.

She stares at me.

I shrug again.

—My bet is all the little piggies got called home as soon as Digga hit Coalition HQ.

—And if not?

I point at the basement door.

—If not, that's plan B over there. Your call.

She pulls the door open and we step into the alley, Ben and Delilah waiting to see if we get gunned down from the rooftops. We don't. And we don't get shot up on the street when we come out the front of the Cure-owned building that faces onto Seventy-second. And the Impala is where I left it on First Avenue. And I haven't lost the key in all the business of the night. And there's still a couple hours to daylight.

A small collection of miracles.

None of them a cigarette.


You can't kill the worm.

Wound it, it'll never be as bad as the hurt it does itself with every bite. It'll just keep chewing. Digesting itself over and over again.

Calling the cops, sending them into Queens. Blowing it wide. Does that rip a hole in the side of the worm? Will blood run from it? Or does something like that make it stronger? More madness.

A sudden fun house mirror skew to the world. Everyone looking at the new reflection, asking, *Do I really look like that?* Your friends and neighbors, seeing them with those new eyes, *Who are they? What are they?*

How bad will it get?

How fast?

Figure it will get as bad as it can possibly get as fast as humanly possible.

Figure it this way. With or without Amanda's research, once they have actual Vyrussy Vampyres in their labs, someone will come to the same conclusions that she did. So if our very existence doesn't push the madding crowd over the edge, the idea of rewriting the history of life with sanguivores as the wellspring should be good for at least one holy war.

Then again, I'm maybe not the one you want sitting judgment on humanity. People being inclined as they are to see their own natures in everyone else. A world full of me? Who wouldn't push the button?

The worm.

You can't kill it.

It can only kill itself.

—I know about you.

I ignore that.

—As much as he talked about Percy, he talked about you almost as much.

I ignore it some more.

—He made you sound like the world's baddest man. John Shaft with white skin.

In the front passenger seat, Lydia turns and looks at me when she hears that.

—Go ahead and smile, Joe, no one's ever going to flatter you more than that.

Next to me in the back, Delilah shakes her head.

—Just said that was the picture my dad painted, I didn't say it was accurate. Look at you. Look like you were something made to be beat on. It's like nothing he ever told me was true. Like it's just one big mess of craziness is all it is.

She shakes a fist at no one.

—I will not stand for more craziness.

I tug on the stump of my left ring finger.

—Girl, you got yourself into a world of craziness the minute you fucked a Vampyre, the rest of this is just what comes with the package.

Delilah slaps Ben's shoulder and the Impala veers slightly.

—You have nothing to say to that?

Ben straightens the wheel and keeps his eyes on the road.

—Baby, I'm new to the whole experience myself. If I was comfortable with the way things are done, I wouldn't have been looking for someone outside the infected community. To my eyes, it's all been crazy. Being infected. Meeting you. Getting into the whole undead scene with you. 'Cause you know I love you, and the role-playing is fun, kinky, but talking like that all the time, it wears me out a little. And now. Becoming a dad. *Crazy* is the least of it.

Delilah sniffs.

—If you don't care to embrace your true self, you need not be burdened by myself or the child.

—Hon, that's not what I.

She raises a hand.

—I'd prefer silence.

Lydia leans into her headrest.

—More craziness.

I rasp my whiskers with my fingernails.

—Price of admission.

●   ●   ●

There's another price to be paid.

—You are so full of shit!

—Delilah, my dear, I was only trying to reassure myself that you were safe.

—Fuck that! I'm not talking about that! I'm talking about all your bullshit about these people!

Ben ducks the pointed finger as it swings his way.

—Baby, I'm not sure that's the kind of language you mean to be using.

Her finger changes into a flat palm that she shoves an inch from Ben's nose.

—Ben, baby daddy, shut the fuck up unless you want the remaining romance in this deal to go running down the drain.

Ben shuts up and takes a step back.

She turns to Chubby.

—Have you ever spent any time with these psychos? They. You made it sound like an adventure!

Chubby has his arms extended, showing his palms, fingers pointed down, supplicant.

—I was trying to entertain.

—I was a kid, for fuck sake!

—Entertain a very advanced child with very mature tastes.

—Don't blame me for this shit.

—I am not. Your mother and I, our business. Of course your own interests were exotic. A bedtime reading of *The Cat in the Hat* was hardly in order.

She gives him the palm treatment.

—Just. OK. I don't want to. Because I will just get.

She steps to him and shoves as hard as she can, failing to budge him an inch.

—We almost died! Over and over we almost died! And my baby, they would have killed my baby!

Her shoves turn to slaps, smacking his face side to side.

—You and your bullshit ideas of what being a dad is. Trying to show off. You and your secrets. Bullshit, bullshit, bullshit!

Slaps turn to fists and Chubby has enough.

Grabs her by the wrists.

—Woman.

Ben steps to, draws a look from Chubby, and steps off.

Chubby pushes his face close to his daughter's.

—You wanted adventure and romance. I obliged. You showed up with your young man and your predicament, and I gave you my best advice and counsel. Get rid of them both. Boy and baby. Because you are my daughter and I want what is best for you. But you are not a little girl, you are all grown up. Making your own decisions. That you judged reality by your bedtime stories bespeaks your own personal weaknesses. That you chose to indulge a predilection for dramatics, which is excessive to say the least, bespeaks your desire to dodge responsibilities. Now you have seen all this, what would you like me to do? What can I do to make up the past for you? Can I tell you a fresh fairy tale? One with a happy ending for you and Ben? From what I understand, that will not be coming true. We'll need to hide you both, more than ever. You and your baby. You will be a mother soon. Time to stop worrying about the past. Time to worry about the future.

She twists free, stares at him.

—Hide my baby?

She shakes her head slow to the left.

—Never.

Slow to the right.

—This child is meant for the light.

Chubby's hands flutter at his sides.

—Delilah, dear, I'm not suggesting you live in a cave.

—Yeah, you are.

He looks at Lydia.

She's leaning against the wall, next to the assault rifle she took from the Cure house.

—You're telling them they have the love that dare not speak its name. And a baby that's going to have to learn to pass. And that's not the way it has to be.

Chubby slips a thumb in the armhole of his vest.

—This is a family matter, Miss Miles.

—*Mizz* Miles.

She comes away from the door.

—Throw those diminutives around, but don't slap them on me.

Chubby looks at me.

—Joe?

I shake my head.

—No way, I'm not in this.

Lydia goes to Delilah.

—We can use you.

She puts a hand on Delilah's belly.

—This baby, whatever it is, this baby says we're all the same. It says infected and uninfected, we're all human. It forces them to look at us and see people, not monsters. This baby, it's not a symbol, it's a fact. And it, and you, both of you together, if you come with me, you can save lives. Just by being there and letting people see you and see what you made together.

Chubby wipes a hand down his face.

—Madness. Madness.

Lydia stays with Delilah's eyes.

—It is not safe. It will not be safe. But it isn't a safe world. All we can do is try and make it better.

Delilah's eyes are wide and shiny.

She holds her hand open to Ben, he takes it, she pulls him close.

—This is a child of destiny in troubled times.

Chubby throws up his hands and walks away.

—Babbling, incoherent madness.

Delilah puts a hand on her belly.

—I will not hide this light.

She takes a step, pulling Ben along.

—Come, Benjamin, we are not welcome here.

Chubby takes a step after them.

—Delilah. Some small ounce of sense, please.

But she's turned away, opening the office door.

—Lydia Miles, we will go with you. She will speak to the world, and our child will lead.

Ben glances back at us.

—I.

She pulls at his hand.

He lets himself be pulled.

—I'm a dad, man.

Both disappearing down the hall.

Delilah's voice raised to declaim.

—We can shine a light. Our baby can be a light.

Chubby stands at the corner of his desk, moves toward the door, has another thought, turns back, stands lost in the middle of the room.

—Impetuous. That has always been her nature. Impetuous, passionate, romantic. Not a patient or a realistic bone in her body.

He looks at Lydia.

—And you encouraged her.

Lydia picks up the assault rifle.

—I just told her the right thing to do, she made up her own mind.

—Yes, a starring role as mother of the messiah baby, how could she resist?

Lydia waves him off.

—I'm guiding a revolution. You, Freeze, you're trying to make yourself feel better about being a crappy dad.

He moves to a corner, stands there, looking at photos on the wall.

Lydia comes to where I'm slumped on the couch, she puts a hand under my chin and forces my head up and takes a good look into my eyes.

—For a girl. Joe Pitt blows up the world, for a girl.

She shakes her head.

—I wish I knew.

She lets go of my chin and straightens.

—I wish I knew.

She turns and walks away.

—I wish I knew where I could find a girl like that.

I watch her walk, favoring the side where the bullet's stuck in her, carrying the assault rifle on her shoulder.

Tomorrow she'll be on TV. Standing with her people around her. Delilah and Ben right up front. Trying to put a human face on what they're pulling out of that hole in Queens.

And she'll be lucky to live one more day past that.

I raise my good hand.

—Lydia.

She doesn't look back at me.

—Save it.

—Just gonna say you can take the Impala.

—I already was.

And walks out the open door.

She does make it through the next couple days without dying or being thrown in a cage, she'll go back underground. Fighting a new kind of fight. But I don't need to tell her that.

After all, she kept the gun.

That lady, she wants to find a girl worth blowing up the world for, she should maybe look in the mirror.


—Do you think Delilah will come back?

I shrug.

—Beats me.

Chubby is still looking at those photos on the wall, a little girl.

—She'll come back.

He looks at the floor.

—Of course she will. Once she sees. How hard it is. She'll come back.

I push myself out of the corner of his couch.

—Don't count on it.

He scuffs his foot against the lay of his shag carpet.

—No. I won't. I won't.

I start to gut myself up for standing.

—Anyway, all I need is for you to tell Evie I did my bit. I got the kids here safe. They didn't want to stay. Too late for me to do more.

He scuffs again, drawing a cross in the carpet.

—Yes.

I lean and grab the side of his desk and pull and my bowels don't fall out of my ass so I'm not dead yet.

—And I could use a ride over to Enclave.

He rubs the cross out.

—About that.

I'm lurching to the door.

—Don't give me grief at this stage, Chubs. You don't have to linger, just drive me over, push me out, and drive away.

—Joe.

I look at him.

He's holding one hand to his cheek.

—I'm sorry, Joe.

I put my back against the wall, trying not to slide down it.

—Chubby?

—Very sorry.

—What did you?

He pulls his hand down his face, dragging the cheek, giving himself a cant.

—I never spoke with Evie.

I start to slide.

He pulls his cheek lower.

—She doesn't know anything about Delilah and the baby. She never.

I'm on the floor.

Chubby looks like the side of his face that he's touching has melted under his hand.

—She never said you should go looking for them.

He lets go of his face and it pulls itself back up.

—As far as I know, she doesn't know that you're alive.

I stay on the floor.

I could pull the piece I took from the Cure house armory and shoot Chubby, but I don't much see the point of it. Said from the beginning that I owed him one. Just because I thought I had extra reason to go looking for his daughter, that doesn't mean the debt wasn't reason enough. Figure I may have thrown in the towel a few times if I hadn't had that extra motivation, but that just doubles his smart for making the play he made.

I lift a hand.

—Doesn't matter, Chubby.

I feel for a smoke, can't find any, remember I never got my tobacco back from Ben.

Oh well.

Chubby comes over, takes my hand, pulls me up.

—If there's something I can do, Joe. Money. I. Anything is what I mean.

He puts a finger alongside his neck.

—Joe, anything to make it right.

I push him off, stand on my own two.

—Hell, Chubby, when the night started I was living underground. I was feeding on dregs. I was hiding from the world and acting like I had an idea of what to do next. But all I really was was in the dark. Look at me now.

I brush at some filth on my tattered jacket.

—A night on the town. Visits with old pals. Rousing adventure.

I fit the zip and pull it up until it snags and stops at my sternum.

—I'm a changed man.

I drag my fingers through my hair.

—You want to do something for me. You can make a couple phone calls, bring some people up to date on the new state of things. And in the meantime.

I sweep a hand at the door.

—You can take me over to see my girl.


Last hour. Dark before the dawn. Empty city. A quiet waiting for the next big thing in the new day.

We drive through it.

—I didn't think you would help.

I put my head out the open window to feel the cold air.

—When you're right, Chubby, you're right.

He leans from the backseat of the Riviera and taps Dallas's shoulder.

—Up here.

Dallas changes lanes, takes the car around the corner onto Greenwich.

Chubby settles back into the seat.

—I don't want to shirk my responsibility for the deception, but it was in fact Percy's idea.

—Percy.

He takes out his humidor, looks at it, removes the cap and pulls one of the cigars half from the humidor.

—As you must have gathered, I embellished a bit when I told Delilah those stories. From a very early age she's had such macabre taste. Her mother had read to her the original Grimm's tales. Heels chopped from feet, eyes pecked out, children sacrificed. I am myself no stranger to lurid material. Some of the most baroque scenarios my films have been based on were those I penned myself.

He pushes the cigar back into place.

—I even wrote one that was Vampyre-themed. But thought it better to leave it unproduced. There was no telling whose ire it might have raised.

He recaps the humidor.

—But I allowed my whimsy full freedom when I had occasion to tuck Delilah into bed. Thanks to the estrangement between her mother and myself, those were rare occurrences, and I hoped to leave an indelible impression. One that would outlast the charm of whichever of my ex's current infatuations might be lurking about.

He waves the humidor.

—I told stories that were appropriately grotesque, but tended toward full and happy resolutions. Percy was a kind wizard who drifted in and out of my narratives, guiding a pair of star-crossed naifs. One of them Vampyre, one not.

He shoves the humidor into his jacket.

—A common-enough trope. Am I entirely responsible for putting the idea in her head? Please. Popular vampire fiction is rife with such relationships. It is a rampant cliché of the genre. What is *Dracula* if not the story of an undead's hopeless love for a mortal?

He cuts the air with the edge of his hand.

—Can I be solely to blame that she took it quite so to heart?

The storefronts along Greenwich flick past the window. I stick a finger under my eyepatch and scratch the scar.

—You're her dad.

He looks at me.

—What has that to do with it?

I bare my teeth as a cramp ripples through my belly, exhale as it passes.

—I don't really know, Chub, but it seems daddies have a bit of an impact on their daughters. Or so I've heard. Could just be a rumor.

He rubs his forehead.

—Yes, yes, of course, yes. These things start early and run deep. Of course.

He wipes his mouth.

—But the past is prologue. And I was saying?

I cough on something in my throat. Maybe a loose piece of my throat, I can't say.

—Percy. Why the hell did you get me involved?

He looks at the roof of the car.

—Percy said I should.

I groan.

Chubby shakes his head.

—When I first called, the children were actually *with* him. I was prepared to go uptown and attempt to speak some form of reason to them. Ferry them to an underground location somewhere away from Manhattan while the troubles here sorted out. I am not without resources. I could have found means to keep Ben supplied. And the baby, whatever its needs may turn out to be. I was to go and fetch them myself.

He lifts his hands from his knees, drops them.

—At the last moment Percy called and told me it had become more complicated. The children had run off. Delilah had been disillusioned by what she found in both Percy and the Hood. She was talking about *shelter in the dragon's very den*. Well, that was clear enough. Still, I said I could go myself. But Percy said he'd heard troublesome rumors about the Cure house. Unsafe.

He scrunches the material of his slacks.

—He told me to send you.

He looks over at me.

—Honestly, Joe, I had no idea where to find you. I doubt it would have occurred to me to look for you at all. But Percy said it needed a tough hand. Said you were the fit for the job. And I could hardly argue.

—How'd he know where to find me?

—I can't say for certain. He said he knew someone keeping tabs on you down there. You mentioned someone watching us when we were in the tunnel. Perhaps?

I think about the old man of the underground. I think about Percy. Enclave and Enclave.

—Yeah, that fits.

He pats his 'fro.

—Still, I told him I didn't think you'd help.

He looks out the side window.

—And he mentioned a girl. Sketched a few details. Gave me a name. Mentioned Enclave.

He turns to me, tears, trembling chins.

—Joe, if it hadn't been my daughter, Joe. If it hadn't. I would never have. Not just because I have more sense than to cross you.

But because. I wouldn't want to lie to a man about something like that. Not a man I know. Not a friend. Joe.

He wipes his eyes with the back of his hand.

—Just. My daughter. That's why.

He catches a sob, huffs it out.

—I didn't want to cause you all this trouble.

He draws a loose shape in the air with his fingers.

—I'm sorry, Joe.

I look out the windshield. We're coming up on Gansevroot. I move my feet around, making sure I can still do that. Legs seem to work. Arms. My brain keeps drifting in and out of fog banks. But that's hardly new. I could keep myself clear, I'd never have fallen for this deal.

Too late now. I was reeled in, cut open, gutted, and there's nothing left but the grill. No reason not to just put myself on it. It's only fire. And you can only burn once.

I stick my head a little farther out the window.

I point.

He sees it, taps Dallas.

—Here.

Dallas wheels us around the corner of Little West Twelfth Street.

—You sure, Joe?

I lean against the door.

—Make those calls, Chubs.

—Of course.

I pull the door handle.

—I'm glad you got to see your daughter, Chubby.

He nods, half laughs.

—Yes. Precious minutes.

I push the door open an inch.

—See you around.

—See you, Joe.

Dallas cuts the wheel, rubber breaking traction on the cobbles as he makes his u-turn, and I tumble myself from the car, rolling off the momentum until I rest in the gutter, watching Chubby's Riviera whip around the corner back onto Greenwich and out of sight.

Alone again. I close my eye to enjoy it for a second.


Got any regrets?

The thing you did? The thing you passed on doing?

I never played that game much. I take something back here, take a little extra there, next thing you know I'm watching one set of bodies rising from their graves, and another set going into the ground. Been a long time since I did anything that mattered when it didn't involve dying for someone. Some folks I've been happy to put away. Some I've been OK with seeing them get another day or two. Most I don't having feelings one way or the other. So why go back and tinker with things that can't be changed anyhow.

But, sure, I got regrets.

Most all of them are tangled up with this lady.

Got one in particular that sits on me.

Like to get it off.

Means opening my eye and crawling out of this gutter and finding out if she'll talk to me long enough to hear what I got to say.

Thought of it, it almost makes me wish I was back in the basement with the monsters. I was scared then, but it was just my life I had to lose.

•  •  •

—Oh, man, you OK, man?

I open my eye and look at the club kids, boy and girl, matching androgyny to go with their matching homburg hats plastered with Gucci logos and matching bug-eye pink-tint sunglasses and matching loops of fluorescing plastic around their wrists and necks.

—Oh, man, G, they laid a pounding on you.

One of them holds up a camera and snaps a picture.

—I'm putting this on my page.

She looks at me.

—That cool with you?

The other one is dialing.

—Hang on. 911 on the way.

—Give me a cigarette.

He stops dialing.

—G, you probably don't want to smoke messed up like that.

The girl is crouching next to me, holding her phone at arm's length so it gets us both in frame.

—Could kill you, a cigarette right now.

—Yeah, a cigarette could kill anyone. Jam a lit cigarette in someone's eye, it could leak infected pus back into their brain and they could go crazy and die eating their own shit.

They both stare at me.

I put out my hand.

The girl hands me a cigarette, pinching it between finger and thumb, holding it as far from herself as possible. I take it and put it in my mouth.

—Light.

The boy finds a Bic in his pocket and lights me.

—Now fuck off.

They do.

It's a fucking American Spirit Light. Tastes like my ass. I tear off the filter and it tastes like half my ass.

I get out of the gutter and pull the piece from under my jacket and drag myself up the steps of the Enclave warehouse loading dock and, dispensing with a polite knock, I grab the handle on the outside and pull the big white door open, rolling it to the side in its tracks, and I step inside.

Grateful again to Predo for the fingers he left me. Index and middle. The smoking fingers. Letting me take the butt from my mouth and carry it comfortably. Leaving my other hand free for the gun.

A gun and a smoke.

Ask for more, you're a greedy bastard.

I don't get to keep the gun for very long.

While I have it, I take in some of the sights. Such as they are. Rows of mats on the floor. Workbenches against the walls. Some big industrial sinks. Kitchen area where I happen to know they boil the bones of their dead before sucking out the marrow. Staircase leading up to the loft where their sleeping cubicles line a long center aisle. Small balcony up there overlooking the floor dotted with the light of scattered candles. Lockers where they store whatever kinds of goods they own. Rags. Cups. Marrow-sucking straws, maybe. Weapons. The cutting and cudgeling variety; they're not big on firearms here. Couple big drains in the floor. Sewer cap in the corner where they dump the occasional dead body or apostate. Took a ride down the tube once myself. Mostly for being an unlikeable asshole.

All that stuff is much as it always has been. More of everything these days. More than when Daniel was running the show. Signs of all the new Enclave since the Count started expanding the ranks. Geeking them up for the revelation.

Whatever shape that might take.

Supposed to be, one of them will achieve a final adaptation, perfect consumption by the Vyrus. All earthy cells eaten and replaced by Vyrals. The Vyrus understood by them to be from somewhere else. Other than this universe. Another plane.

Whackoness.

Supposed to be, the one who starves himself in perfect discipline and doesn't die of it, that one will show the others how to do the same. And, made into creatures from another plane, nothing, not even the sun, will harm them.

Cue the crusade.

You die, I die, everybody dies.

Except Enclave.

How it is my girl came to be here is, well, I brought her here. Wanted to keep her from dying of AIDS. It worked, but it created issues. Complicated issues. And I got turned out for being a lying sack of shit who barely told her a word of truth from the night we met.

Speaking of regrets.

So I take in the place, trying to figure what I might say. Trying to figure how long I have to say it before I fade to black. Trying to figure if I'll get a crack at settling just one more score.

And I almost trip over part of someone's rib cage and catch myself before I fall and stumble across a hunk of someone's thigh and just get my balance and have to jump to keep from stomping on a pile of seven livers and that's all the grace I can muster and I go down with a tangle of gristled spines under me and find myself looking up at the beams crossing under the shallow peak of the sheet-metal roof where an upside-down forest of chains have sprouted, each carrying the flower of a dead and rotting Enclave.

—We've been separating the chafe.

I roll toward the voice, gun first, and that's when I lose it, something white winking close, taking it from me, and winking back into the dark.

I open and close my hand on the emptiness that used to be the gun, then bring my other hand to my face and take a drag and thank fuck they took the piece and not the smoke.

—Hey, Count.

Spindle thin, wearing just the slacks from his white suit, a belt wrapped almost twice around his waist, and a matching vest that slips half off the high point of one of his shoulders, the Count strolls into the light of one of the candles.

He's carrying a twenty-inch bush blade from the end of a scythe, bringing it like a blood-crusted talon to his forehead; the tipping of a hat.

—Joe.

He lowers the blade, sniffs the air.

—You smell like you're just about ready for the pot.

I'm one of them.

Not by choice, just how Daniel called it.

Daniel said you were Enclave, that was a sealed deal. It doesn't wear off. Even if you don't want to play, you're in the game. Can I say it another way?

*When you're a Jet . . .*

Like that.

I never had any use for it. Gave me room to tap Daniel for a little news of the world. Gave me a bolt-hole once or twice. Mostly it was just strange baggage to be hauling around.

But if not for the Enclave thing, Daniel never would have baited me years back. Starved me out. Drew me to the edge and pushed me into the deep end. Never would have cared to find out if I could cope. Never would have sent the Wraith to make a killing and keep me alive. And if none of that had ever happened, I wouldn't know just how close I am to over, and what to do when it happens.

Course it also means they'll be eating my marrow pretty soon. Just hoping to keep one fucker from tucking in.

He grazes my forehead with the tip of the scythe blade.

—What did I tell you, Joey Joe Joe Joe?

He drags the tip from brow to brow, scraping bone.

—Told you never never come back. Utterly clear on the concept, man. Nothing vague.

He strikes a pose, pointing the blade in the air.

—I remember it like it was yesterday, man. Said, *You go out, you don't come back.* Pretty sure I put a distinct verbal period at the end of that sentence. But, hey, give the benefit of the doubt. You tell me, did I mumble?

I got about two inches left on my smoke. I suck away a quarter of that.

—No, you were clear enough, just that I don't take you seriously. You being a bad cliché and all.

He nods.

—Yeah, OK, yeah. I'll bite.

He squats next to me, resting the point of the blade on my chest.

—Tell me how it is I'm a punch line? Cuz I live for this kind of shit.

I suck a little more smoke.

—You're a punk kid who got infected and named himself Count. Textbook asshole.

He smiles.

—Ever tell you the last name I picked for myself?

I wave my butt.

—Vlad?

He shakes his head.

—*Count*.

I study the last of my cigarette.

—OK, I'll give it to ya, that shows a little sense of humor.

—Count *Count*. You get it, right? You've seen *Sesame Street*?

I lift a hand.

—I get it. It's not bad.

—Cuz I can laugh at myself, is the point.

—Sure.

He taps his own chest with the blade.

—I'm not the type takes himself all serious.

I nod.

—So laugh at this.

I jam the cherry of my last cigarette into his eye.

Nasty little hiss, drip of blood and something else rolling over his cheekbone, and him just sitting there and staring at me from the eye that I haven't turned into an ashtray.

Then he opens his mouth wide, drops his head back.

—Ha! Ha! Ha!

He brings his head up and plucks the butt from his eye, looks at it, and flicks it away.

—You know.

He reams drippings from his eye socket with a knuckle.

—Truth is.

He wipes the knuckle on my jacket.

—I barely even use my eyes anymore.

He closes the good one. The other has blistered over, covered in a cluster of tiny bubbles of skin.

—Everything is so lit up at this point. My senses? I feel, like, micro-changes in air pressure on my skin. Hear things. Smell like a hunting dog. My sense of taste, man, I wish I had a couple bottles of nice wine in here.

He runs a fingertip over the concrete floor.

—And the tactile. Telling you, I had any kind of sex drive left, it would blow away any crazy rave ecstasy orgy I ever got my ass into at college. On the subject of the senses, let me ask you.

He stabs the tip of the scythe blade into my biceps, through, until it tinks against the floor.

—You feel that?

I look at the blade, no blood welling around it, like a giant scalpel stuck in a corpse.

He pulls it out.

—No.

He rises.

—You are faaar gone, my main man. But that's not news.

He points the blade down at me.

—You got fat. Old. Tired. Beat. You are beat. I'm not just talking about you being all cut to chunks, I'm talking about how tired your story is. Man alone. Yojimbo. Get out of the middle of town and let the big boys do business. Only big enough for one operation. We aim to be that operation.

He swings the blade.

—Time to cut down the old and make way for the new. Know what the new is.

He runs his fingers down the ripple of his ribs.

—The new is lean and sleek. It is hungry. It is wild. It is dangerous to the old. New is always dangerous to the old. And you, Joe Pitt, you never read the headline. You met me and you just saw *punk kid*. What you should have been seeing is what the dinosaurs saw when they looked at the sky and spied that big meteor dropping on their heads. Know what they thought when they saw that rock?

He points up.

—Thought, *That is gonna hurt.*

He raises the scythe blade over his head.

—What you thinking now, Joe?

He brings the blade down and puts it in my stomach.

Goes through, pins me to the concrete, don't feel the cut, but I feel the cold of the steel, feel that because it's the only thing colder than the meat of my dead body.

And what I'm thinking is, *Man, I'm glad I died before he did that.*


I died about the time he started talking about how old I am. Was. Whatever. It's hard to figure what tense to use. Mix in the fact this is the second time I've died, it could get confusing in a hurry if I tried to think it all the way around.

So I don't.

I don't think around. I don't think up, down, in, out, over or under. My thoughts, they become a straight line. He's talking, and his words, what I'm seeing, the past, any kind of future, the concrete under my back, it all collapses into a sheet of black that becomes a horizon before it drops over my body and sucks me inside.

And I think just one last thing.

*Damn, I didn't get to see Evie.*


And I fall up and out the other side of the black sheet.

Everything expands until it is touching me everywhere and I feel the Enclave back in the shadows, watching, count their numbers by the way the air shifts when they breathe. All sound amplifies until I can separate the vibrations in the air as they strike my eardrums and name the key to which each is tuned, harmony and dissonance of the Count bragging, city waking outside, wax melting from a candle across the warehouse. Smells untwine, each has a color, fabric, leads to a source that I can see in my mind. I taste the rotting meat dangling overhead, the flaking rust on the upper curve of the Count's blade, the night's accumulation of grime on my clothes. I see into the dark, how the Enclave move without the purpose and control they used to own, jittery, gnashing, I see there are more of them hanging from the rafters than walking the floor. But that's not for me, the pot, a dangle from the ceiling. I've got better ways to die.

My eye is open, looking at the blade in my middle, and I raise it and see the Count, and I look at the stairs that lead to the loft, and I see the beautiful ivory girl sitting on a step at the middle of the stairs, a cluster of Enclave around her.

And I tell her what's on my mind.

—Hey, you look great.

She smiles.

—Kill him for me, Joe.

The Count looks at her.

—Get back in your place, bitch.

I stand up, rising, letting the blade cut deeper, until I am on my feet and it is sunk to the haft, the Count's knuckles pressing into the edges of the wound.

It's happening fast. Happening in the spaces between my heartbeats. I'm down and I'm up and he is looking at me and I am stepping backward and punching him in the wrist and now I am standing five feet away from him, the blade still in me, but it is my hand on the haft, pulling it free.

The wound in my belly seals as the steel comes out.

I show the Count his blade.

—Lose this?

He shows me my gun.

—Lose *this*?

I charge.

He shoots.

My thoughts are chasing themselves, trying to keep up with the pace of events. Thinking of Predo's death, my thoughts are trying to make my body veer, but I am not faster than bullets and the Count has fired twice, and two bullets should be enough to keep me down while he finishes me, but he's shooting from his hip like a gangster and he may be hot shit with a scythe blade but he's probably never fired a gun in his life and he just plain misses and throws the gun to the side.

—Fuck this shit.

And I'm going to cut his head off with his own blade and he drops under the flat arc as I swing for his neck and shows me what he's learned since he came here, squatting and pivoting, one leg extended, going for my legs, that are not there as I hop and realize I've put myself in the air and he comes out of his squat and puts both fists in my chest before my feet touch ground and I twist away from the impact but it still feels like two tiny trucks driving into me and I flip backward out of the air and tumble and my face goes into concrete followed by the rest of me and I can feel the Enclave shifting and coming at us, circling and as I'm rolling to my back I realize I've lost the scythe and the Count comes into view scooping it from the ground where I dropped it and I keep rolling as he brings it down like a pick again and again chipping the concrete and leaving divots closer and closer faster than me the tip skittering across my ribs and my hand goes inside my jacket for the amputation blade and that slows me too much and the scythe splits ribs and rips my lung and punches out my back and he hauls on it and it tears my side open and I have my feet and I have my own blade and I feel the Vyrus swarm my wound's gaping hole like a million tiny electric shocks trying to close it up and we're at the middle of a circle of Enclave where I will die and I lunge at the Count and he spins away from me and the scythe cuts as he steps past me and my hamstring is plucked so I go to one knee and he's just better at this than I am, just faster and stronger and used to living at the edge of the Vyrus, and I'd really like to see the look on his face when he finds out his whole world has been destroyed and it was me who blew it to hell.

But I don't think I'm going to get to.

The curve of his blade is so perfect for harvesting.

It travels flat and smooth, a little sharper and it would be slicing through the dust in the air as it comes for my neck.

And I see that I am on a stain in the concrete, a shape I remember, left there when I laid Daniel on this spot and watched him die. I remember Daniel. How he liked to tease me with hints. Suggestions that I was supposed to replace him. Never taken seriously. I remember him telling me the Wraith was something Enclave summoned from someplace else. Remember the old man of the sewers, the old man whose real name is Joseph. Remember how Daniel only called me by the name I was first born with, Simon. Remember old crazy Joseph of the sewers telling Simon that he'd seen a Wraith summoned. Saying that the Wraith was what we become. Remember seeing that blackness in his eyes. Swimming under the surface. I remember dying in that long-ago basement. Dying because I'd been without blood too long. Because my supply had been stolen. But not dead long. Coming back, Vyrus bringing me back, emptying me out to live, forcing me to live, just long enough to get it the blood it needed to live. Remember being on the verge of dying, Vyrus dying too, and the Wraith. Freezing a man through. Cold like space. At the end. And Daniel saying they summoned the Wraith. And Daniel, I get this idea of him in my old apartment, stealing the last of my blood. I get an idea of Daniel, for years, trailing me, walking in my steps and in my scent, erasing traces of himself. I see Daniel, telling me again, they summoned the Wraith. Telling me again that he starved me, to watch me die, to see if I could survive it, and telling me he sent the Wraith to save me. And I get this idea of myself in that basement, cold like dead, black-eyed, doing something inhuman. Something that wouldn't have been the strangest thing I've ever done.

I see the Wraith.

And.

I'm.

There.

World breaks around me, scrambles, reassembles, and I'm back in the school basement. Holes leaking blood. Naked Doctor Horde about to shoot me. Black at the edge of my vision. Vibrating, writhing, black. And bits of it break off and drift over my eyes.

And I see Amanda in the corner. She's going to die if I die.

And I think of Evie. She doesn't know who I am.

And I don't want to die.

So I do.

Something.

My fingers curl, corkscrew, twist into Horde's skin, bloodless, piercing, and frost creeps over him and the room pulses with every heartbeat, black, white, black, white, and the black retreats and I close my hands and they are empty fists and my eyes clear and Horde is dead and there is nothing in this world that could have killed a man like that.

The Wraith.

I see the Wraith.

And I see myself.

And the blade is closer.

My hands are on the Count's stomach.

I feel the dark before I see it. And then it's in my eyes. Filling my eyes. And I know how to do this. How to become this.

Even if I don't understand what it is.

Black comes down and the first bullet goes in his back and comes out his chest, opening a blossom of bone cartilage and blood and he starts to turn but a garden of similar flowers bloom there and the scythe shaves some of my scalp as it veers upward and he is thrown into me and I can almost see through the gaping hole that was his chest, right through to Evie, holding the gun that he threw away, pulling the trigger until there's no point in it anymore.

Black floats away. My thoughts clear.

—That's my girl.

The Count spins from me, screwing himself into the ground, screams rising and falling like a dying rabbit singing scales, one word over and over.

—Kiiilll, kiiiillll, kiiilll, kiiiiiiiilllll!

But no one does.

—Tell you, buddy.

I feel the hot wind as he comes out of the sewer cap.

—Tell you, looks to me like something is being decided here.

Enclave are shifting.

He comes into view.

—Kind of a power struggle, looks like to me.

The smell of him is freezing everything. Enclave going still.

Mad old man, a ripple on the air, his words a shiver.

—Remember me?

He moves and everyone moves now, around him, creating distance.

They remember. The Enclave killer. They remember.

He paws the floor with his feet, digging in.

—What's lacking here these days.

His hands flash open and closed.

—Is a little discipline.

Which he starts to dispense.

And I have just enough in me to roll my head to the side so I don't have to see it.

All I can see now is Evie, walking to me, one hand alongside her face, shielding her eyes from what the old man is doing.

She kneels next to me, shakes her head.

—I hate fights, Joe.

I'd tell her she shouldn't have fallen for a fighter.

I'd tell her it's only because I love her that I make such a mess.

But she's got her mouth on mine, and I want that to last as long as it will, this kiss, here in the slaughterhouse, I want it to last till I die.


I dream a green and pink egg. It cracks, black ink leaks. Something is writhing inside, forcing its way out.

Amanda looks up from her microscope.

—Once it's out, you can't put it back in.

I look at the egg in my hand, the black dripping into my palm, the thing inside pushing the halves of the shell apart.

Terry spins the hand crank on his mimeo machine, turning out handbills for a protest.

—Let it, I don't know, let it out, but make sure you keep a handle on it, let it out when its energy is aligned with your own desires.

I'm holding the egg in both hands, black dribbling onto the floor, a few fragments of shell falling away.

Predo sits at his desk, flipping through a file marked TOP SE-CRET.

—Close that thing up, Pitt. You are not suited to making decisions of this scope.

I'm cradling the egg in both arms, knees bent under the weight, rocked from side to side as whatever's inside thrashes about.

Hurley pats the end of an ax handle into his palm.

—Step on da damn ting dere, Joe. Best not ta take any chances wit it.

It's on the floor and I'm balancing it, keeping it from rolling over on top of me, a flood of black running off it and pooling over my shoes.

Percy takes a drag from his Pall Mall.

—That's a problem you got there. Thinkin' on that one, gonna give your head a hurtin'. Askin' me, I say use it, before it use you.

I'm backing away from the egg, watching the shell shatter.

The Count looks up from the miniskirted teenager he's making out with.

—Yo and just fuck it or whatever. What he will be will be.

The shell is breaking open, it's coming out.

Daniel studies the sun through an open window.

—Simon.

I run to him.

—Daniel, what the hell is that?

The shell crumbles to the floor and a worm, glossy in the black blood of its birth, bursts out, its own tail in its mouth.

Daniel glances at it, shrugs, returns his attention to the sun.

—Got me. I've never seen such a thing.

—But you know everything.

He shakes his head.

—I fake a good game, Simon, but I'm just making it up as I go along.

It eats itself and grows and eats itself and grows and I back into a corner and someone puts a hand on my shoulder and I turn and look at Evie.

I shake my head.

—Baby, you're not dead.

She nods.

—OK, well, neither are you.

Which is news.

I wake up with blood in my mouth.

I swallow and lick my lips.

—More.

Evie pushes the cup against my mouth and I drink the rest and lick the inside clean and nod and suck it from my teeth.

—More.

She holds the cup upside down.

—All gone.

I wince.

—Shit. I need. I'll never make it without.

I feel for the wound the Count opened in my side and find a deep gnarled dent, slivers of bone poking through fresh skin.

—That's not as bad as I thought.

Evie shows me an empty two-liter soda bottle with an interior glaze of tacky blood.

—You've had quite a bit.

I roll my head to the side, we're still on the killing floor, but the killing looks like it's done. New bodies scatter among the parts that had fallen from the hanging corpses. And living Enclave, in rows, unmoving, facing the old man at the front of the ware-house, like they used to do with Daniel.

But the old man's not Daniel.

—OK, buddies, tell you what for and then some. Living up here, listening to ten kinds of bullshit. Buddies, forgetting what we're made for. Made for killing and death. Made for the dark. Made to become strong in the light. Make a religion out of that when it's supposed to be life. Do you doubt me?

He picks up a corpse in each hand and shakes them back and forth.

—Do you doubt me?

No one seems to doubt him.

He drops the corpses.

—Buddy over there.

He points at me.

—Buddy over there, he's cracked your world in half. Let in the sunlight. Trust me he has. You don't know it, but you're standing in the sun right now. Buddies, everyone can see you now. And look at yourselves, are you burning? Do you melt?

He stomps, tosses his head around, screams.

—I can feel my skin being eaten by the Vyrus!

He plants himself and a grin slashes his face.

—I like it!

He starts walking through them, pulling them to their feet.

—Buddies, this is not where we live. Playing church games. We live in our natures. True to ourselves. We're in the sun, and it's not killing us, not a one. Only thing that kills us is one another. That's over. Buddies, we're going down now. Live like dark things live. Discipline doesn't grow because you nurture it. It grows be-cause you need it to live. And you!

He's standing over me and Evie.

—You two.

He smells the air around us.

—You two got dead all over your smell, buddy. You ain't gonna last.

I push myself up on my elbows.

—None of us are.

He gives his cat cough.

—Oh, buddy, look into my eyes.

He bugs them at me.

I look.

And I see it there.

—It doesn't scare me.

He slides his lids closed, slides them open.

—And why should it, buddy, it's just who we are.

He looks at Evie, grunts, nods.

—Yeah, buddy, I see, I see. I'm old, but I'm not gone. I see.

He waves a hand, flickers off.

—You cling to that life as long as you can, it'll drag you down, both of you.

He's at the sewer cap, waving the Enclave down into the ground.

—Told you before, buddy.

He clambers down himself, only his head visible.

—You belong down here.

His head drops.

—With us.

And quiet. Creak of dead-bearing chains above, slow trickle of blood. And the breathing of my girl.

She turns from the sewer cap and looks at me.

—Always interesting when you pay a visit, Joe.

I wave a hand at the havoc.

—Got to be the life of the party, that's just me.

She puts a hand on top of her bald head.

—I shot the Count.

—Baby, you killed his ass.

She hugs herself.

—I never killed anyone.

She hugs herself harder.

—God, that felt good.

She holds up a hand.

—Not just anyone. Him. Killing *him* felt good.

She smiles.

—Reeeally good.

She hides the smile with her hand.

—Awful. I'm awful. Terrible.

—Naughty even.

She takes her hand from her mouth.

His own fault. Such an asshole. Such a titanic asshole. Two years. Two fucking years in this place with him. Constant back-and-forth. Just trying to keep some kind of stability to the whole thing. And he just keeps bringing in more Enclave. Kids clearly not capable of adapting to this life. Pushing all the limits of what we can bear. And then he started these gladiator matches. Pitting them against each other. Said it was to *strengthen the whole*. He just pulled that stuff out of his ass. He just.

She draws up her knees, rocks back and forth.

—I couldn't. I couldn't stop it. Not without. My people, there weren't enough of us. So. I could have tried. But. We all would have. And then what? Because no one would have been here to keep things.

She stops rocking.

—*Normal.*

She laughs.

—Yeah.

She puts her head on her knees.

—I was so lonely.

She closes her eyes.

—I was alive. I wasn't dying anymore. I was alive. But I was so lonely. And I thought to myself sometimes, *If I was back in the hospital, Joe would come see me.*

She opens her eyes.

—I was so lonely.

She unwraps her arms, touches the wound in my side.

—Hey.

I wince.

—It's OK.

She puts a hand on my stomach.

—Joe.

—Baby. I need to. I'm. Sorry. I think.

She pushes a hand under my shirt.

—I was so lonely.

She runs fingers along the healing scar in my stomach.

It hurts, but I don't stop her, I just try to get the words out before I can think about them anymore.

—There were these kids, and, they were in a hole, and, I didn't. I could have, like you here. I could have helped. But I didn't. And then I gave up. I went and hid. Kids. But. I don't want to lie. Because. Baby, I don't care. I don't. I did what I could for them when I could and if I was a year too late for some of them. I don't care. What I care about. What matters to me.

I grab her wrist.

—I'm sorry I lied to you. I'm sorry I didn't tell you what I am.

I touch her face.

—Baby, I'm a killer.

She covers my mouth with her hand.

—It's OK. I am too.

She takes her hand away from my mouth and exhales.

—And, Joe, I'm a Vampyre, we can totally have sex now.

She's not in the mood to wait.

Everything hurts. Nothing feels good.

Nothing but her.


I don't tell her what Amanda said, that we could have been having sex the whole time we knew each other. Something like that could kill the mood. Such as it is. And sure, holding that back after just apologizing for years of lies, that's maybe not how you put your relationship on a healthy new footing. Figure I'm not really looking for a healthy relationship. I just love the girl. So I do what seems the right thing to do at the time. The other stuff, we'll sort that out later.


It doesn't take long.

Who wants to linger over it in a place like this.

—Baby.

She pulls her face from where it's buried in my neck.

—M'tired.

I touch her cheek.

—Favor to ask.

She sits up.

—Don't push it.

I kick off the jeans that are still around my ankles.

—Got anything I can wear?

—Well, white's not really your color.

—I'll manage.

She stands.

—Anyway, I have a jacket that's all you.

She starts for the stairs, picking her way, naked, through the dead.

I stand myself up, my body mostly shocked still to be here.

—Another thing.

She's on the stairs, waiting to hear it.

I give it to her.

—We got to get out of here.

She looks around the place.

—Well, I didn't plan on staying at this point.

—Yeah, but I mean the Island.

She folds her arms.

—Manhattan?

I raise my hands.

—I know.

—Leave Manhattan?

I drop my hands.

—I got to ask you to trust me on this.

She frowns and raises a finger.

—You ask a lot, Joe Pitt.

—I know.

She unfolds her arms, swats the air, turns and climbs the stairs.

—I won't go to Jersey.

I don't say anything. I just stand there. And look at her ass. There's not much left to it, but what's there is choice.


I'm at the door.

White painter's pants, white T, white boat decks, and my old black leather jacket. Not the palette I'd choose for myself, but I make it work. Evie's dug in her basket and found white tights, white jersey skirt, white V-neck sweater, white hoodie and white Chuck Taylors.

We're a pair.

—It took me so long to feel like a New Yorker.

—Baby, I get it. But an island has tunnels and bridges. Tunnels and bridges can be blocked.

—I know.

—Not like my first choice is someplace where the bars close at midnight.

—I'm not complaining, Joe. I just.

She looks out the door at the streets starting to show signs of morning.

—I love this city.

—Yeah. Me too.

The street rumbles, I look up to the corner, and thirteen bikers in top hats, aviator goggles and long duster coats round onto Little West Twelfth and roll up to the loading dock.

The lead rider lifts the goggles from his eyes and lets them hang from his neck.

—Joe.

—Christian.

He puts a hand at his ear, like he's holding a phone.

—Got a strange call. Said you'd been up to some crazy shit. Said getting lost was a good plan. Said you were the man to talk to about finding a lost place. Said find you here.

He lowers the hand.

—Can't say I'm pleased about any part of that.

I limp onto the loading dock, packing nothing but attitude.

—Got a problem with it?

He puts a hand in the pocket of his duster, comes out with a pint of Old Crow.

—No one told me I'd live forever.

He takes a drink, screws the cap back, tosses it to me.

I offer it to Evie.

She takes it, flicks the cap with her thumb and it spins up and off and onto the ground and rolls away.

—Fuck yes.

She drinks.

—Man. Whiskey.

She hands it to me.

—Almost as good as blood.

Christian fake-shades his eyes and squints at her.

—How'd you lay your hands on that one, Joe?

I take a drink, pass him the bottle.

—You know me, lucky in love.

He shakes his head.

—Not sure I like the idea of you riding with us sporting that look.

Evie gives him the finger.

—Says the man in a top hat.

He nods at me.

—Hang on to her, Joe.

I've got her hand in mine, it's a two-finger grip, but that's what I got to work with.

—That's the plan.


A Duster named Tenderhooks lends us his bike, climbs up behind Christian to a chorus of whistles and limped wrists. Evie hikes her skirt a little and gets behind me.

And we ride.

Over the bridge there's a lady who runs the Bronx. Chubby did as I asked, she'll know we're coming. She did like Chubby asked, she'll have a place for us to hide out the day. And she'll have made a call of her own. They listened to her, she'll have a tribe of filed-teeth savages standing by. Match the Mungiki with the Dusters, put them on one side of a thing and anything else on the other side of a thing, I know where I'll put my money.

Close to the Island, but we'll be good for the one day.

After that?

What do you do when you leave home?

Figure you put it together. New world. No telling which way it turns on its axis. When it faces the sun, when it turns away. A whole new clock to the day and the night.

New rules.

Terry and Predo, even Digga and Enclave, things running on their rules, I knew where I stood. In the middle. No future. And no room for the lady behind me on the bike.

Want to make room for yourself, knock down what's there.

I want room for two. I got no other reason to be if it's not her. If it's not because she knows me. She knows what I am inside. Vyrus or Wraith. Whatever you believe. Killers both. She knows what I am now.

And the girl likes me that way.

I gun the throttle and she wraps her arms tighter around my middle and all the holes that got stuck in me the last night ache like hell and I hit it again to make her hold tighter still.

It just feels better that way.

A few blocks from the bridge I pull to the curb outside a deli. When I come out I have five packs of Luckys. I peel one open and stick a smoke in my face and my girl digs my old Zippo from my jacket pocket and gives me a light.

Some moments, they're worth what you go through to get there.

Engines gun, rattling windows and setting off car alarms, a noise that lets everyone know they're better off getting a door between them and the street.

**TRANSCRIPTION CONTINUED**
**DO NOT COPY**

I'm a mess.

Five, six years back, I was a guy about forty who looked in his late twenties. Nothing pretty, but in one piece.

Look at me now, I look like a guy about fifty who looks like a guy in his forties. Knee is never gonna heal right. Big toe, my fingers, my eye, those won't be coming back. The hole the Count put in my side, that's gonna leave a mark. Feels like I'm maybe going the rest of the road on no better than one and a half lungs. And the *half* is seriously in question. Get some blood in proper amounts the next couple days, that might help things along, but I'll be a mess no matter this, no matter that. Had enough blood to soak in a tub of it, it couldn't put me back as I was.

And odds are we'll be looking at trickles of blood for a bit.

Once the night comes and we start moving, it will be fast and low. Things are gonna be shaking out hard, and until they settle down, we'll need to stay out from under anything big that might fall on us.

Evie, she's rigged for lean times. That's all she's done the last two years. Never got the full Enclave skeletal look going, but she's pared down to the sinew. Likes it that way. Likes the way it feels. Says it feels natural. Says I'll get used to it. Says I got it in me to live that way too. Says Daniel called it right about me.

The way he fingered me as the future of Enclave.

She says I showed Enclave how to live in the light. Showed all of us. Exposing the Vyrus, it pushed us all into the light. Like the old man was saying. Evie says it's just like the Enclave always wanted, we're in the light, but we're not burning. She says prophecy isn't literal, it's figurative.

I figure that's bullshit.

Her, she's mostly saying it to watch me squirm, laughing at me the whole time. But only half laughing. She takes it more serious than me. Two years in there, living in Daniel's old room, reading his journals. She read all of them. Going back to before he was Enclave. Before he was even infected. She says she has a different perspective on things.

I haven't said anything about what happened in the warehouse. With the Count. I haven't asked her if she saw anything before she pulled the trigger.

Working on how to phrase it.

*Hey, baby, before you shot him down, did it look like my eyes turned black and I pushed my fingers inside him and froze him to death?*

But I took a look at his body. I touched it. And it was cold. Colder than even a dead body has a right to be.

So what.

So if the Vyrus is where life started, then what? Because it had to come from somewhere, yeah? Amanda, you little crazy twist, the ideas you put in my head.

It isn't *literal*.

Enclave and what they believe, not literal. So what's it mean when you say you *summon* something? Does it mean you prod some slob till the Vyrus in him mutates again?

Christ it all hurts my head.

Evie says all that Enclave stuff started as practical lessons for survival. Says the whole fasting deal has as much to do with fitting into the *ecosystem* as it does anything else. Says it's all like that at its heart.

Whatever.

I say I like a full belly.

But we'll just let it play out.

Some rumbles on the news: Long-range camera shots from Queens. The gravel quarry. SWAT vans, fire trucks, black-and-whites, some dark sedans. Some cops huddled in a prayer circle. Another cop bent over puking, his partner standing next to him in tears. Some cell-phone video of blanket-draped figures being led into ambulances and commandeered school buses from the depot next door.

Rumor starting up on NY1 is about a secret way station for East European white-slave prostitutes.

Could be a cover story given out by the cops, could just be the shit people make up. Doesn't matter, it won't last. The truth wants to be free is what Terry said. This truth will break out the hard way. Then it will go mad dog in the streets.

Look at the clock, running low on daylight. Ready to sleep a little. But Evie's right, I need to finish this last recording first. Besides, doesn't look like there's any room for me to stretch.

Crowded tight.

Esperanza got the call from Chubby, rigged up the upper floors of the abandoned house she squats in. Window boards and the like. Kind of stuff she never did before so as not to draw attention in a neighborhood that festers with superstition. But she figured this hideout will be blown soon anyway. Now she's got Mungiki, Dusters, odds and ends of her people that she gathered up. Me and Evie. Don't know which was more terrifying, watching the Mungiki and Dusters square off and sniff at each other, or watching Evie and Esperanza do a stare-down.

Best thing about leaving at sunset will be keeping those two apart.

Esperanza's not sure what she'll do. Off the Island, her people have a better shot at laying low than the folks other side of the bridges, but *anywhere* in the city will be a tough place to be. She's thinking about hooking up with Lydia. Safety in numbers. From where I am that will just make it easier for them all to be scooped into cages and labs. But I think that way.

Whatever she does, the Mungiki will join in. They follow Skag Baron Menace. And Menace loves Esperanza. Deal done.

Christian's got no confusion in him. The Dusters are for the road. Biggest question they're gonna face is do they break up the gang and have a shot at staying under the radar, or do they ride tall and feed as a pack and go out in a blaze of glory? I read the look in Christian's eyes right, there'll be some headlines about crazed biker gangs in a few small-town papers the next weeks. And then maybe one big national headline about how they go down hard and take a lot of law along with them.

Christian likes being hard.

I get that.

No idea what Digga will do. I maybe had a twinge about sending him to raid the Secretariat just before I blew the whistle on everything. Kinda hung him out there away from his home base, set him up to have to scramble some. But we're all scrambling. And when I get to feel too bad about it, I think about the hole in Queens and those kids and I feel better knowing the kind of hit Digga and his rhinos laid down on the Secretariat. I like picturing Digga going in with his pit bulls all juiced on anathema, Vyrus blood-crazed and hungry, running the halls and eating what they kill. No telling if that's how it went down, but it makes a pretty picture.

Digga is smart, he'll have cleared out the Coalition armory, put wheels under his people and drove them to Yonkers or some similar wasteland to wait out the first day. Morning will find them in a new diaspora, scattering over Upstate and New England. But he might just take all those guns, seize control of the Columbia campus, and start negotiating for resettlement to a neutral location. They take a few dorms, they won't lack for eating.

Lydia I don't think about too much.

Think about that gun she hung onto.

Hang onto that gun, girl. And don't wait too long to see if the other side greets you with open arms before you decide if the right thing to do is to pull the trigger.

I look at my bad hand and feel that hole in my side and I get thinking on Chubby's kid. The price I paid to save the blood of a pregnant woman. All those pieces of me. And in the end that blood may get spilled out anyway. Delilah and Ben and their baby.

Either they're the future or they're gonna die young.

Crazy kids.

Tired. Up all night getting shot and stabbed and bit, up all day talking into this mike.

Part of a package. Something me and Evie are gonna drop in the mail. Still debating an address. Cops, government, newspaper. Esperanza says post it on the Internet. Haven't thought it all the way around to figure for sure the best thing.

This tired, I don't think clear. Not that I ever do. But we got to deliver this message, and be sure it gets heard.

The message is, I'm dead.

Evie's dead.

We're in the grave.

Whatever lists you're making when you start interrogations and investigations, you mark us *Accounted For.*

DOA.

We could make the road our home, we could settle down, but we're dead either way.

And we want to stay dead.

Saying, if someone in some town wakes up in a strange place with a telltale hole in his arm, feeling woozy, light a couple pints, and it gets reported to the local heat and it gets kicked up to whoever is going to be in charge of Vyral enforcement or whatever it ends up being called, saying that's a report that should be filed under *Do Not Fuck With This Shit.*

Let me spell it out.

Lydia kept the USB drive with all Amanda's proof that the Vyrus exists. Including a file that breaks down and explains her

*Vyrally activated bacillus.* That vial of spun aluminum with a sticker on the side. I got a look at that sticker. Almost laughed myself dead when I read it, the name little Amanda gave her creation.

*Ouroboros.*

You laughing yet?

Laugh at this.

I kept it.

Someone had to.

I sure as hell wasn't going to leave it lying around. Something like that in the wrong hands, who knows what they'd do with it.

But me, I'm dead. Nothing I can do. Only way I could pull the cap from that bottle is if someone picked up a shovel and dug me from the dirt. Someone scraped the clay from off my coffin and found me and my girl lying side by side and stuck a couple stakes in our hearts to make sure we stayed in the ground, that's the only thing that could rouse me.

Wake the dead, and I'll let loose the worm.

Figure that's all there is to say right now.

Got the rest of the story down already. Going back just enough years to give you a picture of what you're dealing with.

Talking about me right now.

Not talking about the Vyrus, the Wraith, who made what and how and is the Vyrus a metaphysical key, the origin of life, or just a nasty bug. Not talking about did Daniel really summon a creature from another dimension to shadow me and save my life. Not talking about do we become the Wraith when we die, or is it in us all along. I'm talking about making you clear on what's important. Because all that stuff, let me sum it up for you: There's more things in heaven and earth.

Put it a different way: Who gives fuckall?

What I'm talking about is *me.*

'Cause like I always said, I was this way to start. Nothing made me who I am. Nothing made me what I am.

I'm a killer.

You're either the kind who can drink blood to survive, or you aren't.

And you're either the kind who would free the mad worm at the heart of the world, or you aren't.

So back off.

Hey, while you're at it, hands off those kids and their baby.

Mean, they should get a shot at life same as everyone else.

Yeah.

And just leave me in my grave.

Me and my girl.

Or you'll find out what kind of a mean son of a bitch I really am.

Please turn the page
for a preview of
Charlie Huston's

# SLEEPLESS

Available from
Ballantine Books
Spring 2010

PARK WATCHED THE HOMELESS MAN WEAVE IN AND OUT of the gridlocked midnight traffic on La Cienega, his eyes fixed on the bright orange AM/FM receiver dangling from the man's neck on a black nylon lanyard. The same shade orange the SL response teams wore when they cleared a house. He closed his eyes, remembering the time an SLRT showed up on his street at the brown and green house three doors down. The sound of the saw coming from the garage, the pitch rising when it hit bone.

Techno-accented static opened his eyes. The homeless man was next to his window, dancing from foot to foot, neck held at an unmistakable stiff angle, flashing a hand-lettered sign on a square of smudged whiteboard:

BLESSINGS!!!

Park looked at the man's neck.

The people in the cars around him had noticed it as well; several rolled up their windows despite the ban on air-conditioning.

Park opened his ashtray, scooped out a handful of change, and was offering it to the wild-eyed sleepless when the human bomb detonated several blocks away and the explosion thrummed the glass of his windshield, ruffling the hairs on his arms with a rush of air hotter than the night.

He flinched, the change falling from his hand, scattering on the asphalt, the tinkle of it hitting and rolling in every direction, lost in the echoes bouncing off the faces of the buildings lining the avenue, the alarms set off when windows were shattered and parked cars blown onto their sides.

By the time the coins had stopped rolling and the homeless man had gotten down on his hands and knees to scrabble for his scattered handout, Park was reaching under his seat for his weapon.

The Walther PPS was in a holster held to the bottom of the driver's seat by a large patch of Velcro. Clean, oiled, and loaded, with the chamber empty. He didn't need to check, having done so before he left the house. He took it from its holster and dropped it in the side pocket of his cargo pants. It was unlikely any of his customers would be this far west, but it would be typical of the universe to send one just now to see him with a sidearm clipped to his waist.

Climbing from the car, he closed and locked the door, secure in the knowledge that the traffic jam would not be breaking up before sunrise. He was working his way through the cars, all but a very few of them sealed tight now, their occupants rigid and sweating inside, when the street was plunged into sudden darkness.

He stopped, touched his weapon to be sure of it, and thought about Rose and the baby, asking the frozen world to keep them safe if he should die here. But the darkness didn't invite any new attacks. Or if it did, they were yet to come. More likely it was an unscheduled rolling blackout.

He edged between the cars, watching a man in a sweat-twisted suit pounding the horn of his newly scarred Audi, raising similar protests from the cars around his. Or perhaps they were intended to drown out the screams coming from the flaming crater at the intersection.

Those flames were the brightest illumination on the street now, almost all the drivers having turned off their engines and headlights to conserve gas. He could feel them on his face already, the flames, baking the skin tight. And he remembered the cabin in Big Sur where he took Rose after they first knew about the baby, but before the diagnosis.

There had been a fireplace. And they'd sat before it until nearly dawn, using what had been meant as a weekend's supply of wood on their first night.

His face had felt like this then.

He tried to recall the name of the cabin they had stayed in. Bluebird? Bluebell? Blue Ridge? Blue something for sure, but blue what?

Blue Moon.

The name painted just above the door had been Blue Moon. With a little star-accented teal crescent that Rose had rolled her eyes at.

"Are we supposed to think we're in fucking Connecticut, for Christ sake?"

He'd said something in response, some joke about not cursing in front of the baby, but before he could remember what it was he'd said, his foot slipped in a great deal of someone's blood, drawing him back to the present, and the flames here before him.

The wiper blades on an Hummer H3, one of the few vehicles with intact glass this close to the blast, were beating furiously, cleaner fluid spraying, smearing blood, batting what looked like a gnarled bit of scalp and ear back and forth across the windshield, while the young woman inside wiped vomit from her chin and screamed into a Bluetooth headset.

Looking at a man on the edge of the crater, his entire jawbone carried away by a piece of flying debris, Park only wondered now at the instinct that had made him take his weapon from the car rather than his first-aid kit.

■　■　■

IT WASN'T THE first human bomb in Los Angeles. Just the first one north of Exposition and west of the I-5.

The sound of the detonation rolling across the L.A. basin and washing up against the hills had brought me out to my deck. One expects the occasional crack of gunfire coming from Hollywood on any given night, but the crump of high explosives in West Hollywood was a novelty. A sound inclined to make me ruminant, recalling, as it did, a pack of C-4 wired to the ignition of a VC colonel's black Citroen in Hanoi, as well as other moments of my youth.

Thus nostalgic, I came onto the deck in time to see a slab of the city, framed by Santa Monica, Venice, Western, and Sepulveda, wink into blackness. Looking immediately skyward, knowing from experience that my eyes would subtly adjust to the reduction in ground light, I watched the emergence of seldom seen constellations.

Under these usually veiled stars, the city burned.

Only a small bit of it, yes, but one of the more expensive bits. A circumstance that would no doubt have serious repercussions.

It's all well and good in the general course of things if Mad Swan Bloods and Eight Trey Gangster Crips want to plant claymore mines in Manchester Park or for Avenues Cyprus Park to start launching RPGs across Eagle Rock Boulevard, but suicide bombers less than a mile from the Beverly Center would not be tolerated.

Uncorking a second bottle of Clos des Papes 2005, I rested secure in the knowledge that the National Guard would be shock-trooping South Central and East L.A. at first light.

Nothing like a show of force to keep up the morale of the general citizenry in times of duress. The fact that the display would be utterly misdirected and only serve to brew greater discontent was beside the point. We had long passed the stage where the consequences of tactical armed response were weighed in advance. Anyone with the time and wherewithal to put a map on a wall and stick pins in it could see quite clearly what was happening.

I had such a map, and said wherewithal, and many pins.

If red pins are acts of violence committed by people traditionally profiled as potentially criminal perpetrated against those who have not been so profiled, and yellow pins are acts of violence perpetrated between peoples traditionally so profiled, and blue pins indicate acts of violence carried out by uniformed and/or badged members of the soldiering and law enforcement professions upon peoples so profiled, one can clearly see patterns of tightly clustered yellow pins, encircled by blue pins, concentrated to the far south, east, and north of the most prime Los Angeles real estate, which is, in turn, becoming pockmarked by random bursts of red pins.

It is, on such a map, the vastness of the territory devoted to yellow-on-yellow acts of violence and blue responses in relative proportion to the wee acreage dotted with red, that should give one pause.

It looked, upon little or no reflection, like the pustules of a disease spreading inexorably against the feeble resistance of a failed vaccine, carrying infection along the arteries of the city, advancing no matter how many times the medics raised the point of amputation up the ravaged limb.

That it was a symptom of a disease rather than the disease it-self was an irony I never chuckled at. There being little or no humor to be found in the prospect of the end of the world.

But I did appreciate it. The irony, and the fact that the disease that was killing us ignored the classifications and borders that de-fined so clearly for so many who they should be killing and why.

The disease didn't care for distinctions of class, race, income, religion, sex, or age. The disease seemed only to care that your eyes remain open to witness it all. That what nightmares you had haunted only your waking hours. The disease considered us all equal and wished that we share the same fate. That we should bear witness as we chewed our own intestines, snapping at what gnawed from the inside.

It wished that we become sleepless.

I could sleep.

Choosing, that night, not to.

Choosing, instead, to pour another glass of overrated but still quite good Rhone into an admittedly inappropriate jelly jar, and to settle into an overdesigned Swedish sling chair to watch that small, expensive fragment of the city burn.

Herald, I knew, of worse.

# 7/7/10

TODAY BEENIE SAID something about Hydo knowing "the guy." What's encouraging about this is that I didn't ask. Hydo called for a delivery and I went over to the farm to make the drop (100 15mg Dexedrine spansules). He asked if I wanted a Coke and I hung around long enough to scroll through my texts and map my next couple deliveries. Beenie was there, making a deal to sell some gold he'd farmed, but mostly just hanging out

with the guys. Hydo passed around the dex to his guys and they
all started speed rapping while they hacked up zombies and
stuff. One of them (I think his name is Zhou, but I need to
check my notes) started talking about his cousin going sleepless.
The other guys all started telling their own sleepless stories.
Beenie asked if I knew anyone. I said yes. They all talked some
more, and the one guy (Zhou?) said he put an ad on Craigslist to
trade a level 100 Necromantic Warlord for Dreamer to give his
cousin, but the only response he got was from a scammer. That's
when Beenie looked at Hydo and said, "Hydo, man, what about
the guy?" Hydo was in the middle of an exchange in Chasm
Tide. His front character was on his monitor in the Purple
Grotto, getting ready to pass off the gold to a Darkling Heller as
soon as one of the guys confirmed that the PayPal transfer had
come through. But everyone stopped talking right after Beenie
spoke. Just Hydo talking to the Darkling on his headset, telling
him he'd throw in a Mace of Chaos for another twenty euro. He
was acting like he hadn't heard what Beenie said. But he gave
him a look. And Beenie started shutting down his MacBook and
said he had to roll. I pocketed my phone and finished my Coke
and said later.

Beenie was my first in with the farms. I met him at a party on
Hillhurst. He knows a lot of people. They like him. If he says
Hydo knows "the guy," it might be true.

In any case, I didn't say anything. I just walked out of the farm
behind Beenie. We talked while he was unlocking his Trek and
putting on his helmet and elbow and knee pads. He said he was
looking for some opium. He has this thing for old Hollywood
and read somewhere that Errol Flynn described smoking opium,
"like having your soul massaged with mink gloves." Now he
wants to try it. I told him I'd see what I could do. Then he

pedaled north on Aviation, probably headed for Randy's Donuts. I made a note to ask around about opium. Made another note to look over my list of Hydo's known associates.

Finished deliveries.

A suicide bomber on the way home.

I did what I could. Not much. I think I stopped a boy's bleeding long enough for him to get to the hospital. Who knows what happed to him there. Traffic got messed up for miles. Once the EMTs and paramedics showed up, I spent most of my time passing out water. A lady thanked me when I saw her fainting in her car and got her a bottle.

A witness said the bomber was a woman, a New America Jesus insurgent. He said he knew she was a NAJi because she screamed "something about Satan" before she blew herself up. He also said she was staggering like she was drunk. NAJis don't drink. A Guard told me that looking at the size of the crater she left, she was probably staggering under the weight of the bomb. He said that kind of blast was what they got in Iraq from car bombs.

I said something about how at least he wasn't there anymore, and he asked me if I was "fucking joking."

Almost noon before I got home.

Francine had to leave Rose alone with the baby.

She was in the backyard with her laptop. There was gardening stuff lying around, but she was logged into her Chasm Tide account, playing her elemental mage, Cipher Blue, trying again to get through the Clockwork Labyrinth on her own.

The baby was on a blanket next to her, under an umbrella, crying.

As I came up, Blue was being dismembered by a skeleton made of brass gears, wire and rusting springs. Beenie says no one gets

through the Labyrinth on their own. You have to join a
campaign, but Rose refuses to try it that way. Which isn't
surprising.

She closed the laptop and grabbed a garden trowel and started
stabbing the dry earth, digging at the roots of one of the weeds
that's taken over the garden. I picked up the baby and asked
how she had been and Rose told me she had just started crying
again right before I came home. Said she hadn't cried for hours
before. But I think she was just saying that. Then she started
talking about her grandma's garden, the topiary, vegetables,
citrus trees, strawberry patch, and the rosebushes she was
named for. She said she wanted the baby to have a garden to
grow up in, learn about how seeds turn into plants. She had a
packet of marigold seeds she was going to plant. I held the baby
while Rose talked, and she stopped crying a little. Rose stopped
talking and looked at me and asked what was on my clothes and
I had to go in and clean up and when I set the baby down she
started crying again.

I called Francine while I was inside and she said she was sorry
for leaving, but she needed to get her kids to school. She said
Rose didn't sleep at all. She said the baby might have slept, but
her eyes never closed. But she was quiet for a couple hours just
after midnight. I told her I'd see her tonight and got in the
shower. There was stuff under my nails that was hard to get out.
Then Rose got into the shower with me and asked me to wash
her back and I had to tell her she had her clothes on. She
looked at me and looked at her clothes like she didn't get it.
Then she got it and started crying and told me she was sorry. I
held her. She cried and the baby cried.

I'll go see Hydo tonight.

Maybe he really does know the guy.

CHARLIE HUSTON is the author of the Henry Thompson trilogy, the Joe Pitt casebooks, and the bestsellers *The Shotgun Rule* and *The Mystic Arts of Erasing All Signs of Death*. He lives with his family in Los Angeles.

ABOUT THE TYPE

This book was set in Fairfield, the first typeface from the hand
of the distinguished American artist and engraver Rudolph
Ruzicka (1883–1978). Ruzicka was born in Bohemia and came
to America in 1894. He set up his own shop, devoted to wood
engraving and printing, in New York in 1913 after a varied
career working as a wood engraver in photoengraving and
banknote printing plants, and as an art director and freelance
artist. He designed and illustrated many books, and was the
creator of a considerable list of individual prints—wood
engravings, line engravings on copper, and aquatints.